POL CHECK... ...REE QUICK
BR...

"Go, go, go!" shoute...

The three men of Able Team cha... ...their guns at their shoulders, gliding in a combat ... ...t gave each of them a stable firing platform. Their weapons barked; there were still a few men left mobile after the Osprey's attack. Most of those in the cafeteria now, however, were dead or dying. A few moaned. The floor of the cafeteria was awash in blood.

"Clear," Lyons said.

"Clear," Gadgets responded. He turned to Pol and his eyes widened. "Pol! Your six!"

Pol spun around, dropping low, trying to get himself out of the line of fire. The man drawing down on him held an AR15. Pol snapped off a shot that punched through the man's thigh, toppling him, causing him to lose his grip on his weapon.

"Secure that guy!" Lyons ordered.

Pol was already on the move. He dashed to the wounded shooter, kicked the man's gun away and put the barrel of his own M4 under the man's chin.

"Do not move," he ordered. "Do not attempt to take any hostile action or I will blow your brains all over this floor."

DON PENDLETON'S

STONY

AMERICA'S ULTRA-COVERT INTELLIGENCE AGENCY

MAN®

TRIPLECROSS

A GOLD EAGLE BOOK FROM
W⊕RLDWIDE®

TORONTO • NEW YORK • LONDON
AMSTERDAM • PARIS • SYDNEY • HAMBURG
STOCKHOLM • ATHENS • TOKYO • MILAN
MADRID • WARSAW • BUDAPEST • AUCKLAND

Recycling programs
for this product may
not exist in your area.

First edition June 2014

ISBN-13: 978-0-373-80445-0

TRIPLECROSS

Special thanks and acknowledgment to
Phil Elmore for his contribution to this work.

Copyright © 2014 by Worldwide Library

TRIPLECROSS

PROLOGUE

Siachen Glacier Region, Pakistan

Hakim Janwari shivered under his winter-camouflage BDUs. He pulled his face wrap tighter, flexing his fingers within his gloves, worried about the frostbite that crept, almost like a disease, from man to man. So many had been affected. He personally knew five men who had lost entire fingers. Janwari lived in constant fear of coming home to his wife less whole than when he had left her.

If he came home at all.

He adjusted his goggles. Already they were encrusted with ice again, making it difficult for him to see. His legs felt leaden as he struggled to raise his boots, to take step after step, to march onward toward a goal he no longer understood on a field of battle he did not care about.

Ahead and to his left, barely visible through the wind-driven snow, a Chinese-built Type 88 main battle tank struggled to move forward. The tanks simply were not built for this terrain. The cold and the driving snow created a deadly, icy paralysis in man and machine alike. The cold was killing both, slowly but surely, here at the top of the world.

The Siachen Glacier region was called the world's highest battleground for a reason. Pakistan and its hated enemy, India, had fought each other here intermittently for more than three decades. What they were fighting to achieve,

Janwari could no longer say. What his government thought it earned by sending men and weapons of war into this frozen hell, Janwari was afraid to ask.

He could feel his legs beginning to grow warm. That was a bad sign. Cold was the only constant here. The illusion of warmth signified his body trying to compensate. It was the first sign that it—that *he* was succumbing to the dreaded cold. He knew the process well by now.

From within his parka he struggled to remove the rugged GPS unit. The aluminum housing of the electronic box made him wince even through his gloves. It was so cold. Everything was so very cold.

He was forced to scrape another layer of frost from his goggles before he could read the GPS unit. What it would tell him, he already knew very well. He and the men of his unit were just beyond the Line of Control, sometimes called the Berlin Wall of Asia, somewhere between the Karakoram and Ladakh ranges and below Karakoram Pass. They had not yet crossed over into Shaksam Valley.

The Line of Control was the demarcation between territory held by India and territory held by Pakistan in what was once Jammu and Kashmir. This landlocked "princely state" had once boasted a Maharaja, whose pretensions of neutrality had not lasted much longer than the 1947 Indian Independence Act. This was when British India was officially divided into Pakistan and India.

Torn by localized rebellions and plunged into armed conflict, the region had been ripped apart from within by insurgents who favored either India or Pakistan. The legacy of Kashmir was one of violence. Recently, an uneasy ceasefire had been called, and held, for some months. But that was over now.

The coordinates finally resolved. The GPS device was sluggish. It was difficult to acquire a clean line of sight to the satellites overhead through this weather. Janwari supposed he should be grateful he was able to take the reading at all.

He was not. The coordinates were not nearly different enough. They should have covered three times as much ground during the waking hours. They had made very poor distance in this weather. Janwari had begged his superiors by radio to allow the men to camp, to seek the relative warmth of their storm shelters, while waiting out the worst of the current weather. But the higher-ups would not listen. They had told him to carry on, to follow his orders.

He did as he was told.

From the pouch on his waist he took one of the last of his flares. He was not sure what they would do tomorrow, when the last flare was used. Perhaps he would be reduced to firing in the air and hoping his men could hear the shot over the howling wind. At the moment he was too cold to care. He popped the cap on the flare, held the tube away from his body and pulled the release cord to fire the flare. He could not smell the acrid fumes through the snowstorm.

The glowing green star that floated to the ground on a silken parachute was almost beautiful. He watched the flare descend, willing the ache in his shoulders to go away, knowing that if he was not within shelter soon, the cold would take the ache and everything else readily enough. Too readily he understood the siren song of the deathly cold. It sang to a man about the end of pain. It told a man everything would finally be all right. It was the easiest thing to do…simply let go, close your eyes and let the cold take you.

Janwari forced himself to open his eyes wide. No. He would not give in. He would not let the glacier have him. He would not die in these frozen mountains.

To his left, Hooth and Gola began setting up the shelter.

Simple as it was, it was harder in the searing cold. Still, they were practiced. Their lives had revolved around this ritual for the past five days, plodding through pointless "patrols" and then setting up the portable shelter every night. Often Janwari helped them, although strictly speaking, they were his subordinates and he was not required to do so. This night he could not bring himself to move from the spot on which he was now rooted. He waited as they erected the shelter, then followed when they beckoned him to enter.

Once inside, Hooth switched on the LED lantern. It was feeble, both from cold and because the batteries were not fully charged. The lantern was solar with a crank backup. Later, after they ate, they would draw lots to see who cranked it this evening. There was never enough time, before sleep beckoned, to charge the lantern fully.

Gratefully, Janwari took off his pack and let it fall to the floor of the shelter. From his shoulder he took the Type 56 Kalashnikov-pattern assault rifle and placed it next to the pack. Many Pakistani troops were issued the excellent Heckler & Koch G-3 battle rifle. There weren't enough to go around, particularly here. He and his men were forced to make do with the Chinese-produced AK clone. Most of these, like Janwari's, were wrapped in strips of white adhesive-backed cloth tape. The tape on Janwari's weapon was dirty and worn.

As Janwari took out his bedroll and began to spread it across his third of the shelter, Gola was already lighting a can of Sterno. The three men huddled around the wisp of flame, spreading their parkas to catch the scant heat. Gola began working on a can of soup with his pocketknife, sawing away at the top of the can. If Janwari counted correctly, this was the last of the smuggled cans Gola had crammed into his pack before they'd left their base camp near Rawalpindi.

"'The land is so barren,'" Hooth said.

"'The passes so high,'" Gola continued.

"'Only best friends and worse enemies come by,'" Janwari recited, finishing the traditional quote about the inhospitable land in which they found themselves. Gola smiled as he shifted the can of soup atop the Sterno can. The heat had to be burning his fingers, at this point, but he did not seem to mind. It was also possible he could not feel his digits. Janwari made a mental note to check Gola for frostbite.

"It is not much of a ceasefire," Hooth said. "Walking in circles in the cold."

"You have said the same thing every night for five days," Gola said. He stirred the soup with the blade of his pocketknife. "I believe we all know your opinion on the subject by now."

"It is better than fighting," Janwari said. "But not much."

"And you have said the same, as well," Gola accused.

"Shall I complain that the soup has been the same for five days?" Janwari asked. He allowed himself a smile as he pried his frosted goggles from his stiff, frozen head wrap.

"We should all be grateful," Hooth said. "I suppose. But this marching to nothing…"

"Crawling to nothing," Gola corrected.

Snow pelted the shelter. They would be forced to unfold their shovels and dig out of the snow in the morning.

"Yes," Hooth said. "Crawling to nothing." He looked to Janwari. "When will the patrol be released? When can we return to base?"

"I cannot get anyone at Command to acknowledge my

requests," Janwari said. "Always it is the same. 'Return to your scheduled patrol route. Follow your orders. Stop asking questions.'"

"They say this?" Hooth asked.

"They imply this," Janwari said. "One learns to read what is meant and not what is said."

"It is ready," Gola said. "The soup is as warm as I can make it." As cold as it was here, that meant simply tepid by normal standards. But Janwari's mouth watered at the thought of a meal that was not rock-hard, frozen protein bars or the unappealing rations issued by his military. From his pack he took his canteen cup. Gola and Hooth were already prepared with their own.

Outside the shelter the howling winds were growing even stronger. The fabric of the little tent was whipped to and fro. Hooth shook a fist at the walls, then rubbed his hands together.

Gola poured the soup expertly. He divided the amber liquid among their cups. Janwari gulped his, knowing that in only minutes the soup would lose what little warmth it contained. Gola sipped his more deliberately, while Hooth followed Janwari's example.

"I am thinking of a place," Gola said.

"No, not this again," Janwari replied. He put a hand to his ear. "Did you hear that?"

"I will play," Hooth said. To Janwari, he said, "The storm is very bad. The worst yet. We will be beaten half to death with balls of ice before this is over." Turning back to Gola, he spread his hands as if describing a scene. "Is it a warm place, Gola, full of beautiful women in indecent bathing suits? A place where they bring you tropical drinks with umbrellas in them?"

"Yes," Gola said. He frowned. "You should not have guessed it so quickly."

"Why not?" Hooth asked. "You think of the same place every time. As do we all, I think."

"Someplace warm," Gola said wistfully.

"Someplace full of pretty girls," Hooth reminded him.

"My wife would be jealous," Janwari noted. "And she is already beautiful. I wish only to get home to her. I do not begrudge either of you your dancing girls and your beaches."

"They are not dancing girls," Gola corrected. "Merely women in very tiny bathing suits. If they dance, it is simply an added benefit."

"Have you leave coming?" Hooth asked. "I have some."

A surge of storm wind made the shelter vibrate around them.

"Neither as soon nor as long as I would like," said Gola, shaking his head. "Were it up to me, I would—"

"You would what?" Hooth said.

Janwari looked to his subordinate. Gola had stopped and now stared, wide-eyed, at the dwindling flame of the Sterno can. "Gola?" Janwari asked. "What is it?"

Gola shook his head, slowly. He put his hand over his stomach.

Cold wind whipped through the tent, causing the cooking flame to gutter. Janwari cursed and reached for the flap of the shelter. "It has come unsealed again, like before. Help me with this before we are turned to icicles." On his knees in the tent, he maneuvered past Gola.

The chill wind issued from a tiny circular hole in the tent. The hole was at chest level to the kneeling men within.

Janwari's eyes widened in horror. He looked to Gola. Gola took his hand away from his stomach.

Gola's palm was covered in blood.

As the other two men watched, crimson spread across the white winter camouflage of Gola's uniform. He pitched forward into the can of Sterno, spilling the rest of his soup. The entry wound in his back was small, almost unnoticeable.

"Get down!" Janwari screamed.

Hooth was too late. As Janwari flattened himself to the floor of the tent, automatic gunfire pierced the tent from two directions, shredding the fabric, spraying Hooth's blood across Gola's corpse. The thick, warm liquid specked Janwari's face and back and as he waited for the fusillade to subside.

Snow blew through the tattered shelter freely now. Janwari crawled to Hooth's body and put two fingers against the man's neck. There was no sign of life. Gola, too, was dead. Janwari crawled to his pack, ripped it open and removed the heavy radio.

There was a bullet hole in its face.

Janwari cursed his poor fortune. Scrambling to drag on his goggles, he threw his face wrap haphazardly around him and took up his Type 56 assault rifle. Then he was plunging outside into the heavy snow, into the driving wind, as another barrage of automatic gunfire raked the shelter behind him. Gola and Hooth were each ripped from boots to skull by the merciless bullets. If they had not been dead already, they surely could not have survived that.

It took Janwari precious seconds to realize he had lost his bearings in the snowstorm. What could he do? He had no means to call for help, no idea who was attacking and no idea from which direction the invaders had come. He saw only the shelter beginning already to blow away in pieces, and the bloody corpses of the two men whom he had counted as friends.

"Damn you!" Janwari screamed into the wind. "Damn you all!"

Only when he brought up his Type 56, felt the cold bite

of the metal and wood of the rifle on his skin, did he realize he had forgotten his gloves. Screaming, he brought the rifle to his shoulder anyway, bracing himself on one knee as he sought targets in the snow-swept darkness.

Suddenly the night was bright with harsh, green-white luminescence. The flares that drifted down from the sky now were not those of Janwari's unit. These were more powerful, clustered for effect. They were meant to reveal, not to signal. They were meant to cast powerful light on what was now a killing field.

Janwari braced himself. He had not noticed the first salvo of flares, not within the circle of light in his shelter, but that had to be why the enemy gunfire had died down. They had fired flares, done their horrible work while the flares came down, then waited to fire another salvo. That meant the killing would resume any moment—

There! The yellow-orange blossoms of muzzle-flashes were unmistakable in the partial darkness. In the wind and the snow he could not hear the blasts. The icy gales of the glacier swallowed the sounds of war, smothering any hope he had of warning the others. He could see the other shelters dotting the camp area. Several of these had been shot apart. The snow around them was dark red with blood. Janwari's heart leaped into his throat at the sight of it.

Feeling the ache of the cold radiate from the grip of his rifle through his palm and into his wrist, he triggered the Type 56, squeezing one shot at a time from the weapon. He could not see what he was aiming at; he could see only the muzzle-flashes of the enemy guns. He hoped his rounds would have some effect.

To his relief he saw several more blooms of fire from among the bloodied shelters. More of his unit were responding, were returning fire, were fighting for their lives. He took a step forward in snow that was now up to his calves. His legs were so warm he could barely feel them. He did not care.

A hot shell from his Type 56 struck him in the face and snaked down inside his parka. He felt the sting on his neck. In his mind he was counting; soon he would be out of ammunition. When his rifle ran empty he would have only the well-worn Tokarev pistol in the flap holster on his belt. The weapon was buried deep under his parka in attempt to keep it from freezing up completely.

Think, he told himself. What will you do when you run out of ammo? What is your plan?

Janwari forced himself to put one foot in front of the other, plowing his way through the snow like an icebreaker in frozen seas. Slowly, dimly, he became aware of disturbances in the snow around him. Pocks in the snow cover were left as fist-size mounds were churned up all around him.

He was taking fire.

He threw himself into the snow, desperate for something to use as cover, anything behind which to hide. The white expanse felt like razor blades where it touched the exposed skin of his face. He raised his rifle and pulled the trigger back, spraying out the last of his magazine, knowing the gesture was futile.

Through the wind he heard the engine of the Type 88. The tank was moving, however slowly, through the storm. He changed course for it, letting his rifle fall. It was too heavy and he had no ammunition. His Tokarev would have to do.

Numbed fingers found the butt of the pistol. The metal of the weapon, even taken from under his parka, should have made him scream from the cold. He didn't feel it. His left hand felt like deadweight as he struggled to drag back the slide of the pistol.

He stumbled and fell. When he finally managed to struggle to his feet, he was completely disoriented. Where was the tank? He did not know why he hadn't thought of it before. The tank had a radio unit he could use. He just needed to get to it. It was possible the tank commander had already used it, but he couldn't be sure.

The light from the flares above began to die. The flares were descending into the snow, where they were extinguished. In the darkness, he could see more weapons discharges. But now he could not remember in which direction the enemy lay. He pointed his pistol into the screaming winds but didn't fire it. In the darkness everything was shadows.

One of the shadows moved.

He heard the rumble of the tank's bogeys, heard the rattle of its poorly maintained engine. Crawling now, he forced himself to stand, plunging forward, staggering, falling.

He collided with the tank.

The armor was slick with ice. He smelled smoke and something worse, something oily and vile. As he tore flesh from his frozen hands scrambling up the side of the war machine, he realized that black smoke was pouring from a crater in its flank. It had been hit with an antiarmor weapon of some kind. He thought the Type 88 was supposed to have reactive explosive plates…but he wasn't sure. It didn't matter. He found the hatch and threw it open.

The tank commander was dead. Janwari didn't climb inside as much as fall to the floor of the chamber within. The commander was the only body there; the rest of his crew had not made it inside. There was a great deal of blood pooled around the dead man. He had been shot, probably more than once, before reaching the relative safety of the machine.

The enemy could fire another antitank missile at any moment. The tank was an obvious target. Janwari thought about taking control of the turret, trying to swing it around to bring the Type 88's main gun into play. He knew the basic procedure. Every man in the unit did.

Fighting was not as important as alerting the rest of the military to what was taking place here. He reached for the radio, which was intact and, as far as he could tell, powered and ready.

His hand struck the console.

Janwari looked down at his arms. Only then did he realize that he couldn't feel his hands, couldn't feel his fingers. He tried to grip the console and could not. He kept striking it instead, his hand a block of frozen, swollen meat that would not obey his mind's commands. No! He had waited too long in the cold without gloves. He could not manage the dexterity required to switch on the radio.

The hatch above him opened again.

Janwari looked up. The circle of sky above was once more illuminated in the harsh green glow of the enemy's flares. He could see faces above him, could see the uniforms his enemy wore. They looked down at him, dispassionate, almost bored.

They wore the uniform of the Indian army.

Janwari wanted to raise his Tokarev and fire at them, but his pistol was gone. His hand was a frozen, useless claw. He screamed at the soldiers staring at him.

One of the Indian men dropped a grenade inside the tank and threw the hatch closed.

The grenade rolled across the deck near Janwari's feet. He tried to grab it, tried to scoop it up, thought of carrying it back to the hatch, forcing the hatch open and throwing the deadly bomb back toward the Indians.

But of course he could not. His hands wouldn't work.

He had just long enough to wonder how long the fuse on the grenade might last.

He had time to think the words, I don't want to die. Not like this.

And then he was finally warm, for just a moment, before he was nothing ever again.

CHAPTER ONE

Indian-held Kashmir

"Does this place have a name?" Calvin James asked.

David McCarter, the lean, fox-faced Briton and former SAS operator who was leader of Phoenix Force, gulped the last of a can of Coca-Cola, crushed it and tossed the can behind the passenger seat of the MRAP. From the driver's seat, James shot him a disapproving look, which McCarter met with a measured stare. Finally the lanky black man from Chicago's South Side allowed a wide grin to split his features.

"According to the chart," Rafael Encizo said from the rear of the MRAP, "it doesn't. This village isn't even supposed to *be* here." He checked his satellite phone again, which was patched to a feed from thermal imaging satellites overhead. The delay was considerable, but what the stocky Cuban-born guerrilla fighter was observing was essentially a real-time top-down image of the target coordinates. "I'm showing a huge drop-off near one corner of the village, though. Probably part of the natural mountain formation."

"Got it," James said. "I'll try not to drive us over any edges."

Phoenix Force, the covert international counterterrorist team headquartered at the top-secret Stony Man Farm, had split its five members between the Farm's two prototype MRAP vehicles.

The MRAPs had been modified and customized by John "Cowboy" Kissinger, the Farm's Armorer. Each Mine-Resistant Ambush Protected vehicle was a four-wheel-drive armored personnel carrier with a V-shaped chassis designed to deflect explosives. The armor offered protection against 7.62 mm armor-piercing rounds and even rocket-propelled grenades. The body of the MRAP was, in fact, touted as "blast proof," although McCarter had his doubts about that.

Powered by Caterpillar C-7 diesel engines coupled to Allison automatic transmissions, the heavy vehicles boasted 330 horsepower. They had both driver's-side and passenger's-side doors, as well as rear hatches for the troop compartment, while a roof hatch allowed access to the armored machine gun mount on the roof. McCarter's MRAP sported a 7.62 mm M-240 medium machine gun, while the vehicle behind it mounted a MK-19 automatic 40 mm grenade launcher.

In the rear vehicle were the stolid, soft-spoken Canadian giant, Gary Manning—Phoenix Force's burly demolitions expert, once a member of an antiterror squad of the Royal Canadian Mounted Police—and T. J. Hawkins, the youngest member of the team. Hawkins had been both a paratrooper and an Army Ranger before he was recruited to Phoenix Force.

McCarter took his own secure satellite phone from his web gear and reviewed the mission data once more. It contained, among other things, a file that listed a series of coordinates. These were all sites at which the Pakistani and Indian military forces had come into conflict, despite a ceasefire that was supposed to portend peace and prosperity for the region. That had been the general idea, anyway. McCarter had about as much faith in political rot such as that as he did in the supposedly bomb-proof hull of the vehicle in which he sat. Promises were nice, but as an American president had once said, "Trust, but verify."

A pair of thermal imaging satellites over this part of the world had been "borrowed" by Aaron "the Bear" Kurtzman and the Stony Man cybernetics team, re-tasked to monitor the upper Kashmir region and its bordering territory. It was through those satellites that the Farm was tracing the pattern of military skirmishes between the neighboring countries. Yet both nations claimed it was the other country doing the initiating. Neither would admit to having taken part voluntarily.

The President was worried about the stability of the region. Responsibility for shoring that up fell to Phoenix Force.

The assignment was simple enough. Phoenix was being sent in as a spoiler. They were to find an area, or areas, of localized Pakistani-Indian conflict, then neutralize that conflict to the best of their ability. McCarter had no illusions about what that meant. Apparently some UN peacekeeping troops had already been sent in, per a resolution from the United Nations itself, in an attempt to enforce the ceasefire. A good deal of power players in the international community, McCarter gathered, had been involved in getting the Indians and the Pakistanis to stop shooting at each other over Kashmir. The "world community"—a term that had always struck McCarter as ridiculous—had decided to send in several units' worth of joint peacekeeping forces.

The soldiers had never returned. Not alive, anyway.

Whether by the Indians, the Pakistanis, or caught between the cross fire of the two, the UN troops had been ground to pieces in this cold, mountainous battleground. Now Phoenix Force, outnumbered by an order of magnitude, was being sent in to meddle in the same nasty business. There would be no friendlies on the field. The troops of both India and Pakistan could be expected to shoot to kill, to ask any questions after the fact. McCarter was not going to let Phoenix Force be taken out so easily. That's why they were traveling in the armored MRAPs and loaded for bear where their personal weapons were concerned.

Each man of Phoenix Force was equipped with his usual pack and kit, including an earbud transceiver connecting him, through his satellite smartphone, to the other team members. Each man also had a modular Tavor assault rifle with a 40 mm grenade launcher under the barrel. The GTAR-21 rifles were equipped with quick-acquisition reflex sights and 30-round magazines. Their cyclic rates had been adjusted by Cowboy Kissinger, who rated them at roughly 800 rounds per minute.

In addition to the Tavors, each Phoenix Force team member had been issued a Ka-Bar-style full-size, fixed-blade combat knife and a Glock 19 handgun, although McCarter had insisted on a Browning Hi-Power. He and Kissinger had argued about it for quite some time, in fact, as Kissinger rightly argued for standardization among team members. McCarter simply could not abide any other pistol. He fought best and hit most accurately with the Hi-Power. He refused to compromise unless absolutely necessary.

Gary Manning, as the largest member of the team, had also opted to carry a heavy RPG-7 launcher and a supply of HEAT, or High Explosive Anti-Tank, warheads. These would provide them with additional range and better penetration when attacking enemy APCs. Anything more than an armored personnel carrier, such as a tank, would generally be too well armored for the RPG to touch, but they would, as one of McCarter's old SAS chums had been fond of saying, "burn that bridge when they came to it." The warping of the old turn of phrase was deliberate. McCarter always pictured running across a flaming bridge with gunfire at his back.

Certainly his life with Phoenix Force was no less "interesting" than that.

"Interesting" indeed described the situation in which Phoenix found itself. It would be caught between two hostile forces, neither of which would hesitate to shoot the team down and leave their bodies in a mass grave. At the same time, McCarter had spent enough time in the business of war to know that the troops against which Phoenix would be arrayed were just mortal men. Some would be decent human beings. Others would be less so. That was the hell of war, and the reason that no man took up arms unless he had to. McCarter would take no pleasure in taking out Pakistani or Indian troops in putting out this brushfire conflict, but he would do it because it was necessary.

Then, too, there was the fact that the UN peacekeepers had been slaughtered. It would probably be impossible to verify who was most responsible for that, but if McCarter had to guess, his combat instincts told him both sides had probably factored into it. While many people made fun of UN peacekeeping troops and their baby-blue berets and helmets, McCarter had served with joint task forces before. He knew that, just as those on the enemy side of the battle lines, the forces making up a UN team were only as good, or as bad, as the soldiers pulled into service to do the job.

He'd seen the rosters of the dead, thanks to the Farm's excellent intelligence-gathering. Good men and even a few women had died as part of that peacekeeping force. The most likely scenario was that they had been caught in a cross fire between the Indians and Pakistanis. That would have resulted in the kind of carnage documented by the search-and-rescue team the UN had sent in.

Precisely where Phoenix Force was headed.

Where previous soldiers had failed, Phoenix Force would succeed. It was what they did. It was how they lived. But McCarter would not be glad to put down the rabid dogs that would get in their way. It was a necessary service, one that had to occur. But a man took no pleasure in killing rats that carried disease. He simply eliminated the rats because they were dangerous.

This was the most complicated part of Phoenix Force's rules of engagement. Technically an attack on forces fielded by India or Pakistan was an act of war. But both nations had repeatedly claimed they were not tasking armed forces to engage in conflict in the region. Somebody was lying or everybody was lying, but "the forms had to be obeyed," as Brognola was fond of saying. Everybody had to play the game as if they believed the other bloke was telling the truth. The absurdity of it made McCarter want to grind his teeth.

Calvin James brought the MRAP to a halt. Manning, in the rear vehicle, did the same. Through the viewports the men of Phoenix Force surveyed the small village ahead, which lay across a winding, barely visible road of dirt and rocks.

"Comm check," McCarter said. In his ear, the voices of the other teammates sounded as they counted off. There was the slightest of delays when James and Encizo spoke compared to the transmission of their voices in McCarter's earbud. That was the satellite delay. It was very slight, but worth understanding. Timing was everything in combat. No, McCarter corrected himself. Timing and flexibility.

Enough wool-gathering, he told himself. It was time to put things in motion.

"All right, mates, let's roll forward. Make for the center of the village. Gary, follow us and break right when we reach the halfway to center point. Circle around on the right flank and keep that MK-19 warm."

"Roger," Manning said.

"Put it to the floor, Calvin."

"Oh yeah," Calvin James crowed, shifting the MRAP into drive. The powerful vehicle lurched forward, its heavy run-flat tires kicking up plumes of dust that matched those of the following truck.

"Ten o'clock," Encizo said, watching through his port. "I've got two—no, three running from structure to structure. I saw at least one slung rifle, probably an AK."

"Copy," James acknowledged.

"Break left and follow him, Calvin," McCarter directed. "Gary, proceed as we discussed. We'll meet up back at the center of the village."

"Affirmative," Manning said.

The "structures" on either side, as the MRAP threaded its way down a side passage between the buildings, were a curious mixture of stone and "shanty modern" construction. Anything that could be employed to bolster the dwellings against the cold and wind had been done. There were sheets of corrugated metal and even layers of tarps lashed with wire. Windows, if there were any, were shuttered slits carved in the exteriors. No structure was more than a single-story tall. Many buildings, which McCarter guessed to be the older ones, exhibited less haphazard construction from stones and mortar. As they drove deeper into the village, the stone buildings began to predominate, which made sense.

Something struck the hull of the MRAP.

"What was that?" Encizo demanded. "It was the right rear panel. Was that a rock?"

"My money's on gunshot," James stated.

"I think it was a rock," Encizo argued.

More impacts struck the hull, and this time there was no mistaking the hollow metallic chatter of Kalashnikov-pattern assault rifles behind the fusillade. Encizo grinned as James shot him a glance and held out his hand, rubbing his fingers against his thumb.

"Where's my money?" James asked.

"We didn't get to that," Encizo said.

"Technicalities, technicalities," James said. He urged the MRAP faster. "Which way you want to go, David?"

"Circle this stone hut on our right," McCarter directed. "Rafe, get on the phone and have the Farm patch us through to the Pakistanis and the Indians. Give them our coordinates and ask them if they've got forces here."

"We're really going to play this game?" Encizo asked.

"Just think of them as very fast rocks until we hear otherwise," said McCarter.

"Whoa!" James shouted. "Contact front!"

The armored personnel carrier that rolled across their path bore the crossed-swords insignia of the Indian army. A machine gun turret at the top of the APC was wheeling in their direction.

"Back, back, swing left!" McCarter shouted.

"Aye-firmative," Calvin said. He hit the gas and the MRAP hustled back in a flurry of gravel and dirt plumes.

"One, this is Two," Manning said through the transceiver link. "We are taking heavy small-arms fire. Elements of the Pakistani military are coming up on our flank. I saw a tank with a green insignia. Swords under a crescent moon."

"That's Pakistan, all right," said McCarter. He looked back to Encizo. "Got that, Rafe? It's a party and everybody's invited."

"India says they don't have any units at these coordinates," Encizo reported. "No word from the Pakistanis yet."

The MRAP shook as an explosion nearby kicked up dirt and debris.

"That's a grenade launcher," Encizo noted.

"Keep her moving, mate," said McCarter. "Stay mobile. Keep the speed on until we get confirmation."

"David, we are moving in your direction," Manning reported. "Coming up on your four o'clock. They're herding us your way and we need to respond with force."

"That is a no-go. Repeat, a no-go," McCarter declared. "Two, use of force is not yet authorized."

"Understood," said Manning. "But if we don't get word soon we may be overwhelmed. Sooner or later they're going to hit us with something our armor can't take—"

Whatever else Manning said was lost in the noise and vibration of McCarter's MRAP. They were taking machine-gun fire now, and nothing of too small a caliber. McCarter didn't think it was .50-caliber BMG or anything as potent as that, but neither was it something light. The MRAP's armor was up to the task so far, but he did not want to push it.

They had a lot of mission ahead of them before this was over.

"Bring us around," McCarter ordered. "We need to link up with Two and then find a quiet corner."

"Not that way!" Encizo shouted. James was starting to turn into what was a crowd of soldiers in cold-weather gear. They were using the corners of two of the older stone structures for cover.

"Back it up, back it up," McCarter urged.

James did so. But now the passage behind them was

blocked by the Indian APC. Again the MRAP shook under its turret gun.

"Rafe? Any word?"

"Coming in now," said Encizo.

"Well?" James demanded.

"Pakistan states…" Encizo said, listening, two fingers to his earbud.

"You are *killing* me, mate," McCarter said.

"No units at these coordinates," pronounced Encizo. "I repeat, the Pakistanis disclaim any involvement in conflict at these coordinates."

"Rafe," said McCarter, "get up there."

"On it!"

As James maneuvered the MRAP to get it out of the APC's line of fire, McCarter saw the second MRAP rocket between two buildings. More slowly, what the former SAS operator swore was a Type 88 Main Battle Tank pursued Manning's MRAP.

"Gary, on your six!" McCarter said.

The only answer was the thunder of the automatic grenade launcher atop Manning's vehicle. Several of the stone buildings on either side of the second MRAP were damaged as the explosions from the hail of automatically released 40 mm grenades filled the unpaved street with dirt, rocks and shrapnel.

Another metallic clatter, closer this time, banged the roof of McCarter's vehicle like a drum. That was Encizo on the machine gun in their own turret. Shooting the gap between two buildings that were little more than corrugated tin shacks, James managed to cut the angle close enough to get Encizo in a position to fire on the APC. As McCarter and James watched through their viewports, Encizo's machine gun fire blew apart the man in the APC's roof turret.

"Run parallel to them," McCarter said. "Get us past

and then over. We need to cut left and help Gary with that tank."

"I have a pit," Manning said over the transceiver link. "Very large. Looks like a garbage dump."

"That's just what the doctor ordered," said McCarter. "Can you hold position near the edge long enough to lure the tank in? Get them heading at you under steam?"

"Holding," Manning confirmed. He paused. "Incoming fire is heavy. The tank is closing on us. Bringing main turret to bear."

"Go, Calvin," said McCarter. "Go."

"The APC is coming up behind us," Encizo said through the link. "I'm trying to brush them off but their nose armor is too heavy." The MRAP shook as Encizo milked a steady stream of rounds from the machine gun up top.

"No, that's good," said McCarter. "Rafe, let them come. Keep up a good show, but don't stop them following. Gary, get ready. When we hit your tank we're going to need you to push forward, circle around and give the APC a shove. And get ready with that automatic grenade launcher again."

"Ready," Manning said.

"Here we come," said McCarter.

"Troops, contact left, contact right!" Encizo announced.

Soldiers were coming up on either side as McCarter's MRAP closed on Manning's with the tank between them. The tank was still rolling, perilously close to the cliff edge that Encizo had noted on the way toward the village. Its momentum was what McCarter was counting on.

Encizo traversed left, then right. His machine gun mowed down first one rank of troops, then another, tearing them apart with brutal efficiency. McCarter winced as he watched the men go down. The human body was never meant to withstand that kind of antipersonnel onslaught.

"Brace yourselves," said James.

"Gary! Now!" McCarter shouted.

The nose of McCarter's MRAP hit the rear of the moving tank, shoving it to the side. The Type 88 was much heavier than the MRAP, but the truck was no slouch in the mass department. It had enough power, coupled with the tank's motion, to shove the right set of tracks over the edge of the cliff.

The tank's weight and momentum did the rest.

The Type 88 went over the cliff.

"Calvin, punch it!" Manning said through the link.

James put his foot down. The MRAP again lurched forward, and the nose of the enemy APC shot past it with Manning's MRAP shoving it forward. The big Canadian had finished his loop and come up behind the APC to repeat the maneuver. Both enemy vehicles were now tumbling into the pit down the cliff face.

"T.J., fire!" McCarter ordered.

Hawkins unleashed a full-automatic barrage with the MK-19, covering the pit with 40 mm grenades. The explosions that resulted turned the garbage dump into a roiling, fiery lake. The smell, even through the protection of the armored vehicles, was like nothing McCarter had experienced.

And just like that, it was over. Nothing moved in the village. The men of Phoenix Force listened, but the only sound was the crackle of the flames in the hell-pit they had created.

"Check your flanks, mates," said McCarter. "We'll need to patrol on foot with the MRAPs as cover. If there's anything to be found in this village, we have to find it. And that means photographs. Whatever we can send to the Farm for analysis."

"Roger," came Manning's voice.

"Got it," said Hawkins.

Encizo climbed down into the cabin of the truck. "Loud and clear," he said.

James turned to McCarter. "That," he said, "is an awful stink."

"Get used to it, boys," McCarter warned, "because my bet is that it's going to get worse before we're done here."

CHAPTER TWO

Stony Man Farm, Virginia

Aaron "the Bear" Kurtzman sat huddled with a "tactical battle mug" of his industrial-strength coffee. The milled aluminum mug, which Barbara Price had called a "flagon," had been a gift from a special operations team with whom the Farm had partnered some time back. The funny thing about the mug was that it bore a set of milled rails, identical to those on an M-4 carbine. The men of Able Team and Phoenix Force had, off and on, teased the cybernetics genius about the best optics to mount on his coffee cup.

Kurtzman, for his part, was unruffled by their good-natured ribbing. He had been the head of the cybernetics team at the Farm since the Special Operations Group had first set up shop in the mountains of Virginia. He had not, however, always been in a wheelchair. That was the result of an attack on the Farm, one that had taken a heavy toll on the men and women of the SOG. Kurtzman, for his part, had simply gone on doing his job. He did not discuss his disability and had never once complained about it to anyone, as far as Barbara Price knew.

Price, for her part, looked through her briefing folder. The Farm's honey-blonde, model-beautiful mission controller checked the array of switches set within the briefing room's conference table. The flat-screen monitor at the far end of the room was already up and running. A scrambled satellite link between Washington and the Farm showed Hal Brognola's desk in his office on the Potomac in Wonderland. The big Fed was not himself at the desk, but he would be. He had excused himself briefly to speak with some government functionary or other in the hallway. When he was done he would secure the door to his office—on which was printed, simply, Hal Brognola: Justice—and rejoin them for the briefing.

On a second monitor, this one opposite one side of the conference table, the men of Phoenix Force were assembling in front of their own portable satellite uplink. Wherever they were, it looked cold through the rear viewport of the MRAP crew compartment. David McCarter, leader of Phoenix Force, was peering into the uplink camera, looking annoyed. Calvin James and T. J. Hawkins sat to either side of him.

Encizo and Manning were not visible on screen. They were, no doubt, guarding Phoenix Force's position in hostile territory, probably from the turrets of the armored vehicles. Price did not like to think of the five-man team operating largely without support across so much open ground, but that was the job that Phoenix Force did. She loved every one of the men on that team like older brothers.

A disturbance in the corridor outside the briefing room indicated that Able Team was on its way. It was Hermann "Gadgets" Schwarz who entered first. As was often the case, he was locked in some sort of deeply philosophical argument with Rosario Blancanales, his teammate. Blancanales was known as "Pol," short for "the Politician." The soft-spoken, gray-haired Hispanic was, in fact, a former Black Beret, not to mention an expert in the psychology of violence and the application of role camouflage. Schwarz was, as his nickname "Gadgets" implied, Able Team's electronics expert. His work had contributed to quite a bit of the equipment fielded by both Able and Phoenix, including the earbud transceivers that kept the teammates in constant voice contact while on missions.

Behind Blancanales and Schwarz, his huge fist wrapped around a foam cup of black coffee, was Carl "Ironman" Lyons, leader of Able Team. The big, former LAPD officer dwarfed his teammates simply through bulk. He was powerfully built and moved with all the subtlety of a bulldozer.

"I'm telling you," Schwarz said to Blancanales, "every adventure movie where the hero gets caught and then has to fight his way out is automatically cliché. A bad guy catches a good guy, what's he going to do? He's going to kill him or he's going to torture him, but either way our hero isn't going to get free."

"But real people have escaped terrorist captors and home invaders in real life," Blancanales countered. "People who didn't even have any training. In your movie the hero is always a tough guy or someone who's ex-military. Or both."

"Exactly my point," Schwarz said.

"Gadgets, do you realize you say, 'Exactly my point,' every time you start to lose an argument?"

"Exactly my point," Schwarz repeated.

"So a trained, albeit fictional military or law-enforcement hero can't do what a real-life civilian can do."

"Exactly my—"

"Here," Blancanales said. From his pocket he took a red-dot sight. "I can't get this to illuminate. I changed the battery and everything. I think it's broken. Why don't you uphold that science-whiz reputation you have and see if you can't fix it?"

"Isn't this Cowboy's department?"

"Cowboy and the armory are backed up," Blancanales said. "I know you can help."

"Did this come off Aaron's coffee cup?" Schwarz said, grinning.

"Don't start," Kurtzman grumbled. "My revenge will be swift and terrible."

"Why's the hero getting caught in the first place?" Lyons put in. That surprised Price, who usually thought of him as the straight man for Schwarz's banter. Obviously, Lyons and Blancanales were a bit taken aback, as well; they both turned and eyed Lyons curiously before Schwarz managed a response.

"Well, we've all been…" Schwarz looked sheepish.

"What?" Lyons demanded. "Caught by the enemy?"

"You've got to admit that the sheer number of times that—" Blancanales began.

"If we're all ready to start?" interrupted Hal Brognola.

The assembled Stony Man operatives turned to regard the larger-than-life satellite image of Hal Brognola. The head of the Sensitive Operations Group was chewing an unlighted cigar and looked as harried as he always did.

Not for the first time or the hundredth time, Price worried about the amount of stress the man was under. A lot of world power plays fell under Brognola's watch. Still more of those turned into fires that the SOG was tasked to put out.

Such as the one they were about to talk about.

"You are go, Hal," said Price. "Phoenix is live and connected."

"Ready and waiting," McCarter acknowledged. "We can't sit here for too much longer, though. Our hind ends are hanging in the wind."

"Understood," Brognola noted. He cleared his throat. "To put it bluntly, a series of military skirmishes between what seems to be Pakistani and Indian forces are driving our intelligence assets batty. Neither government admits to deploying military assets in the region."

"And that region is?" Lyons asked.

"In an around the disputed territory of Kashmir," Brognola explained. "As you know, due to a rather complicated series of political maneuvers more than half a century ago, the two nations have, arguably, been in a state of low-grade war ever since. They simply do not like each other. Over the years the conflict has flared up and then died down. It's gone on like that, hot and cold, for decades. Recently, a ceasefire was brokered by the Man and several high-profile diplomats with plenty of political capital in the United Nations. It was a big deal."

"I remember seeing that on the news," Schwarz said.

"What makes any lessening of tensions between Pakistan and India so important," Brognola continued, "is the fact that the two nations are among the eight nations of the world who have, or who are believed to have, viable nuclear weapons. The United States, Russia, the United Kingdom, France and China you know. Israel has long been suspected by the rest of the world to possess defensive nukes of its own, and while they won't admit it, we wouldn't be SOG if we didn't know that, yes, they do. North Korea, for all its problems, has been a nuclear power since 2006."

"If their tests aren't hoaxes," McCarter said. "This is a nation that builds ghost cities on its borders to make the South believe it's not mired in poverty."

"Nonetheless," Brognola said, "the relatively short list underscores just how dangerous it is to have India and Pakistan rattling sabers at each other. The conflict destabilizes the entire region, but if it goes too far…"

"One of the two is going to start thinking they don't want to wait any longer to see what their nukes can do," Lyons finished.

"India tested their Pokhran-1, code-named 'Smiling Buddha,' back in '74," Price said. "Pakistan went nuclear later, but they're not new to the game. They conducted a string of underground nuclear tests in '98, as retaliation for India's Pokhran-2, or Operation Shakti. The message on the part of both nations was clear—we've got the means to wipe you out. Either because of that threat or despite it, the two have skirmished with each other but never gone all the way. The President is concerned that if things keep going as they are, all-out war is assured…and we think we know why."

"Neither India nor Pakistan will take credit for voluntarily committing forces to the border conflict," Brognola said. "Both countries claim their own patrols have come under unprovoked attack. As you can imagine, any one of these attacks can be construed as an act of war. Our thermal imaging has mapped out a series of border conflicts between what we at first believed were elements of the Pakistani and Indian armies. We were right…and we were wrong."

"Okay, I'm officially confused," Blancanales protested.

"During the mop-up of a clash with what we took to be both Indian and Pakistani uniformed soldiers," Brognola explained, "Phoenix Force took digital photographs of as many of the dead soldiers as they could. Those photographs have been analyzed at the Farm."

"We've run the identities of the soldiers through our databases," Kurtzman put in. "Many of them have no file on record. The ones that do, however, have something very specific in common." He tapped a few buttons on the keyboard built into the conference table. A pair of images came up on the wall screen next to Brognola's image. The two men depicted were both dark of skin and wearing military uniforms.

"The heavyset man is Ibrahim Jamali of Pakistan. His thinner, hawk-nosed counterpart is India's Siraj Gera. Both men were or are generals in their respective armies. But there's more."

Kurtzman took the cue and tapped several more keys. Now a grid of images appeared. The faces were much alike and too small to be particularly memorable, but the text below each image indicated that the file photo belonged to a man found dead by Phoenix Force.

"The men you see here were all found dead at the scene of a battle in the Kashmir area. During the conflict, both sides targeted Phoenix Force. What all of the men listed here have in common is that they're dead."

"Naturally," said Lyons.

"No, not after the battle," Kurtzman said. "They were *already* dead."

"Those that weren't officially listed as dead are criminals or mercenaries," Brognola clarified. "A few have been declared deserters. None are officially traceable to their governments."

"Shadow companies," Lyons concluded. "Private armies."

"That's right," Brognola said. "We believe that Pakistan and India have lost control of Generals Jamali and Gera, and that both men have crafted military forces loyal to them. Most likely they've simply misappropriated the units over which they initially held control, and then bolstered those forces with expatriates and other mercenaries. In other words, gentlemen, they've gone rogue."

"To what end?" Schwarz asked. "What are they trying to accomplish?"

"That's the question of the day, mate," McCarter said through the satellite link. "While we were mopping up this village we found something that makes the rest of it seem fairly tame."

Brognola nodded. Kurtzman tapped another button and this time the image of a balding man in a suit and tie appeared on the screen.

"This is, or was, one Arthur Hughbright. He was fifty-one years old. Until two years ago he had never held a passport. He has no criminal record. He was married, with one child, a freshman at William and Mary. He has consistently filed his income taxes and, according to official government records, he grossed nearly two hundred thousand dollars last year."

"Not exactly the dossier of an international man of adventure," said Lyons.

"No," said Brognola. "What Hughbright did do, however, was write a book that, in trade circles, is considered a bestseller. Specifically, he wrote an industry text on innovative geo-location methods for deep-mining techniques. When he died, he was working for a company called Earth-Gard, which is based right here in the United States."

Kurtzman looked at McCarter. "Show them," he suggested.

McCarter nodded and, next to him, Calvin James held up a suitcase. Inside the suitcase was an array of electronic equipment, none of which was recognizable to Barbara Price.

"What is that gear?" Schwarz asked, looking on with interest. "I don't recognize it."

"That's the problem," Kurtzman said. "We're not entirely sure. Until we can courier it back here and take it apart, we're going to have to consider it an unknown."

"The suitcase was found with Hughbright," McCarter added.

"This square was in Kashmir?" Lyons asked.

"He was," Brognola confirmed. "He was also killed there, most likely by accident, and almost certainly in the cross fire created when the military contingents controlled by Gera and Jamali tried to catch Phoenix Force between them."

"He looks like he caught shrapnel from an exploding piece of masonry," said McCarter. "It wasn't pretty."

Kurtzman nodded. "We had to use a computer algorithm to reconstruct his dental work and then compare it to records of—"

"I don't think we need to go into the details," said Brognola, interrupting. "Let's stipulate that the results were quite graphic. But this begs the question, what is an American mining expert doing in disputed territory on the borders of India and Pakistan? What is his connection to Gera and Jamali? And what is the equipment he was carrying with him?"

"I'm going to go out on a limb here," Lyons began, "and guess that it had something to do with 'innovative geolocation methods for deep-mining techniques.'"

That provoked a snicker from Schwarz.

Price shot the electronics expert a withering glare. "Yes," she said. "The thought had occurred to us, as well."

"EarthGard specializes in beryllium mining," Kurtzman said. "You've heard of it but, if you were like me this morning, you've never bothered to learn what it's for."

"It's a rare metal," Schwarz said. "It has applications in the aerospace and defense industries, among others. Highly lucrative."

"Yes," Brognola agreed. "If EarthGard is somehow involved in finding and mining beryllium in the Kashmir region, it would explain why a piece of ground that has been the subject of a relatively cold war for the past decades is now a hotly contested proxy battlefield."

"Meaning it was worth fighting about before," Lyons said, "but now that there's money in it, the area is finally worth *having*."

"Precisely," Brognola said. "Both Gera and Jamali have siphoned men and equipment from the regular armies of their respective countries. If we are interpreting the pattern of battles and the protests by both nations accurately, both men are using their rogue military elements to attack legitimate patrols fielded by India and Pakistan. This is bringing both countries to the brink of war. Initially, the Man thought—and I agreed, when we sent Phoenix to Kashmir in an attempt to put a stop to the border flare-ups—that war between India and Pakistan was the whole point. But given the discovery of Hughbright's body, there is another theory in play."

"Gera and Jamali are trying to carve out their own little fiefdoms," McCarter proposed. "They're not hitting elements of the enemy military to cause a war. They're hitting them to get them out of the way. Both men see the other side as an obstacle to control of the region. And they know their governments aren't really in a position to mount an effective resistance. Not with their governments bickering and the region so geographically isolated. So they're just going to make Kashmir too costly to hold while they take it from within. But each would-be warlord is in the other's way."

"Yes," Brognola confirmed. "That seems likely. It accounts for what would otherwise be simply suicidal behavior. And it's all we have to go on until we learn more about the EarthGard angle."

"Here it comes," Schwarz said quietly.

"Shaddap," Lyons muttered to him.

"Able Team is going to investigate EarthGard's extensive network of mining sites and business offices here in the United States," Price stated. "We've prepared a list of these, ranked in terms of size and relevance."

"The cyber team has also worked up a full history on EarthGard as a business," Kurtzman said. "We haven't found anything dirty so far, but we've only peeled back a couple of layers. I've been working Akira and Carmen all night to see what we can learn, but it is slow going. EarthGard has a lot of very state-of-the-art security at the virtual level...which probably tells us something right there." Akira Tokaido and Carmen Delahunt were, together with Huntington "Hunt" Wethers, the rest of the Stony Man cybernetics personnel. "We'll keep on it," Kurtzman promised, "and update the teams in the field as we learn anything of value."

"What's the outlook for local assistance?" Lyons asked. "How many toes are we going to be standing on?"

"Conceivably quite a few," Price admitted. "Jack Grimaldi is standing by with an Osprey troop transport. He'll take you where you need, quickly and with a minimum of bureaucracy, so you can check your target list and then move on to the next without any unnecessary entanglements."

"Hit and git, as they say," Blancanales quipped.

"Exactly my—" Schwarz started to say again, gesturing with the red-dot sight. A look from Lyons stopped him.

"We've generated a priority target list for Phoenix Force," Price continued. "All of them are locations on the India and Pakistan borders that we calculate will be attractive to Gera and Jamali, either strategically or symbolically."

"What's our goal?" McCarter asked.

"You're to chip away at the enemy until the threat posed by Gera and Jamali has been eliminated," Brognola answered. "As long as those two are stirring up trouble in their bid to control the region, the threat of full-scale, even nuclear, war between Pakistan and India remains real. It's our hope that you can neutralize the two generals. If you can render their forces incapable of mounting further campaigns against one another or the border, then we can step in with UN support and renegotiate the ceasefire."

"Everybody join hands," Lyons scoffed, "and sing 'We Are the World.'"

"Something like that," Brognola said, frowning. "Look, I realize we're asking a lot of both teams. Phoenix has before it a particularly broad mission, and we have no idea just how deep the EarthGard connection may go."

"Something about that name bothers me," Lyons said. "It sounds like that 'green' hippie group we took down a while back."

"There is evidence that EarthGard has ties to some radical environmentalist concerns," Kurtzman said, "at least so far as their charitable and political giving goes. But nothing about the company we've learned to this point indicates anything along the lines of eco-terrorism or anything like that."

"Still," Lyons conceded cautiously, "I don't like it. But I guess I don't have to. We're on it, Hal."

"And we're moving out," McCarter said. "Priority target list received."

"Good hunting, David," said Price.

"We'll do our best," said the Phoenix Force leader. He nodded to James and, a moment later, the satellite image cut to static and then a blue override screen.

"Phoenix will be more or less on its own," Brognola told those in the conference room, "beyond the reach of either India or Pakistan until they get closer to resolving the military threat in Kashmir.

"Here in Washington, I'll be running interference for

you and coordinating through Barb to make sure the locals know you have the highest federal authority. But that's no guarantee you won't meet with at least some resistance from 'friendly' authorities."

"No worries, Hal," Blancanales said. "We've played the game before. We'll try not to break too much that you might have to pay for."

"It isn't you I worry about, Pol," Brognola said. He cast a meaningful glance in Lyons's direction. The big ex-cop chose that moment to study an imaginary spot on the ceiling, whistling tunelessly to himself.

"We'll keep you informed, Hal," Price said.

"Good," Brognola said. "Good luck, Able. Keep an eye on them, Barb." He cut the connection.

"Let's move, boys," Lyons said, standing. "We've wasted enough time on our behinds."

"Jack will be waiting for you at the landing pad area," Price directed. "Cowboy has prepared a full complement of gear from the armory."

"That's what I like to hear," Lyons returned. He strode out of the room with Blancanales close behind. Price moved to follow, but before she did she stopped and watched Schwarz. The electronics expert looked left, looked right and then leaned over the table. He then clipped the red-dot sight to Kurtzman's coffee mug.

"I'd check the windage and elevation on that before you fire it," Schwarz said, grinning. He left quickly.

As she walked down the hall after the chuckling Schwarz, Price thought she heard Kurtzman talking to himself in the conference room.

"Swift and terrible," Kurtzman muttered to himself. "Swift and terrible."

CHAPTER THREE

Twin Forks, Utah

The black GMC Suburban waiting at the tiny airfield was a rental from a national chain that Carl Lyons recognized. He assumed that a local courier, coordinating through the Farm, had arranged for the vehicle to be left for them. In both hands he carried heavy black duffel bags, as did Schwarz and Blancanales. Each was full of weapons and ammunition, including loaded magazines, grenades and other explosives. When Lyons reached the truck he set the bags down in the gravel and began searching the nearest wheel well.

The magnetic key box was in the second well he tried. He slipped the key out of the box and put the magnetic holder back where he had found it. An electronic fob was included. He used it to unlock the truck.

"The exciting life of a covert counterterrorist," Schwarz said as he walked up and dropped his bags.

"Be sure to drop the one with the C4 charges in it extra hard, Gadgets," Lyons said.

"Good thing the detonators are in the other bag," the electronic genius said without missing a beat.

"Thrill as they carry heavy things from their plane to their car!" Blancanales intoned, imitating a movie announcer.

The "plane" in this case was a Bell Boeing V-22 Osprey,

on loan from Special Forces. The VTOL troop carrier was armed with a 7.62 mm GAU-17 minigun. The retractable cannon was belly-mounted and featured a video-equipped remote-control slaved to a display on Jack Grimaldi's helmet, much like the nose-cannon setup used by Apache gunship crews. The multibarrel cannon was more or less stock, as Cowboy Kissinger referred to it, but the Stony Man armorer had worked with Schwarz to adapt the video and camera equipment so that Grimaldi could fire the minigun while piloting the Osprey.

The massive twin-rotor craft was capable of transporting far more than just the three men of Able Team and their gear, but portions of the interior cargo space had been converted to include auxiliary fuel tanks. These and the weight of the heavy multibarrel cannon in the ship's belly reduced the aircraft's cargo capacity considerably. It was still more than sufficient, though, to get Able Team and their weapons where the three men needed to go…and it had the range to move them around the country with speed and maneuverability.

"Everybody get your gear in order," Lyons said, although the instructions were unnecessary. The three men of Able Team had executed enough missions together that they could work together without speaking, practically reading each other's minds. Lyons put two fingers to the transceiver in his ear. "Comm check. Check one, check two."

"I read you," Grimaldi said in the Osprey. "Check-ins will be by the book, gentlemen. Your transceivers should give you enough range that I can live vicariously through your adventures while I sit here warming the pilot's seat."

"Roger that, Jack," Lyons said. "Pol? Gadgets?"

"Loud and clear," Blancanales said. "Of course, you're also standing next to me."

"Two by four," Schwarz said.

"Don't you mean five by five?"

"A two by four is what it would take to knock you down," Schwarz said.

Lyons looked at him. "Gadgets," he said, "I never know what the hell you're talking about."

"Story of my life," Schwarz answered.

"Get in the truck, Gadgets," Lyons said.

For this mission, Able Team was operating under full cover of their Justice Department credentials. They wore civilian clothes—Lyons, his familiar bomber jacket and jeans, Schwarz, a T-shirt and cargo pants with a windbreaker, and Blancanales, khaki slacks with a button-down shirt and a blazer. Their weapons were their usual individual kit. Each of them had a spring-assist folding combat dagger. Blancanales carried a Beretta 92-F and an M-4 carbine, while Schwarz wore a shoulder holster that carried his Beretta 93R machine pistol. Lyons, for his part, carried his trusty Colt Python in .357 Magnum. His massive Daewoo USAS-12, as well as a healthy supply of 20-round drum magazines, was one of the items weighing down his duffel bags.

Lyons drove the GMC from the airfield with Schwarz navigating. The GPS coordinates were fed to all three team members' satellite smartphones. Gadgets simply called up a local map interface and gave the turns to Lyons. A commercial GPS unit would be a liability; the coordinates stored in such a unit could conceivably be an intelligence problem after the fact. The smartphones, by contrast, were encrypted.

They had driven for some distance, making their way to the first of the prioritized EarthGard properties, when Lyons said, simply, "Utah."

Looking out his window before turning back to his smartphone, Schwarz said, "Yep. Utah."

"Are you playing Furious Birds or some crap?" Lyons said, glancing at Schwarz's phone.

Schwarz looked up. "These phones can run more than one application simultaneously—"

"You *are* playing," Lyons said. "What's it called?"

"Maniacal Blue Jays? Aggressive Waterfowl?" Blancanales queried from the backseat. "Gadgets, did you get past the brick level yet?"

"Don't help, Pol," Lyons said.

"Turn left, Ironman," Schwarz said. An enormous road sign they were passing read EarthGard Beryllium, LLC, Next Left. Lyons shot Schwarz a look but said nothing. He spun the wheel over.

The team made its way up a long, winding dirt road. The curve of the road suggested a very large circle, which of course it was; the mine was at the center, and no doubt this was the primary means through which earth-moving equipment and other heavy industrial machinery was moved to and from the mine. The headquarters building was a large affair—larger, Carl Lyons thought, than it probably needed to be for an operation as relatively simple as taking ore out of the ground. He had been noticing the sentries as they'd traversed the winding dirt drive. When he saw the guards grouped outside the building's entrance, he decided it was too much to be coincidence.

"Doesn't it look like they have an inordinate amount of security for a mining operation in Utah?" Blancanales asked.

"I was just thinking that," Lyons said. "Pol, grab one of the smaller duffels and tuck your M-4 and my shotgun in there. Make sure we've got plenty of grens and extra mags. Gadgets—"

"You're going to make me carry it, aren't you?"

"Yes," said Lyons. "Yes, I am."

A sign at the entrance to the main building parking area proclaimed EarthGard a "carbon neutral enterprise." Lyons pulled the big Suburban into a parking slot marked Visitors: Reserved For Hybrid/Eco-Friendly Vehicles. As he climbed out of the GMC, a trio of security guards in black tactical gear was already converging on him. Blancanales came around to stand next to Lyons, while Schwarz, with the duffel bag, took up a position on the other side of the truck.

"Awfully militarized for local security," Blancanales whispered.

"Yeah," said Lyons. "That too."

The three guards were large, bearded men with the experienced, self-assured look of independent contractors. Lyons did not get an "amateur security guard" or "wannabe cop" vibe from them at all; what he perceived was the type of lethal potential that men of violence, men experienced in warfare, could sometimes sense in each other. Their uniforms also put Lyons's sixth sense for combat on alert. They were wearing a commercial brand of "tactical" clothing—including distinctive pants with slash rear pockets and cargo pouches—that were extremely popular with contractors in the sandbox abroad. The front man of the trio wore expensive, mirrored, wraparound sunglasses that cost a week's pay for most people. The hook-and-loop nametag on his uniform shirt read Kirkpatrick.

Each man held an M-4 carbine worn on a single-point sling.

The two men behind Kirkpatrick were Conyers and Gomez. And if those were their real names, Lyons would eat his shoulder holster. While Kirkpatrick and Conyers looked the parts their names implied, Gomez was clearly

Asian, not Hispanic. He was very big for an Asian man, easily massing as much as his partners did.

"These are back-breakers," Schwarz whispered from the other side of the Suburban. "No way is the operation here legit." The electronics expert spoke quietly enough that his partners could hear him through their earpieces, but the security team would not be able to listen in.

"Can I help you gentlemen?" Kirkpatrick asked.

"Justice Department," Lyons said, flashing the credentials Brognola had issued to the team. "We're investigating an international commerce issue."

Kirkpatrick exchanged glances with Conyers. Gomez, for his part, simply stared at Lyons as if he could bore a hole through the big ex-cop with nothing but a hostile look.

"I'm going to need to see a warrant," Kirkpatrick said.

"This identification is all the warrant I need," said Lyons. He wasn't really the authoritarian type; he respected the Constitution as much as the next guy. But something was off about these characters and he wasn't going to play along. The fastest way to get them to cut to the chase was just to push their buttons until they revealed what they were after.

"No entry to unauthorized personnel," Kirkpatrick said At the words "no entry," Gomez and Conyers began to fan out in an attempt to flank Able Team.

I don't like where this is going, thought Lyons, but I can't say I'm surprised.

"Maybe you don't understand, Slick," Lyons said. "We're with the Justice Department. To go higher than us you have to have a word with the President. Something's dirty here in Denmark and we're going to find it. Step aside."

Kirkpatrick's stance changed. Lyons saw it; Kirkpatrick saw that Lyons saw it. Both men knew the hammer was about to fall. The "security guard" was getting ready to bring up his M-4. Lyons couldn't see the selector switch on the weapon, but he had to bet that all three men had their safeties off and rounds in the chambers.

"No entry," Kirkpatrick said, his teeth clenched, "to unauthorized personnel." He moved to take a diagonal step back, which was his attempt to get off the attacking line and bring his weapon into play. Lyons was already moving. As Kirkpatrick tried to raise his M-4, Lyons's Python was in his fist. The snout of the big pistol came up under Kirkpatrick's chin, below his line of vision. It was an old trick, but a good one. Kirkpatrick was already visualizing Lyons's death, already taking up the slack in the M-4's trigger, his expression one of triumph. That changed the moment the barrel of the Python touched the flesh under his jaw.

"Here's my authorization." Lyons pulled the trigger.

The top of Kirkpatrick's head exploded. Lyons pushed the corpse away, watching it fall back as he backpedaled to the only cover available, which was the Suburban. Schwarz and Blancanales had already opened up on the other two gunmen, driving them back toward the double doors of the mining office entrance.

There was a heartbeat's lull in the firefight as the two security guards dove inside the office. Schwarz ripped open the duffel bag. "Carl!" he called.

Lyons held out a hand. Schwarz tossed him the heavy USAS-12 automatic shotgun. He threw Blancanales's M-4 to him and then hooked his support hand through the trigger guard of his 93-R machine pistol, using the fold-down foregrip to brace the weapon.

Schwarz and Blancanales advanced on the double doors, covering each other as they left the shelter of the Suburban. Blancanales reached out and tried the door handle, pulling his hand back quickly lest he lose it to a spray of gunfire from the other side. Nothing happened. The door was solidly locked. The walls flexed slightly, however.

"Talk about cheap construction," Blancanales said.

"It's a prefab trailer," Schwarz said. "Big and modular, probably multiple trailer units interconnected. Flimsy. But the doors are held on good."

"Let's do this," Lyons said. He leveled the USAS-12 at the lower set of hinges on the left side and pulled the trigger. The hinge disintegrated under the barrage of 00 Buck. It took less time to blow the second one; Lyons simply raised the barrel and rode out the recoil. He stepped aside as the door fell off.

Bullets flew from inside. The guards were shooting back, the sounds of their M-4 carbines unmistakable. It was said, and Lyons knew it to be true, that the Kalashnikov had a distinctive metallic noise. This was due in part to all the empty space under its receiver cover, which turned the AK into a metal drum when rounds were cycled through it. But the 3 AR platform and its variants also had a distinctive sound, with which Lyons and the other members of Able Team had become very familiar. If you'd heard it enough you could never forget it.

Blancanales's M-4 had been modified and tuned by Kissinger, as had all their weapons. Blancanales squeezed several long, full-auto bursts. Among the modifications Kissinger regularly preformed was to replace the 3-round-burst mode with sustained full-automatic. The men of Able Team were more than capable of the trigger-control required to avoid wasting ammunition.

"I'd say we've got ample verification of hostile contact," Schwarz noted.

"Affirmative," Lyons said. Noting Blancanales had the

most forward position of the team, he asked, "What's it look like in there, Pol?"

Blancanales waited for a moment, timing the bursts of fire from inside the mining office. When he judged he could risk it, he moved his head just enough to expose his left eye, then whipped his skull back out of the line of fire.

"Our two friends have backup," Blancanales related. "I count two more, all armed. No civilians. No noncombatants anywhere in range."

"Good," Lyons said. "Gadgets, pull two grenades. No, three."

"Three?" Schwarz queried.

"Three," Lyons confirmed.

"Time to blow everybody up," Schwarz said. He reached into the duffel bag, snaked his index finger through the pins of three grenades and popped all three bombs at once. Then he tossed them in quick succession through the doorway.

"Which did you—?"

"Willie Pete," Schwarz said quietly.

"And Hell followed with them," Blancanales whispered.

The white-phosphorous grenades ignited. The screams from within the mining office were beyond horrible. Each grenade carried 15 ounces of white phosphorous and had a burst radius of 34 meters on open ground. Within the corridor of the mining office, detonated simultaneously as a trio, the blasts would create a fiery tunnel of molten death that bored through any human being unfortunate enough to be in the way. The cloud of smoke created was immediate and overpowering.

"Let's move," Lyons said. "Secondary entrance to the west."

"Roger that," Schwarz said.

"Affirmative," Blancanales said.

Under cover of the pall of smoke drifting from the flaming charnel house that was now the main entrance, Able Team took up positions around the west entrance. This door, too, was secured, but the thunderous hammer blows of Lyons's automatic 12-gauge made short work of the barrier. When the three men of Able Team finally entered the building, fire alarms were sounding through the halls. Through the distant screams, Able Team could also hear fire extinguishers being deployed. Schwarz hoped for his enemies' sake that those extinguishers were chemical models and not simply tanks of water. Water would only scatter the hungry white phosphorous, which would burn until it no longer had oxygen to feed it.

The corridor in which Able stood was comprised of offices, each with a name on a faux brass nameplate on the door. There was no reason not to check them. Lyons signaled to his partners, pointing to the next set of doors. The team worked its way up the hall, kicking in the doors on either side as they went, with Blancanales and Schwarz working the entries and Lyons stationed in the corridor for backup.

Something creaked in the ceiling above. "I think we're doing some serious damage to this place," Blancanales said. "It sounds like the roof is coming apart."

"If the fire spreads to the crawl space above the drop ceiling," Schwarz noted, "it will move very rapidly. We need to be careful we don't get cut off."

"I'll shoot us an exit, if it comes to that," Lyons said. "I have slugs if we need them. They'll carve through the pasteboard this place seems to be made of."

There was still plenty of ammo left in Lyons's 20-round drum. He scarcely felt the weight of the heavy USAS-12. The weapon was comforting in his big fists. He liked knowing that he had the option of laying down a cloud of 00 Buck that would shred almost any resistance. Each 12-gauge double-aught shell carried nine pellets, each roughly comparable to a 9mm bullet. To be on the receiving end of most of a drum of those shells was world-changing for just about anyone and anything.

The ceiling creaked again. "That's not sounding good," Blancanales warned.

"Keep moving," Lyons directed. "We're up against the clock."

The sweep of the corridor turned up nothing. It was time to take the party closer to the main entrance, where more EarthGard personnel appeared to be active in trying to quell the chemical flames. The prefab office was arranged like a wagon wheel, with a central hub and multiple spokes. They were reaching the hub, opposite the spoke that bore the Willy Pete conflagration, when something felt wrong.

"Gadgets," Lyons said. "Pol. Look." He pointed. The security camera set in the wall had been turning, but now it was pointed directly at them. Lyons realized what had been nibbling at the edges of his awareness. There were automatic security cameras in every corridor, and these had been moving mindlessly back and forth when they'd first entered the building. But the cameras had been stopping and tracking them, quietly, as they'd made their way through the structure. And if they were being tracked, that meant the enemy wasn't nearly as confused and ineffective as Able Team had been led to believe. It meant the enemy—

Lyons looked up.

"Hit the walls!" he shouted. He shoved Schwarz, who was within arm's reach, against the far wall of the corridor, flattening himself against the fiberboard of the hallway.

Tiles from the drop ceiling rained down, followed by gunfire. The security guards, obviously coordinating with someone operating the cameras from a control area within the mining office, had crawled along above the drop ceiling until they were in position to take out Able Team.

Gunfire chewed up the cheaply carpeted floor. There were three different muzzle-flashes up there. The shooters were braced on the boards that held the ceiling tiles in place. Lyons dropped to one knee, planted the butt-stock of the USAS-12 on the floor and held back the trigger of the mighty shotgun as he walked the barrel from left to right. He emptied the drum while Schwarz and Blancanales pumped bursts of fire into the three men in the ceiling.

Three bloody corpses hit the carpet in rapid succession. One of them nearly striking Schwarz. He started and then looked more closely at the dead man.

"I've got another Asian here," he said. "And over here." He pointed to the second of the three.

"And this one," Blancanales confirmed.

"Okay, this just got weird," Lyons said. "No telling how many more of them could be hiding in the freaking walls or whatever. Pol, time to call in backup."

"Good idea," Schwarz said. "This is exactly like that movie with that woman."

"Gadgets, so help me, if you go off on another science-fiction tangent," Lyons began.

For Grimaldi's benefit, Blancanales said, "G-Force, this is Able Team. Do you—"

Lyons nearly ripped the transceiver from his ear as a burst of feedback brought him to his knees. "Son of a bitch!" he roared. Blancanales and Schwarz were both wincing with pain. "What the hell was that?"

Footsteps in the corridor to their immediate left signaled that more personnel were coming up the hallway toward where they stood near the hub. The footfalls were fast, heavy and purposeful. It was the sound of troops moving in for the kill, if Lyons had to guess.

"That was active jamming," Schwarz said. "Our friends have the means to blanket the RF and shut us out."

"Does that mean what I think it means?" Lyons asked. "I thought these were satellite phones?"

"The transceivers are RF," Schwarz said. "For short range."

"I've got movement!" Blancanales announced. He went to one knee and braced his M-4 against the corner of the hallway junction. "Multiple contacts, coming up fast and using the offices for cover. They're walking up two by two."

"More over here," Schwarz said. He pressed himself against the wall near the spoke opposite Blancanales. "Carl, they've got us pinned between them."

"So we've got multiple hostiles inbound who have superior position," Lyons said. "And our only means of calling in backup is hosed."

"Until we can find the source of the jamming, yes," Schwarz said. "We're completely cut off."

"How does that movie go?" Blancanales asked.

"Everybody dies," Schwarz said.

The enemy shooters charged.

CHAPTER FOUR

Jammu, Kashmir

"That's it," Hawkins said, peering through a pair of compact field glasses. "The dossier on Jamali says his personal logo is the Pakistani military insignia superimposed on a red field."

McCarter, crouched next to Hawkins on the ridge overlooking the small encampment of Jamali fighters, nodded.

"That's how they confuse the issue," Encizo added. "Gera does the same thing. He uses the Indian military symbology, but next to a series of black slashes to signify territory conquered. If you're not looking for the differences you'll just identify their rogue elements as part of the main Pakistani and Indian militaries. It's a nasty tactic. Sure to put the two countries at each other's throats, just as it's done."

"Well, not for too much longer," McCarter vowed. "We're going to put the hurt on them both." He turned to Encizo. "Is the Farm still tracking that contingent of Gera's forces?" he asked.

"Yes." Encizo nodded. "We have real-time satellite surveillance on them. They're a ways out yet."

"Text Barb and ask her if we can get some generic chatter spliced into their local airspace," McCarter directed. "Something that will make Gera's people wonder what's going on and give them the itch to investigate. We can do that, can't we?"

"As long as there's a way for Bear to reach out through the ether and touch them, yes," Encizo said. "Why?"

"I want to draw Gera's people here," McCarter explained. "Give both contingents a bloody nose at the same time."

"What happens if we overplay it?" Manning asked. He was crouched alongside James. The MRAP vehicles were parked in the shadow of a tall stone outcropping that was dusted with snow. Rather than gang-bust their way through the camp below in the vehicles, McCarter had opted for an infiltration on foot. The plan was to destroy the Jamali scouting party from within. This would give them a chance to gather any intelligence there was to be had, while putting them up close and personal with Jamali's forces. Such men operated on the basest of animal levels. They understood fear and they understood strength. McCarter was going to put them on notice by showing them the latter and, in so doing, instilling a healthy dose of the former.

"Concern noted, mate," McCarter said, nodding again. "And you're right—if we don't time this right, we end up caught between the two forces, which nobody wants or needs. So let's be brisk in dealing with Jamali's men. Remember—we want to make an impression."

Manning loaded the grenade launcher of his Tavor.

"Forty mike-mike makes an impression, all right," James said "So do those RPGs you're lugging around." Manning had the heavy rocket-propelled grenade launcher on his back, together with the launcher. He was large enough to be able to carry that load without it inhibiting his mobility. There weren't a lot of men with his combat time who could boast that, even in circles as elite as the one in which Phoenix Force traveled.

"Let's move, lads," McCarter said.

Half crouching, gliding along from heel to toe, the men of Phoenix Force spread out and began descending, traversing the decline and closing on the scouts' camp. Jamali's men had a pair of Toyota trucks with machine guns mounted in the beds. They also had a canvas-covered, six-wheeled troop truck. These were parked at three points around the camp, forming a triangle, while the scouts had erected tents in the intervening space. They had set sentries, too, but not enough of them. McCarter had been watching them walk their patterns and had deliberately timed Phoenix Force's movements to take advantage of a gap in their coverage.

"Grenades, get ready," McCarter said softly. His words left a trail of frozen vapor that crystallized on his face. He pulled his mottled cold-weather neck wrap tighter around his face. The generic camouflage pattern of his fatigues matched that of his scarflike wrap, which was really just a big square of fabric folded over on itself several times. The gloves McCarter and the rest of the team wore were easily some of the most expensive on the market. They were durable and they insulated the hand but did not add too much bulk, allowing the soldiers of Phoenix Force to fight in cold weather without giving up too much dexterity.

Someone within the perimeter of the camp shouted an alarm. Phoenix Force had been spotted. McCarter had been counting on that. They had done what they needed to do, which was put themselves in the scouts' midst before the enemy gunmen knew what was happening to them.

"Fire," McCarter ordered.

His four teammates opened up with their 40 mm grenade launchers. Two grenades each struck the front of the first pickup and the rear of the second. Each vehicle was shoved aside by the explosions. The mounted machine guns were torn and bent and the vehicles themselves were rendered inoperable. The gas tank of one of the trucks exploded in a brief orange fireball.

Phoenix Force broke formation. The veteran counterterrorists ran for cover, threading their way through the tents of the scout camp, firing their Tavors in measured bursts. McCarter no longer felt the cold once the battle started. He stopped feeling anything at all except alert and awake, focused on the battle that now unfolded in front of him.

That was always how combat had been for him: a focusing of his mind to an almost painful acuity, giving him the data he needed to assess the threats before him and deal out force, mete out violence, as was required for the task at hand. Dispassionate, his trainers in the SAS had called it. It was all well and good to be angry, to let anger, even hatred, fuel your battle. But when it came to actually taking a man's life—or the lives of a hundred men, for that matter—you had to maintain your detachment. You had to see them as what they were: targets, obstacles to be removed. That was why McCarter took no pleasure in removing even men like these, brutal though both Jamali's and Gera's rogue forces were reported to be.

It was simply time to remove some obstacles.

"T.J., Gary, left," McCarter instructed. "Rafe, Calvin, right. Flank them and walk them toward the center. I'll come straight up the middle."

A chorus of affirmatives sounded through his transceiver. McCarter used the wreckage of one of the pickups to shield him from enemy gunfire as he took up his position. The flames from the second truck nearby were hot enough that he felt them as he waited on one knee. No time to cozy up to a campfire now, though, he reflected. The smell of gasoline was strong where the closer truck had been wrenched apart.

It was only in the movies that every vehicle was made of flashpaper and nitro, ready to blow up at the first bullet that glanced off its fuel tank. Most of the fuel in McCarter's cover vehicle was now soaking the snow beneath the pickup's wreckage. Even if it caught fire, it would just make McCarter's brief stay that much more comfortable. But even without the risk that his cover would erupt into flying shrapnel without warning, he had plenty of bullets to worry about.

The Pakistanis were fielding Kalashnikovs by the truckload, from what he could see. As he watched, one of the Jamali fighters sprang up from the perforated remains of his tent with an AK in either hand. Screaming what McCarter assumed were bloodthirsty oaths, the fighter blazed away from the hip, bracing the stocks of the AKs between his body and his elbows, letting the muzzle rise carry his twin streams of bullets to hell and gone.

McCarter let his Tavor lie at the end of its single-point sling. He pulled his Browning Hi-Power, thumbed back the hammer and took careful aim.

The dual-wielding soldier was still screaming when McCarter's carefully aimed 9 mm bullet tunneled through his forehead and blew a hole through the back of his skull.

"Close it up, lads, close it up," McCarter said, knowing his transceiver would carry his words to the others. He stood, ready to push forward, cutting through the center of the encampment as he'd said he would.

"David," Calvin James warned, "you've got a wild one headed your way."

"Wilder than dual-wielding assault rifles?"

"On your two o'clock," James said.

But McCarter already saw the Pakistani soldier coming. The man held what looked like a battered Makarov pistol in one hand and in the other...

"Bloody hell," said McCarter softly. "Is that a fireman's ax?"

The other Phoenix Force members began engaging new targets. Automatic weapons fire from the Tavors filled the air, met by diminishing return fire from the scouts.

McCarter hit the snow and rolled as bullets filled the air where he had been standing. His charging attacker emptied the Makarov and actually threw the pistol through the air as McCarter struggled to regain his feet. It was a move the Briton hadn't seen outside a cowboy movie in a long time.

From his back in the snow, McCarter brought up the Browning and fired three times. He struck the attacking soldier in the chest, but the gunshots weren't enough to bring the man down. The Phoenix Force leader felt the air being forced from his lungs as the Pakistani shooter collided with him, crushing his ribs and shouting in pain and anger. McCarter shoved the Hi-Power into the man's torso and pulled the trigger, but the slide was out of battery. He smashed the weapon against the side of the Pakistani's head and pushed with his off hand, rolling them over just as the enemy soldier tried to bring the fire ax down.

The gunfire all around the two men, cutting through the small encampment, increased in pitch. The Briton had seen some strange weapons carried into battle by men who had their idiosyncratic favorites. A fire ax was not the most unusual one he had seen, but it was a rare thing. It was also long and deadly, with a rear spike as long as his hand.

McCarter pushed until he was on top of the enemy. He smashed the Hi-Power against the man's face once more and grabbed the ax, twisting it out of the other soldier's grip. Only then did he see the soldier pulling a combat knife from a sheath at his waist. There was nothing else McCarter could do. If he hesitated, that knife would be in his guts and he would be a dead man.

He brought the heavy blade of the ax down on top of the enemy soldier's head.

There was a sickening crunch. The packed snow around the two men was suddenly red with blood. McCarter bent, retrieved the Hi-Power he had been forced to release and reloaded it. Adrenaline dump coursed through him, familiar and powerful.

"David," James said as McCarter checked his six o'clock and saw his teammates closing on his position. The camp was suddenly quiet. The gunfire had ceased. They had neutralized all the opposition.

An engine roared to life.

The covered troop truck was rolling slowly through the snow, the tires digging for traction, the vehicle picking up speed. McCarter turned, spotted the vehicle and ran for it, shoving his Hi-Power in his belt and raising his Tavor as he did so. He wanted to line up the truck for a shot, but it was already out of range.

"David," Manning warned. "Get down."

McCarter knew instantly what the stolid Canadian had in mind. He flattened himself into the snow, feeling the chill of the crystals against his clothing. Half a moment later the distinctive sound of a rocket-propelled grenade sailing overhead caused him to put both hands on top of his insulated skull cap.

As if that gesture would save me if the RPG wasn't precisely on target, he had time to think.

The RPG round struck the rear of the troop truck, blew apart the canvas-covered bed and physically shoved the truck through the snow. It was a very precise shot…but the RPG had detonated against the flimsiest portion of the vehicle, short of the cab. The truck, now a pillar of orange-yellow fire from behind the cab to the rear of its troop area, continued to plow through the snow. The engine raced harder.

"I don't believe it," McCarter muttered to himself.

The other four members of Phoenix Force joined him, flanking him as they came up from behind. Manning began to load another RPG round, but the truck was out of range.

"We could let them go," Encizo said.

"Chances are," said McCarter, "when Gera's men home in on this area, they're going to be drawn straight to that."

"A flaming troop truck moving through a frozen, desolate wasteland?" James asked. "Who'd notice that?"

McCarter shot James a look. He gestured. "We can go back to where we stashed the MRAPs," he said, "or we can run them down on foot. So let's do both. Calvin, you're with me and Gary. Rafe, T.J., you go get the trucks and bring up the rear. They aren't moving fast and they're heavily damaged."

"Not to mention glow-in-the-dark," Encizo said.

"That, too," McCarter said. "We'll catch up, circle the wagons and make ready to intercept whatever diplomatic overtures Gera's forces are likely to make."

"On it," Encizo said.

"You got it," Hawkins drawled.

As the two men traced their approach back to the armored vehicles, McCarter, Manning and James set out after the burning truck, trotting through the snow at a brisk pace. McCarter was grateful for the activity. It was damned cold out here, even though the weather was calm at the moment. It felt good to put some blood back in his extremities.

"I don't know, man," James said as they moved. "I mean, I'm no Native American tracker or anything. We might lose them."

Ahead of them, the trail made by the truck through the fresh coating of snow was as clear as a highway. Not that much farther ahead, the still-burning truck was impossible to miss, like the light at the end of a train tunnel.

"Somehow," Manning said quietly, "I think we'll manage."

They had not gone far when the sound of the two MRAPs was audible at their backs. The troop truck was growing larger, too; they were gaining on it.

Something didn't feel right.

"Slow it up, lads," McCarter said quietly. The transceivers Phoenix Force wore made it possible for him to issue quiet verbal commands where he might otherwise have used hand signals. He did not have to speak loudly enough to be heard; he only had to speak loud enough that his transceiver picked it up. His amplified voice was then run through the earbuds of the other team members. The transceivers had smart algorithms for screening noise, too, which was why they did not transmit the sounds of gunfire and explosions.

"Yeah, I don't like it," James said. "Seems just a little too easy."

"Let's get down in the cold white again," McCarter suggested. "Gary, join me down here. You're from north of the States. It will be like home." He looked to James. "Calvin, circle them, low and quiet. Take the right side of the truck. It's flaming more than the left. Should obscure their vision."

"Got it." James loped off across the snow, silent as a panther.

"Somehow," Manning said, going prone in the snow with his RPG at the ready and his Tavor slung, "it's just not the same."

McCarter judged the distance from Manning and gave

himself a little more space to stay clear of the backblast from the RPG. He aimed with his Tavor and prepared to fire a targeted burst. Through the futuristic assault weapon's sights, he watched as men began moving in and around the cab of the flaming truck, first jumping down from it, then climbing back in, then exiting again. A quick survey of the surrounding snowy ground, dotted by rocky outcroppings and scarred by natural trenches carved by the wind, showed him that James was nowhere in sight.

"They spotted something," Manning said, speculating. "They saw Calvin but they're not sure. They're probably arguing among themselves. Trying to figure out if what they saw is what they saw."

"Get ready, mate," McCarter said. "I think they were laying for us. Using the vehicle and the fire as cover and distraction. They were hoping we'd walk right into their bullets. When we stopped, it ruined their plans."

Manning had no response for that. The range was extreme for the RPG, and with James not visible, a shot would be unwise. But there would be no denying the explosive power of the RPG when it came time to light up their foes. McCarter spared Manning's pack a glance. The big Canadian still had plenty of firepower for the rocket launcher, and there was more loaded in the cargo areas of the MRAPs.

The gunfire McCarter had been waiting for, the gunfire James, too, had sensed was coming, finally exploded from the truck. There were more shooters than McCarter had anticipated. He judged at least half a dozen men, possibly as many as eight. They must have been crammed pretty tightly in the cab and toward the front of the big truck, because there couldn't have been many survivors of the blast at the back.

A muzzle-flash on their ten o'clock gave away James's

position for just an instant. Silhouetted by the guttering flames of the troop truck, a figure fell into the snow.

Score one for Calvin, thought McCarter. He waited. There was another flash, this time at eleven o'clock. James was on the move, shooting and then changing position. A second body fell from the truck.

That's two, the Phoenix Force leader thought to himself.

McCarter waited long enough to verify that, when James's third shot rang out, he was farther away from the vehicle, not closer. It was then that McCarter reached out and tapped Manning on the shoulder.

"Fire in the hole, Gary," he said.

Manning pulled the trigger of the RPG. The rocket blazed from the tube, made its deceptively lazy way to the target and struck just to the rear of the cab, blowing a hole in the sheet metal and knocking the truck over on its side. A singed door, ripped free of its hinges, flew through the air and landed in the snow between the doomed vehicle and where McCarter and Manning were stationed.

"Rafe, T.J., bring it in. Put yourselves on either side of the truck and get those turrets manned. If the Farm has done its part we won't be lonely for long. Rafe, what's the latest satellite tracking update?"

"They're headed to us, all right," Encizo said through the transceiver link. "I estimate eight minutes, maybe ten, before we've got all the Gera we could ever want."

"Then let's make sure we wrap up the party here first," said McCarter. He got to his feet and offered Manning a hand up. Given Manning's size, the Briton had to put his weight into it.

"You're not getting any lighter, mate," McCarter noted.

"But you're as charming as ever, David," Manning retorted with a grin. "Shall we?"

"Let's," the Phoenix Force leader said. He brought his

weapon to his shoulder and stalked toward what was left of the troop truck.

Nothing moved in the wreckage until the two men were practically on top of it. McCarter didn't see the man who climbed out of the "top" of the truck. With the vehicle on its side, what had been the driver's window was now the only egress through the hole where the door had been. A single Pakistani gunman, his bloody uniform bearing Jamali's modified military crest, half jumped, half fell directly on top of McCarter.

The Briton went down under the weight of the other man. Just as quickly, he surged to his feet, carrying the smaller, lighter Pakistani with him, smashing the man against the burned-out hulk of the troop truck.

As McCarter was slamming the butt of his Tavor down on the skull of his enemy, he was aware of the gunfire around him. Manning was engaging a contact at close range, and while McCarter dealt with his own enemy, he saw James appear in his peripheral vision. The lanky James sauntered up as if he didn't have a care in the world. Steam escaped from the neckline of his cold-weather fatigues. He had been pushing hard. His assault rifle was still in his hands.

"You all right, David?" James asked.

McCarter looked down where he knelt. The Pakistani was dead. He checked his rifle for damage, but there was none that he could perceive. He took the time to eject the magazine, check it, seat it and make sure a round was chambered. Then he stood.

"You couldn't find something a little more unique?" James said.

"What, mate?" McCarter asked, momentarily confused.

"You know, like a garden hoe or maybe a rake."

"What are you on about, Calvin?"

"Dude, you killed a guy with an *ax* a little while ago."

It was then that McCarter realized that, no matter what else happened on this mission, he was never going to live that down.

CHAPTER FIVE

Twin Forks, Utah

Shouting a battle cry that Lyons swore was in Chinese, the gunmen began hurling themselves down the hallway, seemingly heedless of the return fire that would greet them. Lyons unleashed a new barrage from his shotgun, but for every man he cut down, another two emerged from the darkened corridor. With nowhere to go and no options, the Able Team leader decided he would have to take the only obvious exit.

"Gadgets," he said, throwing his shotgun over his shoulder on its sling, "come here."

Schwarz had time to turn and throw the duffel bag on his back before Lyons bent down, grabbed the slimmer man by his belt and one ankle and threw Schwarz bodily into the ceiling. The Stony Man electronics expert squawked as he was thrown, but he got the idea, grabbing on to the drop ceiling struts and clambering into the darkened crawl space.

Blancanales did not need to be prompted. He took a running start and, as Lyons held his hands low as an improvised stirrup, Blancanales didn't so much climb as jump up into the crawl space, using the boost that Lyons gave him by standing suddenly. The two smaller men, in turn, groaned under the strain of hauling Lyons up after them.

"Go," Lyons urged. "Go, go, go!"

Bullets chased them into the crawl space. As they pulled themselves along the metal lattice framing the drop ceiling, the shooters in the corridor below moved into position to spray upward. Raking the tiles fore and aft of Able Team's position, they began punching holes that tracked toward the three men from front and back.

"This is bad!" Blancanales shouted.

"Gadgets!" Lyons called. "Give me CS!" He pointed toward the gap in the tiles behind them.

Schwarz nodded. From the duffel bag he produced several CS gas canisters, pulled the pins and lobbed the gas grenades through the opening. Lyons's nose twitched as the familiar smell hit him. He had never particularly liked tear gas. Which was the point of the stuff, he supposed.

"Keep moving," Lyons directed the other team members. "Backtrack until we get near the end of the building."

The feedback in his ear told him his transceiver was still being jammed. Whatever was going on here at the EarthGard mine, it spoke worlds that the gunmen guarding the place had active jamming equipment readily available. What would justify so much hardware? Assuming the shooters believed Able Team represented the federal government, the guards had been awfully quick to shoot down agents whose deaths could bring a world of trouble down onto the mine.

Not that Lyons intended to die here today.

They reached a split in the crawl space where two prefabricated sections were joined. The connection formed a T-shape that led left and right. If Lyons's bearings were correct, they were headed to the opposite end of the building, with the hub behind them. That put the left turn north and the right turn south. He took the left and glanced back over his shoulder to make sure his men were following.

"Gadgets!" he called.

Schwarz came up alongside him with Blancanales trailing. As they crawled through the ceiling, the footing beneath them became more firm. Lyons looked down and realized the drop ceiling frame had given way to plywood. The terminus of the wing they were navigating had been reinforced. There was no immediate exit.

"Ironman?" Schwarz asked.

"In a minute," Lyons answered. He withdrew the folding combat dagger from the pocket of his jacket and snapped it open. "Dig!"

"Should have made that left turn at Albuquerque," Schwarz muttered. He snapped open his own blade while Blancanales did likewise. All three men began stabbing at the plywood, taking large chunks out of the wood. Soon they had created a hole large enough for the three of them to slip through, although Lyons's broad shoulders would be a tight fit.

"Down?"

"Not until they get closer," Lyons answered. "Did you text the Farm?"

"You thought of that, too?" Schwarz asked, grinning. More seriously he said, "Yes. They're relaying our request for air support to Jack."

"Then we just have to try not to get dead until the air cavalry arrives," Lyons said.

Rays of light from the fixtures below punched through the darkness of their space just short of the exit they'd created. The three men of Able Team rolled aside, pressing themselves against the sides of the upper walls. Schwarz groaned as Lyons's bulk practically crushed him against the vertical boards of the trailer.

"Thanks, Ironman," he gasped. "I didn't know you cared enough to shield me from bullets."

"Shaddap, Gadgets," Lyons said. "And hand me a flash-bang."

Schwarz handed over the grenade. Lyons pulled the pin, released the spoon and dropped the weapon through the hole, making sure to put some spin on it to get it rolling toward the enemy. All three Able Team members closed their eyes, covered their ears and opened their mouths to equalize pressure.

The vibration of the powerful flash-bang grenade shook the plywood beneath them and set Lyons's ears to ringing. The explosion was Able Team's cue to act. They dropped down to floor level, Lyons first, his two teammates following.

Several uniformed guards struggled to bring their weapons up. At least one man's ears were bleeding. All were squinting hard, trying to see through the blinding flashes that had been left in their vision. Blancanales brought his M-4 to his shoulder and snapped off two rounds into the head of each one. He moved like a machine, firing and swiveling, until all the hostiles were down.

"Let's take this party outside," Lyons said. He turned, knelt and emptied the drum of his USAS-12, dropped it, reloaded and repeated the process. The ringing in his ears was worse now, but not so bad that it would stop him from fighting. He threw kick after powerful kick at the ravaged wall until it gave way, creating a hole the men of Able Team could simply walk through.

Lyons's boots hit the arid soil outside.

Behind the modular headquarters building was a mine structure of some kind. Enclosed shafts of wood radiated from the configuration. Lyons assumed there were conveyors inside. He knew little about the actual mechanics of a beryllium mining operation and, insofar as none of those specifics interfered with his mission, he didn't care.

But the shafts above were shifting now and he could hear footsteps on the wood.

"They're on the roof line!" Lyons called. "They're using those conveyors!"

Able Team scrambled to position themselves as much directly below the enclosed shafts above as they could. Gunfire began to rain down on them from the shooters on the roof. Lyons cursed under his breath. That was probably how they'd gotten into the drop ceiling in the first place. The firebomb entrance had driven the security forces to some roof access and they'd circled back around under cover of the building's false ceiling.

All of that added up to something not on the level. Ignoring the fact that these guys were armed to screw all and completely okay with murdering a quantity of unknown law-enforcement agents, there was no way the sheer volume of security here was part of any legitimate operation. Lyons didn't know how valuable beryllium was on the open market, but he had to assume you didn't need a private army to protect it from all comers.

So what was going on here?

They were just scratching the surface of this mission and he didn't like where they were going. He didn't like it one bit.

It was time to take it to the bad guys. "Pol," he said, "give me a rifle grenade into the center of the nearest walkway. My eleven o'clock."

Schwarz reached into the duffel, found the rocket-shaped weapon and tossed it to Blancanales, who affixed the STANAG Type 22 mm rifle grenade to the flash-hider of his M-4. Then he brought the weapon up, aimed and pulled the trigger.

The grenade exploded on impact, shredding the wooden slats of the covered walkway, sending debris and dead men falling from the sky. Lyons barely moved out of the way fast enough. A corpse hit the dirt only feet from his previous position.

Renewed fire began from the remainder of the roof line. Lyons signaled his partners to follow him and then took up position behind a support leg that was nothing so much as a stacked wood-and-reinforced-concrete column. The column was just what the doctor ordered when it came to cover and concealment. The angle, for the roof gunners, was a poor one, while the concrete and wood absorbed bullets nicely.

"Cozy," Blancanales said as the three men put their backs to the column. Gunfire ate away at the opposite side, but it was much wilder now, less focused and directed. There were shouts of outrage mixed in, too, which would be expected from any group of men, even paid mercenaries, who had lost so many comrades in so short a time.

"I swear that's Chinese," Blancanales said.

"There's English mixed in, too," Schwarz said. "One of those voices is as Southern as Southern gets. He sounds like an angry version of that big rooster from the cartoons."

"I say, I say," Blancanales said. "You-all are gonna pay for shootin' my friends."

"Yeah," Schwarz said. "Just like that."

"There are times when I hate both of you," Lyons said.

"We know," Schwarz said. "It's part of your charm."

The next voice they heard, however, was amplified by an electric bullhorn.

"You down there," the bullhorn's operator shouted. "Surrender and you will not be harmed."

"Oh, that's rich," Lyons said. "I guess they top out with warning shots around three or four thousand."

"Some people hold on to resentment," Schwarz said.

"So help me, if you're quoting movies at me again," Lyons said.

"No," Schwarz said, managing to look unconvincing. "I really cherish these firefight moments we have."

"Hate," Lyons said. "Seething, white-hot hate."

"You don't mean that," Schwarz said.

"Oh, yeah?" Lyons started. He stopped when the metal sphere of a grenade bounced to a stop a couple of feet from his right boot.

Schwarz shoved Lyons sideways, into the column. Lyons had time to look down and recognize the threat. Schwarz, meanwhile, had shoved Lyons to "clear the road" for a massive, swing-through kick. He nailed the grenade with his toe and sent it flying from their position. It exploded, throwing clods of soil everywhere, spraying dust on Able Team.

"Thanks, Gadgets," Lyons started to say. "I take back everything bad I just said."

"No, don't!" Schwarz shouted.

"Huh?" Lyons had time to say before another grenade, then another, then a third, rolled to a stop by their feet.

This time it was Lyons's turn to act. He grabbed both Schwarz and Blancanales by their collars and shoved them forward, around the other side of the column. This put them in the line of fire from the roof above. As Lyons propelled them, his partners took the cue and ran for their lives. Bullets were biting at their heels when the three grenades blew, tearing large chunks out of the support column with their trebled destructive power.

Something cracked high above.

Lyons looked up and back as they ran, trying to find an angle at the corner of the headquarters that would make it harder for the roof gunners to track Able Team. What he saw caused him to reach out and grab Schwarz and Blancanales again.

"It jinxes us when you're nice to me!" Schwarz blurted.

"Shaddap, Gadgets!" Lyons yelled again. He dragged his teammates against the wall of the headquarters building as the shaft behind them snapped in two, falling toward them like a redwood before an army of lumberjacks. Concrete shrapnel flew everywhere. The crash of the column was followed by the staccato pings of nails from the walkway overhead. They were being wrenched out under tension as the walkway tore itself apart on the way down. Half the walkway struck the dirt below, bringing with it whatever machinery was being housed inside. This raised a sudden sandstorm of dust and grit and billowed over the Utah war zone and forced Able Team to crouch more tightly against the building.

"You there!" came the voice from the bullhorn.

"There," Lyons said to the rest of the team. "To the north. There's an overcrop where the roof as been patched. Move into the shadow of that. They'll have to reach down and back to target us if they want to try."

Able Team moved.

"You down there," came the megaphone-amplified voice again. The sound of feedback signaled the megaphone had been thrown down. A face appeared at the edge of the roof above them.

"So you've chosen suicide," said Lyons, raising the barrel of his shotgun.

"Don't shoot!" shouted the man on the roof. "My name is Daniels. I'm one of the men in charge here."

"We accept your surrender!" Schwarz called out. Lyons shot the electronics expert a dirty look.

"This is getting us nowhere and it's destroying the place," Daniels shouted down. "They don't pay me enough to fight wars. We're just supposed to be security. You put your guns down and come out, we'll let you walk to your truck and leave. No questions asked."

"Sounds legit," Schwarz said quietly.

"My thoughts exactly," growled Lyons. "They're just trying to get us out into the open so they can shoot us."

"Hey, Ironman?" Schwarz said.

"Yeah?"

"I just had a thought. They're all on the roof."

Lyons looked at him. Then he looked up. "You got an ETA on Jack?"

Schwarz checked his satellite phone. "Twenty," he said.

"Twenty minutes?" Lyons asked.

"Nineteen," Schwarz said. "Eighteen. Seventeen."

"Hey, Daniels!" Lyons called out, a broad smile splitting his face. "What's black and white and red all over?"

Daniels stuck his head over the side of the roof once more. "You've got no chance!" he shouted back. "We outnumber you! My men will swarm your position and you'll all die! Take the deal!"

"What's black and white and red all over?" Lyons repeated.

"Five," Schwarz said. "Four."

In the distance, the twin rotors of the Osprey were audible. Lyons looked at Schwarz, who was texting again.

"Giving him our position?" Lyons said quietly.

"That and typing in 'LOL' over and over again. One. Contact."

"Down!" Lyons ordered. The three Able Team members hit the dirt.

The furious whine of the automatic multibarrel cannon fitted to the Osprey's belly was like the hammering of an angry demon. The 7.62 mm rounds from the GAU-17 ripped through the roof of the mine headquarters, spraying gunmen and fragments of roof tar, wood and drywall in every direction. The men of Able Team crawled closer to the wall of the building, seeking the protection of the steep angle from roof to ground, as pieces of the roof and the men formerly standing on it began to rain down.

The Osprey whipped from side to side, its cannon never relenting. Grimaldi brought the powerful flying machine over the ravaged structure in a lateral strafe that shook the very walls. Lyons could feel the vibration against his back.

"What is it?" Schwarz shouted over the noise of the GAU-17.

"What is what?" Lyons yelled back.

"Black and white and red all over?"

"A mime!" Lyons yelled.

"But that doesn't make any sense!" Schwarz shouted.

"It does if the mime was up there on the roof!" Lyons yelled, but suddenly the whine of the GAU-17 stopped. In the comparative mild noise of the Osprey's rotors above and in front of the mine office, Lyons's bellowed punch line fell flat.

"Wow," Blancanales said. "Just…wow."

"This is why I hate both of you," Lyons said. "Come on."

They circled around the perimeter of the building. The relatively lightweight, prefabricated structure was now falling apart, collapsing in several places. The mine structure connected to it was similarly destroyed. Multiple fires burned, and black, oily flames still billowed near the front of the mine office where the white phosphorous had done so much damage.

Something moved within the wreckage of the building.

"Boys, this is G-Force," said Grimaldi. His transmission came through their transceivers but was marred by static.

"I'm still getting a lot of jamming interference,

G-Force," Schwarz said. "Can you see if you can do something about that?"

"Must be the proximity," said the garbled voice of Jack Grimaldi. "Harder to block me when I'm right on top of you. Let me see if I can't do a little fine-tuning."

The GAU-17 cannon opened up again. Links and shells rained down, clattering on the ground and on the debris of the mining company building, shaking the interior of what was left of the structure. Grimaldi swept back and forth, hosing down the four corners of the building and then lingering along the length of the structure. Finally, when the cannon went silent again, his transmission was clear as a bell.

"I think that's done it, boys," he said. "Whatever jamming equipment they had in there is now in tiny pieces. Just like the rest of the building."

"Don't worry, Jack," said Lyons. "I'll vouch for the fact that you only blew up half of it."

"Credit where credit is due," Grimaldi said. "I... Wait a minute. I have movement, on your three o'clock. Headed away from the building. One man, no weapon visible. Moving as briskly as a wounded man can."

"On it," Lyons replied. "Gadgets, Pol, take up station here. If you see a body that still has a face, take a photo. We need to run these guys through the computers at the Farm and see what they can tell us. If anything moves, put a bullet in it."

"And you?" Blancanales asked.

"I'm going to chase down our runner."

Lyons slung his shotgun over his back and ran with the big Colt Python in his fist. He picked out the uniformed security operative easily enough. The fleeing man was limping badly and leaving a trail of his own blood in the dirt. Judging from the volume, he'd be weakening every minute from blood loss. Before too long this particular fugitive would be lying in the Utah dirt, bled out and pale, dead for good. But if there was any chance of taking a live prisoner, Lyons favored that strategy. The men of Able Team weren't murderers. He would not take a life in cold blood.

"Stop making me run," Lyons called out.

The fleeing figure turned. From the glimpse Lyons caught at a distance, he could see it was Daniels. The man reached for his waistband. When the wounded security guard's hand came up again, he was holding a pistol. Daniels fired, but the shot went wide.

Lyons didn't make the same mistake.

The Able Team leader thumbed back the hammer on his Python, took careful aim and put the site post low over the gunman's belly. He pulled the trigger. The Python bucked in his hand and sent a .357 Magnum hollowpoint round thundering toward Daniels's midsection.

The impact put Daniels on the ground. Lyons watched the man's pistol fly through the air and land in the dirt some distance from him. He approached carefully. Many a good operative had been killed by a seemingly "dead" enemy.

"Don't make any sudden moves, Daniels," Lyons instructed.

When the wounded man didn't respond, Lyons carefully toed him over with one boot. On his back, Daniels was ashen. Not only was his stomach bloody, but his leg was leaking badly and he had another gunshot wound to the upper chest. Lyons hadn't been able to see that chest wound. He knew he was looking at a dying man.

"I'm done," said Daniels quietly. "You've killed me."

"Yeah," said Lyons. "Looks like I have. You don't have to take what you know to the grave, Daniels. I don't know what you'll see on the other side, but it can't hurt to lighten your load some."

The dying security operative managed to shake his head. "I'm just…a hired…gun," he said. His voice was a whisper now. "Soldier. Soldier of fortune. I don't…know anything. Not that would…help."

"And your Asian buddies?" Lyons asked. "Tell me those guys aren't a foreign contingent of operatives of some kind. What are they? Renegade North Koreans or something? Chinese mercenaries? What?"

"Tell me…first," said Daniels.

"Tell you what?"

"The joke…" said Daniels. "What's…black…and white…"

"And red all over," supplied Lyons. "It's a dumb joke. A mime. A mime after you hit it with a minigun."

Daniels didn't say anything. He was still staring up at Lyons, but now he looked at nothing. His eyes were glassy in death.

His face bore the slightest hint of a smile.

CHAPTER SIX

Jammu, Kashmir

"Here they come," James said. He adjusted the focus on his field glasses. "Definitely Gera's forces. The insignia is right. And they're moving at what must be top speed for them, in these conditions and on this terrain. The tanks are junk, from the looks of them. A couple of old T-55s that should have been mothballed back in the eighties. Probably skimmed from the regular Indian army before they were junked or stored. Modern Indian military forces use the Arjun or the T-90, I think."

"I'd call not facing down a modern 120 mm cannon a good thing," McCarter said.

"I see a few Ashok Leyland Stallion troop carriers," James stated. "Standard canvas-covered models. And… Gary, check me on this. Are those Suzuki Samurais?"

"Maruti Gypsies," Manning said. "It's a four-wheel-drive light utility vehicle, made in India by Maruti Suzuki."

"Let's tip a few over," James said.

The three men were situated in a natural depression just forward of the wrecked troop truck. Hawkins and Encizo were ready to leave their turrets and reposition the MRAPs, should it become necessary to withdraw them. The armored vehicles were powerful and durable, but they would not stand up to a T-55. Of course, that was what

Manning's RPG was for. The older T-55s were vulnerable to rocket-propelled grenades fired into their tracks. The explosives were too light to get through the armor in which the tanks were clad, but it wasn't necessary to hull them. All Phoenix Force had to do to take the tanks out of the equation was to render them immobile and then render the gun crews ineffective.

Usually that was done by covering the tank in fire.

James suppressed a shudder at the thought. That was no way to die, even if these jerks were brutal killers. He was satisfied with taking somebody out. He didn't need to make that man's death a memorable horror.

But he also couldn't afford to be squeamish when it came to removing their foes.

As he always did with battle on the horizon, he returned to procedure, checking his Tavor, making sure his grenade launcher was loaded, and dropping a hand to the hilt of the fighting knife on his hip. If anyone asked, he would admit that, yes, he would prefer a straight-up, one-on-one knife fight with an enemy, rather than a protracted gun battle. James had always figured that if you truly wanted to kill a guy, the least you could do was look him in the eyes while the lights went out. His early life on Chicago's South Side had taught him a lot about violence on that personal, direct level.

"All right, Gary," said McCarter. "Time to go to work. Calvin, don't stick your head up to high."

"I'll see what I can do," James said. "Watch your hind ends, both of you."

"Always, mate."

James took aim through his Tavor's optics as Manning and McCarter crept off. They were going to flank the approaching Gera forces. Manning would neutralize the tanks while McCarter spotted for him and kept any enemy gunners off the big Canadian. James was free to attack targets of opportunity while staying mobile, but his line of retreat was directly to the MRAP vehicles. Once he rejoined Encizo, he would drive while the Cuban-born fighter manned the vehicle's turret. Combat was always, *always*, about mobility and flexibility.

The cold air carried the thunderous noise of both T-55 tanks firing their main guns. The rounds landed beyond James's position, uselessly targeting the hulk of the troop truck, scattering what was left of the wreckage to twisted shrapnel. James started moving, staying low, running through the snow in a half crouch, using the rocky, broken terrain to cover his movements while seeking new cover. He could not afford to fall into the pocket of the T-55 guns. The tanks were old, but they were still a formidable obstacle. He would need more distance between him and those machines until Manning and McCarter did their work.

The decline in which he found himself deepened into another natural trench. The terrain here was full of crags, some of which were very dangerous. You had to learn to judge the density of the snow. Gauge wrong and you could step into what you thought was a three-foot drop and find yourself neck-deep in frozen powder with a broken ankle.

The battle began in earnest. From his vantage, James heard the turrets of the MRAP open up. The staccato roar of the machine gun was punctuated by the heavier hammer of the automatic grenade launcher. Pieces of the snow-covered earth around him began to erupt in a landfall of riotous fireworks.

The light utility vehicles began to overrun his position. It was hard not to laugh at them as they passed him; they looked like the kind of miniature sport utility vehicles that were popular twenty years ago in the United States. The things couldn't stay upright worth a damn; their center of gravity was too high and American drivers just wouldn't slow down taking curves in them. James had had a girlfriend for a little while, in fact, who drove one of the miniature trucks. It had been just a passing thing, nothing serious, on those rare occasions when James had some downtime. She'd rolled one of those little Suzukis on the way home one day. It only took a couple of guys who'd seen the whole thing from the street corner to walk over, push it upright, and send her on her way.

As one of the little trucks passed right by James, missing him in his arctic camouflage against the snow, he reached out with the blade of his knife and rammed it into one of the spinning tires.

The impact wrenched the knife from his hand. Air shot from the weal in the sidewall, and the Maruti began to describe a half circle. James hurried along after the little SUV, staying in the driver's blind spot, careful not to give himself away. He let his Tavor fall to the end of its sling and took out his Glock.

He had no worries that the cold would have negatively affected the otherwise unfired pistol. The Glock was an Austrian gun renowned for its durability and its reliability in adverse conditions. Its inventor had, James thought he remembered reading, never designed a pistol before. He'd just sat down and created what seemed most logical. The result was a pistol that did nothing for the user. It had no external safety, no chamber-loaded indicator, no external hammer to rise and fall. It did only what the essence of a gun was supposed to do: it put a bullet through the barrel every time the trigger was pulled.

James walked up on the driver of the Maruti, who was climbing out of the little truck's cab, and put a bullet through the back of the Gera fighter's head. He dropped low on one knee, spun and fired through the open doorway of the vehicle, punching a shot through the open mouth of the shocked man sitting in the passenger seat. Stepping over the corpse of the driver, James climbed into the vehicle, pulled the door closed and slammed his foot down on the gas.

In four-wheel drive, the truck still slipped, pulling to the right as it dragged its flattened rear wheel on that side.

"Boys, this is Calvin," James said. When operating in unfriendly territory while maintaining plausible deniability, the team used first names only when communicating. The transceivers were encrypted, thanks to the work of Schwarz. An enemy intercepting their transmissions would hear only garbled nonsense and static. But on the off chance that the opposition could break that encryption, or in the event that a team member's earbud was captured —with or without the teammate who was wearing it— using first names meant that enemies would have little to go on if they tried to track down the identities of Phoenix Force's members.

Things like that had happened to counterterror and special operations teams before. Many of the very dangerous people the Special Operations Group hunted, fought and killed had vengeful friends and long collective memories. Some of the better financed terror groups and drug cabals were entirely prepared to track down the team members who had hit them…and their families. While the men of Phoenix Force led fairly isolated lives, they all had connections to the rest of the world. Dig deep enough and sooner or later, some lever, some pressure point, could be found.

Security protocols helped prevent that kind of thing from happening.

Right now, however, James had a bigger concern. He

didn't want to get shot by his teammates, nor blown up by a 40 mm grenade or an RPG round.

"I am behind the wheel of one of Gary's Gypsies," James reported. "You can't miss me. I'm dragging around a flat tire. Try not to put a bullet in me."

"Roger that," Manning said. The others acknowledged, as well. Calvin was grateful for that, because he wasn't sure he could wrestle the wheel of the crippled vehicle and also dodge gunfire. Only the fact that the other Gera fighters thought he was one of them had saved him so far. He pulled the wheel as far over as it would go, managing a more or less straight course through the broken terrain, the snow, the ice.

There was an old entrenching tool on the seat next to him. It was covered in ice. He almost pitied these men, working exclusively in this inhospitable place.

Almost.

He saw one of the T-55 tanks to his left. As he watched, a trail of smoke snaked toward the front corner of the vehicle, catching the right-side tread and smashing the bogeys apart in a cloud of yellow-orange fire.

Score one for Gary and David, James thought.

The charging Gera forces had arrayed themselves in what was essentially a skirmish line, fanning out and trusting to what they thought were their superior numbers to roll over and overwhelm their enemies. James pushed his scout vehicle back the way it had come, causing two of the troop trucks to dodge him. He imagined he could hear the drivers of those trucks cursing him out.

James looked down. The radio on the dash of the little truck had come to life. He couldn't speak the language the Indian soldiers were shouting to him through their radios, but he strongly suspected that they were indeed cursing him.

One of the troop trucks stopped and armed men began to climb out of the rear. They carried AKM assault rifles. They made a tempting target, clustered as they were, and there was no way James could get to them in time on foot.

It was a good thing he had wheels.

He judged the arc and pushed his boot down on the gas as far as it would go. The little Gypsy picked up speed. James reached into his coat and began plucking grenades from his web gear, inserting his finger through the pins. When the distance seemed about right, he wedged the shovel between his seat and the accelerator, holding it down. Then he pulled all the grenade pins, dropped the grenades inside the car, and threw himself out of the rolling Gypsy.

The soldiers debarking the troop truck saw the incoming vehicle but didn't know what to do about it. One or two of them pointed. James actually saw them exchange puzzled glances as the truck, rolling on its flattened tire, plowed through the snow and circled around to head straight for them.

Some sixth sense might have warned them. Then again, it was possible their default reaction was simply to empty their AKMs. Whatever the reason, the Indian soldiers began shooting at the Gypsy. James was still counting in his head, hoping he had timed the grenade release correctly.

He had.

The Gypsy exploded as it reached the enemy soldiers. A pipe bomb worked on the pressure principle. The enclosure was what made the explosive powerful. In this case the Gypsy's frame acted like a rolling pipe bomb, scattering the Gera fighters like so many pounds of barbecued meat. James, again, *almost* felt bad for his enemies as they were churned to hamburger by the booby-trapped Gypsy.

The tactic had an unexpected benefit. Other Gera soldiers, both on foot and rolling in the troop trucks, turned their weapons on the remaining Gypsies and began firing into them. The Gera men inside the trucks were killed where they sat; there was no way they could have survived the onslaught. The distraction caused the remaining T-55 to home in on one of the doomed Gypsies, and this gave McCarter and Manning the angle they needed. Another RPG, then a second, hammered the T-55. It took a third round before Manning was finally able to disable the tracks.

Both tanks still had operable turrets, but the men inside were firing blindly, shooting and traversing their turret without any real thought for the effect. Twice, errant rounds from the T-55s created blasts that killed more Gera men. Then again, as small as the Phoenix Force was compared to these soldiers, it was possible the Indians really couldn't tell the difference between friend and foe.

Pressing himself prone into the snow, James decided to play sniper with his Tavor. The optics weren't really meant for extreme long range, but he was a good shot, experienced with the weapon and with combat. He would make do.

One of the MRAPs trundled past him. Encizo, through the windshield, shot him a jaunty wave. He was reasonably sure he could identify the positions of all of Phoenix Force with enough margin of safety to call in mortar fire without killing any of his teammates. That was another of the advantages of fielding a small, elite fighting force rather than a heavily armed mob.

There was a lot less Gera mob than there had been, however.

The enemy had showed little discipline. They had arrived as a mob, attacked using the simplest of tactics and fallen apart as soon as they encountered resistance that caught them off guard. James supposed the Jamali forces were roughly on par, or the two generals could hardly be fighting each other to a standstill. Then again, though, Phoenix Force had seen little of the viciousness that the Jamali soldiers had exhibited. Certainly there had been nobody in this bunch packing his own fire ax.

Something about that seemed odd to James. The Gera people were dangerous, but Jamali's men seemed much more so. How was it that Jamali hadn't managed to wipe out Gera and seize the area for himself?

For that matter, James had seen about as much as he wanted of the countryside. He paused and held his breath, firing off a shot from his prone position that tagged one of the running Gera soldiers in the face. There were more men running around the battle area, firing blindly into the snow or shooting uselessly at the MRAPs. None of the Gera men had managed to field a rocket launcher or an RPG yet.

Encizo's MRAP drove straight for one the T-55s, causing the turret to move his way. James could not help himself. He spoke aloud.

"Rafe," he said. "There's no way that's going to work."

"It might," said Encizo defensively. "They aren't too bright so far. Didn't they shoot up all their own trucks after you took one of them?"

"Still," said James. "I don't think you'd better."

"I'm going to."

"He's going to what?" McCarter asked through the transceiver link. "Gary, what nonsense is Rafe engaged in? Can you see?"

"I think it might work," Manning put in.

"You see?" Encizo said. "You see? Gary's on my side."

"I said I thought it might work," Manning corrected. "I didn't say it would."

The MRAP picked up speed. Now the tank's turret was hurrying to line up the shot. No, scratch that, thought James: both tanks were hurrying to line up the—

"No way," James had time to say as Encizo hit the brakes on the MRAP and arrested its forward motion.

The T-55s fired. They were directly aligned with each other. The tanks hulled each other, putting both machines out of action and sending up plumes of dark smoke to meet the falling snow.

"There is no way that worked," said James.

"Told you," said Encizo."

"Can the chatter, mates," said McCarter. "We've still got some hostiles running around. Let's police them up and regroup for our next stop."

James stood. He turned—

The Indian soldier who crashed into James was screaming something. He was bleeding from the side of his head and, in his hands, he held a combat knife similar to the one James had lost. It looked like a next-generation Ka-Bar, in fact, with a single guard and a synthetic handle. The knife was hard to miss, poised over his face as it was.

The lanky Phoenix Force man fought for control of the blade. And to think, James thought. I wanted a stand-up knife fight. Be careful what you wish for…

He had lost his own blade flattening that first Gypsy's tire. The knife was lost in the snow and would probably never be seen by another human being. The Tavor was pressed against James's chest by the weight of his enemy.

It would have to be the Glock. James wrestled for position, knowing that if he pulled the gun too soon or at the wrong angle, his enemy could wrest it from him and use it against him. Close quarters retention of pistols was not exactly a new topic for James. His knowledge told him that it was always dangerous, to everyone involved. With his left hand, he took a death grip on the attacker's knife hand, hoping the Indian wouldn't think to circle his wrist and carve his way out. Fortunately, James's opponent was fixated on the knife, staring at it, as if by force of will alone he could get it past James's resistance and plant the blade in the Phoenix Force member's face.

There. He had found his moment; he had managed to get the rest of his body between his attacker and his right side. Dragging the snowy Glock from its holster, scraping the earth and his own body with the weapon, he managed to free it and press it against his own torso.

His elbow was up as high as he could get it. He could practically reach out and touch his own right nipple with this thumb. His wrist was locked. It was a classic retention shooting posture, which indexed the weapon against the body and gave the shooter a good chance of hitting the enemy in the pelvic region. The trick was to do this without putting any part of your own body in the way. It wouldn't do for him to shoot the enemy but also perforate himself several times.

James fired three times in quick succession. The effect was like throwing a switch. He essentially blew the enemy off him, making the Indian roll into a ball. That wasn't an uncommon reaction. The Indian's body had just sustained horrible trauma. Just as a man automatically grabbed himself when he cut his own hand, the wounded Indian was grabbing at his wounds, trying to seal himself up, reacting instinctively to the damage he had just incurred.

He died still rolled up like that. James heard his death rattle. The machine gun turret of Encizo's MRAP roared behind him. He checked his six long enough to make sure nobody was sneaking up on him. Then he checked himself to make sure he hadn't sustained a cut or even a stray bullet wound that the cold and his own adrenaline had stopped him from feeling.

Satisfied that he was not badly hurt, James bent and pried the next-generation fighting knife from the dead man's fingers. The blade did not look bloody, but there was no telling where it had been. He plunged the knife into the snow and out again several times, drying the blade on the dead man's pant leg. Then he put the knife in his own sheath, where it fit well.

The battle site was a scorched and smoky mess. The tanks were burning now; something had caused them to catch from inside. It was also possible that Phoenix Force had dropped some incendiaries down the tank's hatches while he was fighting with his knife-fighter friend. It didn't really matter. Here and there, a forlorn Gypsy also sat, bullet-riddled and bloody. There was one troop carrier still intact, although it appeared to be abandoned. A second troop carrier was pulling away and leaving twin sprays of snow in its wake as it powered through the landscape.

"David, David, I have a troop truck withdrawing," James said.

"We have it in sight, as well," McCarter said. "Let him go, Calvin. I've no more stomach for shooting Gera men just now. What a bloody mess."

"Yeah, I heard *that*," James agreed. He walked toward where the two MRAPs were now parked and idling. Dead men littered the snow in every direction. The ground was red now, not white. There were fallen, frozen weapons everywhere.

"Some say the world will end in fire," James quoted. "Some say in ice."

"Yeah," Encizo said through his transceiver. As James approached, Encizo climbed out of the armored vehicle. He looked around as James had done. Then he held up his satellite phone. "The next target on the list," he said for the team's benefit, "is a village named Banihal. Apparently both Jamali and Gera use it as a way-post. We have a lot of thermal traffic showing their forces going back and forth through the place."

"All right, then," said McCarter. "Let's see what we can see in Banihal. It can't be any worse than this parcel of nothing."

"I can't believe this place is worth fighting and dying for," Manning said. His voice was very quiet. Manning was echoing James's own thoughts.

"It isn't," James declared. "Something strange is going on. Why are Gera's forces so much less effective than Jamali's if the standoff between the two has raged for as long as it has?"

"Maybe Jamali's a tactical dunce," Hawkins offered. "That would explain a lot."

"Neither side seems terribly advanced, tactically," Encizo noted. "But they don't necessarily have to be in order to take and hold ground out here. They just have to have balls. They have to have guns. They have to *want* it more."

"Enough," McCarter said. "I agree it stinks, lads. But let's talk about it in the MRAPs with the heaters going. And let's make haste to Banihal."

They piled aboard and James took the wheel.

"Try not to blow us up," McCarter said. "You know how you get."

"Mind if I *ax* you a question, David?" James shot back, grinning, deliberately mispronouncing the word.

"Bloody hell," McCarter said.

CHAPTER SEVEN

Elmore, Ohio

"I've been reading up on beryllium processing," Schwarz announced. Able Team, once more in a rental Suburban, was minutes out from a processing plant located in Elmore, Ohio, which boasted more than one of the facilities. The location was next on their list of prioritized EarthGard holdings. Lyons looked at Schwarz briefly, while Blancanales nodded. "We'll need to exercise some caution," he said. "From what I've heard, we don't want to breathe the stuff."

"The dust from beryllium attacks the alveoli in the lungs, where it gets treated like an attacking organism," Schwarz reported. "Once you're 'sensitized' to beryllium, you can go on to develop clinical, chronic beryllium disease. Its symptoms are similar to pneumonia and there is no cure. Your lungs stiffen up, you can't breathe and you die a slow and lingering death."

"Well, that's cheerful," Blancanales said. Lyons grunted.

"Proper safety procedures, like filter masks, prevent the disease in modern workers," Schwarz went on, "but we want to make sure we don't blow anything that contains the dust. Beryllium ceramics, alloys and metal are pretty safe as long as you're not nearby when you're machining them. You want to hear about the refining process for bertrandite ore?"

"No," Lyons answered. Blancanales opened his mouth,

but the big former LAPD officer said to him, "Neither do you."

"Beryllium ore is crushed in something called a 'ball mill,'" Schwarz went on as if he hadn't heard. "They treat it with steam and sulfuric acid in these big tanks. Then they make it thicker. Sludge is pumped out and the beryllium sulfate is harvested."

"Does this story end soon?" Lyons asked.

"No, there's a lot more," Schwarz retorted.

"Cut to the relevant part, then," Lyons said. "Because I'm bored."

"Actually," Blancanales said, "I think he covered it. Steam and sulfuric acid. Big tanks of it. And dust that will kill us slowly with incurable, chronic, pneumonia-like lung-stiffening."

"That about covers it," Schwarz said.

"I feel like one of those red-tunic astronauts getting ready to phase down to the Planet Doom," Lyons said.

"You…you've never actually watched that show, have you, Ironman?" Schwarz asked.

Lyons stared straight ahead and gripped the steering wheel more tightly, saying nothing for a moment. Finally he said, "No."

"Well I give you credit for making the effort," Schwarz said.

"There it is," Blancanales interrupted. "Reichart Beryllium Processing. According to the dossier, it's a division of EarthGard."

"I don't know about you guys," Lyons said, "but I'm a little tired of this game."

"What game?" Blancanales asked.

"Is that a chain-link fence?" Schwarz asked. "I think that's a chain-link fence around the processing plant."

"The game where we make all nice, tell them we're federal agents and they shoot at us," Lyons said.

"We don't know that's going to happen here," Blancanales said. "They might not shoot at us at all."

"The gate is closed," Schwarz said from the passenger seat of the Suburban.

"The armed security is strange by itself," Lyons noted. "But when the company's got enough armed security that they're fielding a small army, you gotta wonder."

"The gate appears to be locked with a chain and a padlock," Schwarz noted.

The Suburban growled as Lyons floored the accelerator.

"So if they respond to a break-in with gunfire, you assume they're working with EarthGard to try and murder us?" Blancanales asked.

"We don't know specifically that EarthGard tried to murder us," Lyons pointed out.

"That's the cop in you talking," Blancanales said.

"Guys!" Schwarz interjected.

The Suburban crashed through the heavy chain-link, barbed-wire topped fence that secured the perimeter of the processing plant. Lyons, if he noticed, said nothing; he appeared wrapped up in his conversation with Blancanales. "All I'm saying," he went on, "is that if they respond with automatic gunfire, there is almost no way that we are dealing with legitimate security personnel. The average armed guard is little more than a librarian with an attitude. They're civilians, not law-enforcement personnel. They take a licensing course and they carry a gun for which, in most states, they have a civilian permit. I would bet except for, like, Fortune 500 mega-corporations, there isn't a single company within 500 miles whose security guards have full-auto Kalashnikovs and ARs."

Lyons's brow furrowed. Evidently he saw something

through the windshield, as the Suburban sped toward the main building of the processing plant, that he did not like. He reached out and, with one ham-size fist, pushed Schwarz down until the man's head was lower than the dash.

"Uh…Ironman?" Schwarz asked. "Why are you folding me in half?

"Pol," Lyons ordered. "Get down." At the last possible second, he ducked down behind the dash, too, as automatic gunfire raked the hood and starred the windshield.

"We are never getting our deposit back—"

"Can it, Gadgets," Lyons said, hauling the wheel hard over, bringing the Suburban in front of the main doors of the biggest building of the plant. "You used that joke already."

"Are you sure?" Schwarz asked. He pulled his Beretta 93-R machine pistol from under his windbreaker and press-checked it.

"If it wasn't this mission, it was the previous mission," Lyons said. "It all kinda blurs together."

"I know that feeling," Blancanales muttered. He slapped a magazine into his M-4. Lyons, grinning, grabbed his automatic shotgun from behind his seat. He didn't need to check his Python, apparently. Schwarz assumed the big former cop slept with the gun under his pillow at night.

"Let's do this," Lyons said. "I've got shooters on the roof of the main building, both front corners." As if in answer to Lyons's observation, another burst of fire ripped up the gravel drive on either side of the Suburban.

"Let me get that for you," Blancanales said. He shoved open his door, leaned out and fired two quick bursts at the roof. Then he shifted his aim and did the same. The men on the roof were suddenly very quiet.

"Did you hit them?" Lyons asked.

"Two for two," Blancanales answered as they exited the vehicle. "I'll wait with Gadgets while you kick in the doors."

"Why can't you do it?" Lyons asked, sounding more curious than anything else.

"Because I know how much you like kicking in doors," Blancanales said. "We all have our things. Doors are yours. Doors and seedy diners."

"I like a good plate of eggs and hash browns," Lyons said, slamming his combat boot against the double doors leading inside. The lock was strong; it took two more kicks, and a lowered shoulder, before Lyons was finally able to breach the entrance.

"Maybe he lets you do it because it looks like a lot of work," Schwarz said. Lyons opened his mouth to speak. "I know," Schwarz said. "I know. 'Shut up, Gadgets.'"

"Stop right there!" shouted another voice.

Able Team took cover in the doorways on either side of the foyer in which they found themselves. The man who had spoken had taken cover behind a reception desk. He wore a uniform similar to that of the guards at the previous target site. It was generic in nature, probably designed to be forgettable. That squared with what Schwarz thought of as the general philosophy of these EarthGard thugs. They went through the motions of looking respectable, but whatever was going on was just under the surface, easily disturbed and set in motion.

"Federal agents!" Lyons shouted back. "Your men have fired on federal officers engaged in official Justice Department business. Surrender immediately!"

"Let's see some credentials!" yelled the man behind the desk. He held some kind of submachine gun in his fists. Schwarz thought it looked like a 9 mm Colt, an ungainly marriage of the 9 mm cartridge to a short-barreled AR-15 platform.

Lyons, undaunted, took out the Justice Department identification wallet that each member of Able Team had been issued by Brognola. The names on all of the IDs were covers. Schwarz's identification labeled him "Hermann Shoreman," a name that would be changed the next time Able Team stopped at the Farm to resupply or debrief. But while the name on Lyons's ID was fictional, the credentials themselves were completely genuine, drawn up through legitimate Justice Department channels at Brognola's orders.

The big former cop threw his identification at the reception desk. It landed behind the desk with the gunman.

"There," Lyons shouted. "You've been duly introduced. What's your name?"

"Talbot," the gunman said. "I'm not authorized to let anyone into this facility. You'll have to leave."

"Talbot, you're trying my patience," Lyons said. "We're coming in. You're going to stand up, lay your gun on that desk and walk slowly toward me. Do that and you just might live to see lunchtime."

Talbot's response was to hold his Colt SMG above the level of the desk and spray blindly on full automatic. Schwarz and the other members of Able Team leaned as far back in the doorways as they could. Ricochets filled the foyer and the air around Able Team with drywall dust.

When the SMG went empty, Talbot yanked it back behind the desk. Lyons took the opportunity to lean out from behind his doorway with the Daewoo shotgun leveled. He had a fully loaded drum of 12-gauge slugs in place. He pulled the trigger once.

A quarter-size hole appeared in the reception desk at knee height. Lyons walked the shotgun from right to left, methodically punching daylight through the flimsy piece of furniture, creating a line of splintered entry holes that would chop in two anything on the other side. None of the men of Able Team heard a scream. Neither was there any return fire.

A rapidly spreading pool of blood appeared from beneath the desk.

Covering each other as they moved, Able Team advanced. They found the dead man with his empty Colt SMG in one hand and a loaded spare magazine in the other. Schwarz paused long enough to throw the magazine back toward the entry doors. Then he opened the Colt, removed the bolt and threw it in the opposite direction. It clattered on the floor at the end of a long corridor, which terminated in another set of doors. These doors had windows in them, but the windows were smoked and only barely translucent. There was no way to know what was on the other side.

"Remember the beryllium dust," Schwarz warned. "We don't want to put a grenade through any marked doors or bounce one off any of the tanks behind this building. Oh, and the acid. Don't forget the acid."

"Got it," Lyons said.

"Right," Blancanales said.

"I think I like the jokes better, Gadgets," Lyons said. "Let's roll."

The Able Team leader took point, building up speed as he charged the hallway, lowering his shoulder as he barreled into the doors. Schwarz understood the tactic. If you couldn't know what was on the other side, and if you didn't dare prepare the way with explosives, then speed and surprise were your next best tools.

Lyons hit the doors and rolled as he burst through. Schwarz followed close behind. As he'd passed the doors he realized they were now standing in an office cubicle farm, which made sense. The forward area of the main building would be offices for the administrative staff of the plant. The offices appeared to be deserted. The walls of the cubicle farm were the same wood-framed, gray-fabric-covered hamster cages that filled countless corporate offices across the nation.

Lyons paused and held up his hand, signaling for the team to stop immediately. Behind him, Schwarz and Blancanales froze. In the sudden moment of silence that resulted, all three men could hear the metallic sound of a magazine being slammed home.

"Uh-oh," Schwarz said.

The men who stood within the cubicles had been crouched behind the three-quarter-height fabric walls. To a man, they were Asian, and each one of them held a Kalashnikov-pattern assault rifle, many of these bearing black plastic furniture with accessory rails and forward hand grips.

Lyons pushed to one knee and, with the USAS-12 at hip level, blazed away on full automatic.

The noise was incredible. The shots brought answering fire from the Asian gunners, whose AK rifles created a wall of sound and gun smoke as they all started shooting at once. Schwarz pushed Blancanales one way and crawled in the opposite direction, hoping that if the two of them stayed low and did not make a tempting target by bunching up, they could avoid the worst of it.

Motes of gray fluff began to drift down from above. Schwarz had a fleeting moment of alarm in which he wondered if they had released beryllium dust from unseen containment area contiguous to the office space, but then he realized what he was seeing. Lyons's automatic shotgun was shredding the fabric walls of the cubicle farm, blowing them apart and causing the sound-dampening insulation inside to fly in every direction. As Schwarz watched from his spot on the floor, Lyons's slugs carved the Asian gunners to hunks of meat, leaving them bleeding and dying on the carpeted floor.

The thunder stopped. Lyons ejected the empty drum of his shotgun and slammed home a fresh magazine. Judging from the empties on the floor, he had changed drums at least twice during the firefight.

Schwarz stood and, with his Beretta in both hands, checked the wreckage of each cubicle. In one, he found a man struggling to reach his AK on the floor. The wounded man's chest was a ragged mess. It was astonishing that he was even conscious. In minutes, he would be dead. There was nothing that could be done for him. His last few minutes would be painful.

"Hey," Schwarz said. The would-be killer turned his head. As if resigned to his fate, he stopped trying for the AK and looked up at the electronics specialist.

"Wo jiu yaosile, wo bushi ma," the man said. His teeth were gritted with pain and he was very pale. Schwarz didn't know what he'd said, exactly, but he suspected. Judging from the man's face, it was something like, "I'm going to dic, aren't I?"

Schwarz gestured with his pistol. The Asian man looked at the barrel of the Beretta, looked back to Schwarz, and closed his eyes. He nodded, once.

The Able Team warrior fired.

"Clear here," Blancanales announced from the other side of the cubicle farm.

"Clear," Lyons echoed.

Schwarz felt his voice catch in his throat. He coughed once, smacking his fist against his chest. Shaking his head, he announced, "Clear."

A bullet punched through the door leading from the cubicle farm to whatever lay beyond. The members of Able

Team didn't try to use the wall on either side for cover. If the gunmen opposite that door were shooting through it, they could just as easily fire through the adjacent drywall. Lyons signaled for his teammates to follow him and then retraced their steps, heading back to the foyer and out the front door.

"The truck," Lyons explained. "We'll take the Suburban around the back."

The team climbed into the GMC. Lyons hit the gas so hard he nearly spun the wheels on the asphalt, urging the big SUV around the corner of the building. As they came around, they got a good view of the sprawling processing plant. Rows of tall steel tanks sat behind the building, and next to these, cylinders connected to a piping system. Schwarz ticked off in his mind what he presumed the function of each component should be. The tanks closer to their position were probably where leeching with sulfuric acid took place, for example. Large portions of the processing took place in sealed systems to make sure no one was exposed to the dust. This was an industry of which few Americans were aware and still fewer would ever see. Schwarz was impressed by the scope of it.

"There," Lyons said, pointing through the bullet-starred windshield. "That's the part of the building opposite the cubicles at the front. Our boys are there if they're anywhere."

"Assuming they haven't changed positions," Blancanales said. He had been watching through the rear window to make sure they weren't followed. He had not signaled, so he had not seen anything.

"You're not just going to ram the building with the truck, are you, Ironman?" Blancanales asked.

"I thought about it," Lyons said. He sounded completely serious. "But, no." He slammed the brakes and the

GMC Suburban squealed to a stop behind the rear of the main building. "Let's go. Dynamic entry."

"Where are the office workers?" Schwarz asked.

Lyons and Blancanales stopped and looked back at him. "Say that again, Gadgets?" Lyons asked. His expression told Schwarz that the electronics expert had managed to intrigue his team leader.

"It's not a weekend," Schwarz explained. "These are office hours. It isn't late enough for everybody to be at lunch. And we didn't announce that we were coming. We drove a truck through a set of gates that were padlocked closed. And that means that not only were there no civilians in that office today, but none were expected. Why is that? How long has this place been locked down? Have there ever been any administrative workers here? Why aren't we seeing any mine workers or other personnel, just going from building to building?"

Lyons scratched his face with one broad hand. Shouldering the Daewoo12-gauge, he nodded. "You're right," he said. "Something is seriously not kosher about all this. There's good news, though." He walked over to Schwarz, reached into the duffel bag that the electronics whiz still carried and removed a grenade.

"Dynamic entry," Blancanales repeated.

"The good news," Lyons went on, "is that if there are only shooters inside, and no office workers, we don't have to be so gentle." He looked back over his shoulder. "Gadgets, I want credit for this. I wanted to just throw a frag in there and blow the place. Instead, we'll do it the hard way." He advanced on the rear doors of the building, tried them both and found them locked. Taking a step back, he triggered the automatic shotgun, blowing apart the heavy wooden doors' locking mechanism. Then he kicked them in. Popping the grenade he held, he tossed that in, too.

"Smoke out," he said.

The grenade fired. Purple smoke billowed thickly through the open doors. Lyons signaled for his partners to follow him. They joined him on either side of the doors.

"Make a Hendrix joke, I dare you," Lyons said.

"Don't spoil it, Ironman," Schwarz said.

"Go!" Lyons said. He went through the doorway, shotgun at his shoulder, ready to cut down any hostiles he met.

He met some.

The room attached to the cubicle farm was a cafeteria, large and open. The only cover in the room, end to end, consisted of round picnic-like tables with built-in benches. These were of steel and fiberglass, from the looks of them. It was a very modern setup, possibly renovated within the past few years. The rest of the building looked fairly old by comparison. The cafeteria had large, wide windows, probably installed as a retrofit, running nearly from floor to ceiling.

The security guards here had modular AR-platform weapons covered in rails, lights and lasers. Able Team hit the floor, narrowly avoiding the first salvo. The gunmen weren't content to stay and fire from behind cover, either. They were mobile, gliding around the room like professional operators, trying to get a better angle on Able Team.

The purple smoke saved them. It was thick enough that it effectively obscured Able Team's movements. Schwarz scrambled to find some option—any option—that would enable them to get a better position on the gunmen trying to encircle them.

"Carl!" he called. "There, to the right! The kitchen!"

Lyons nodded. Laying down cover fire with his fearsome shotgun, he backed toward the door to the kitchen as Blancanales and Schwarz worked their way through the smoke to get there. Once past the threshold, they took advantage of the sturdiest shelter available: the stainless-steel, waist-high refrigerator and freezer that stood, like an island, at the rear of the kitchen's prep area. Seconds later they came under fire again. This time the 5.56 mm NATO bullets from their enemies' AR rifles clattered ineffectively against the stainless-steel barrier.

"Great," Blancanales said. "We're trapped again."

Their enemies were now moving through the kitchen area, pausing at the halfway point, firing in staggered bursts.

"Seriously?" Lyons asked.

"I'm telling Jack you have no faith," Schwarz said.

"Say the word, gentlemen," Grimaldi said through their earbuds, "and I'll drop in."

"The word is given, G-force," Lyons said. "The word is most certainly given."

The gunmen charged, making for Able Team's shelter, their guns spitting lead.

"This is going to be close," Blancanales said.

CHAPTER EIGHT

Banihal, Kashmir

The village of Banihal was beautiful in a stark, ascetic way. In the shadow of mountain outcroppings that boasted a mixture of snow and low scrub growth, the houses dotted the hillside on either side of a well-traveled pair of dirt ruts that qualified, in this remote region, as a "road." The homes were mostly of stone and brick near the center of the village, some newer and more elaborate than others. The roofs were of corrugated metal. Better houses boasted painted roofs; poorer dwellings were a mottled collection of steel gray and rust brown. All the roofs were relatively shallow and sharply peaked to discourage accumulation of snow, except for the most pitiful of stone dwellings. The poorest had thatched roofs and layered walls repeatedly patched with mortar and mud.

On the outskirts of the village, colorfully painted wooden homes, some of them brilliant red and even fluorescent lime, were clustered in runs of three and four, some practically on top of each other. One such structure, its porch painted bright green, boasted a speaker on the peak of its metal roof. This was a *masjid,* a mosque. The loudspeaker was used to call the village's Muslims to prayer.

The men of Phoenix Force watched through the viewing ports of the MRAPs as they rolled through the outer stretches of Banihal. T. J. Hawkins noted the people they passed. One man, in a beige tunic and matching pants under a heavy woolen coat and colorful scarf, was carrying a long-barreled rifle of some kind. The wooden stock had been ornately carved. He had a pair of goggles on his head and walked next to a similarly dressed man on a horse. The horse wore a hand-woven bridle.

"There's good Ibex hunting up here," Manning said.

"Good what hunting?" Hawkins asked.

"Ibex," Manning said. "Also called the steinbock. It's a species of wild goat. The males can develop amazing horns."

"I'm more interested in the rifle," Hawkins said. "I can't identify it."

"We may get to see the reason for that," Manning said. "If we don't, I'll explain."

"You're on, Gary," Hawkins said.

They passed a few more villagers, most of whom eyed the big armored trucks with a combination of fear and suspicion. A few were mothers, who grabbed their children and disappeared indoors. The children wore a broad variety of Western and local clothing, some of it bizarre, but all of it heavy enough to keep them warm. Knit caps abounded among the younger males.

Most of the adult men they saw were bearded, wearing cloth wraps on their heads. Hawkins thought of the wraps as turbans, but he wasn't sure if that was correct, nor did he know what the local word for them might be. Layers of flowing, long-sleeved garments, some of them very colorful, seemed to be the fashion trend. Women wore a type of head shawl that, in some cases, was long enough to be wrapped around the body like a cloak. Quite a few of these boasted vibrant, elaborate designs.

"One, fall back," McCarter ordered. "I want to cover both ends of the village." He looked at James. "Calvin, when you get to the end of the main drag here, take up station with Rafe on the gun. Gary, I want you to loan me T.J. as backup. Stay close, but give us enough distance that you're not barking up our backsides. The armor is likely to spook the locals and I'm hoping they'll take us to their leader, as they say."

"Roger," Manning acknowledged. He stopped the MRAP long enough for Hawkins to climb out. Then he moved the big vehicle a few houses down the dirt road, repositioning the MRAP so that it wasn't quite blocking the road. It now held a commanding view both into and out of the village on that end. If Manning took the automatic grenade launcher, he could level the center of the village with little effort. Not that Phoenix Force meant the villagers any harm. The opposite was true.

Hawkins took up position behind and to the left of McCarter, his head on a swivel, making sure that nobody took a shot at McCarter. It was a fact that a man's awareness was impaired while the conversational part of his brain was engaged in dialogue. If McCarter was going to play diplomat here in Banihal, he couldn't focus on that task while also protecting his own life. For the next few minutes that job fell to Hawkins, who would look out for them both. The rest of Phoenix Force, in turn, was securing as much of Banihal as was practical.

Hawkins couldn't imagine how some people rode a desk all day, when instead they could be doing work like this.

McCarter walked to what was more or less the center of the village. Several sets of local eyes watched him and Hawkins pass. At some unspoken mark of his own, McCarter simply stopped and stood, one arm steadying his Tavor on its single point sling, the other hooked in his belt not far from the butt of his Hi-Power.

"David?" Hawkins whispered.

"Steady, mate," McCarter said. "They'll come to us."

They did not have to wait long.

The elder who came for them appeared between two of the poorest stone-and-mud dwellings. Another local man trailed behind him, but his posture was deferential. This second man was not a bodyguard so much as…a second? A lieutenant? Something to that effect? Hawkins had the feeling they were essentially being met by their opposite number. He girded himself for what was to come. If an attack was offered, it would be soon. Hostiles would waste no more time than that required to distract the Phoenix Force team members.

The old man wore a yellow head wrap. His face was covered by a snow-white beard, which was stained yellow from cigarettes. He smelled heavily of cloves, in fact. The dark clove cigarettes were very popular in this part of the world.

When the old man stopped a few paces in front of the two Phoenix Force soldiers, McCarter bowed slightly. "Hello," he said. "My name is David. I'm with…the United Nations. I'm leading a peacekeeping effort in the area."

The old man looked at Hawkins, then at McCarter. He spared the closer MRAP a long, skeptical glare, then looked over his shoulder at the farther armored vehicle. He raised one hand to his face and, with dirt-caked nails, scratched his craggy nose.

"This is a lie," he said in English.

Hawkins felt himself tense. If it was going to happen, it was going to happen now. He visualized bringing the Tavor to his shoulder and acquiring targets—

"It is good that this is so," said the younger man. "I am Zia Chodary. This is our elder, Rizwan Baloch."

"Zia says it is good that you are not the United Nations because Zia has no stomach for cowards," said Baloch.

"Can you imagine United Nations' troops in a place such as this? They would be eaten alive by Jamali's men." He paused to spit on the ground. "Even by those of General Gera. They are cowards. What is the word that you have? Without innards."

"Gutless," McCarter said. "I can see why you might think so."

"You," Baloch said. "You are not this 'gutless.' I can see death in your eyes. The United Nations send sheep in pretty blue hats. You have the eyes of lions. Even this one, the young one." Baloch gave Hawkins a hard, appraising glance. "Do you think us fools? He watches your life as you speak to me. If I were to take a knife from my belt and attack you, he would shoot me down. Is this not so?"

Hawkins didn't know if he should respond to that. He looked at McCarter.

McCarter smiled at Rizwan Baloch. "This is so, mate," he said. "This is so."

"Then we understand each other," Baloch said. "If you were with Jamali—" he paused to spit again "—or with General Gera, you would not be speaking with me. You would not be showing me this respect. So what do you want? Who are you?"

"I'm part of an international team," McCarter said. "A team with the same goals as the United Nations. Let's say we're a bit more effective in smaller groups. We have fewer rules."

Baloch grinned. Half his teeth were missing; the other half were yellow. "What is it you want of the people of Banihal?"

"I'm led to understand, mate," McCarter said, "that both Jamali and Gera use this location to transport troops back and forth. And it sounds to me like you know both names pretty well."

"Yes," Baloch said, looking at the ground. "Yes, we do. We are a poor village, Englishman. If we had more for them to take, they would take it. Gera shows us no respect. He comes through, he kills our animals, he smashes whatever is in his way. His tanks have twice killed villagers who were not fast enough to leave the road. He treats us as if we do not exist."

"That must be difficult," said McCarter.

"Life is difficult," the elder said. "Better to be treated like nothing than to be treated like animals. This is what Jamali does." The old man spit in the dirt once more. "He burns our homes. He rapes our women. He takes our food stores. He makes my people suffer. There is little we can do to fight him. We have guns. We have many guns. But he has more. We cannot fight him and we cannot fight Gera. We are so many ants compared to these men."

"What if I told you," McCarter said, "that there's a way you can hurt Jamali? Or Gera? Or both?"

"I am listening, Englishman."

McCarter leaned in, his body language conspiratorial. "We have certain information on the movements of both generals' forces," he said. "But ground intelligence, specifics, could really help us hit them where they live. Our goal is to cause them as much trouble as we can. As much pain as we can."

"You will treat them like animals," Baloch said. "And bring them to heel."

"That's right, mate," McCarter confirmed. "That's the idea."

You want Doru Shahabad," Baloch said. "It is a village not far from here. If you have a map, I can show you."

McCarter removed his secure smartphone from his coat and called up a satellite map. He adjusted the distance and displayed the topography of the region directly around their position. Gesturing, he showed the screen to the village elder. Chodary, behind the old man, exclaimed in amazement.

"Yes," Baloch said. "It is truly amazing."

Chodary muttered something in his native language, shaking his head. Hawkins wanted to laugh.

"The village is here," Baloch said, pointing. At the touch of his finger, the screen enlarged the village area, showing a satellite picture of the cluster of dwellings. Baloch pursed his lips in amazement. "Remarkable," he said. Chodary, behind him, nodded.

"So what is in Doru Shahabad?" McCarter asked.

"The Pakistani forces use it for what they call 'recreation.' Many atrocities are committed there. It is larger than our humble village. It offers them more opportunity to enjoy their brutality. Much to their horror. But if you go there, you can hurt them. You would have our gratitude if you did so."

"I think we can arrange that," McCarter said. "Thank you, Elder."

Baloch bowed. "It is we who thank you, Englishman. And I thank you for the story."

"The story?" McCarter asked.

"I will be able to tell my grandchildren of the day I met a wolf who claimed he was a sheep."

McCarter smiled. Hawkins had to struggle to maintain his poker face.

"With your permission, then, Elder," McCarter said respectfully, "my men and I will—"

Gunfire rang out from somewhere in the village.

Hawkins instantly had the Tavor up. Baloch held up a hand. "It is not a threat," he said. There were a few more shots, followed by the sound of someone shouting angrily. Baloch frowned.

"Is that normal?" McCarter asked. The shouting became much louder. Clearly some sort of dispute was occurring.

"No," Chodary said. "It is not. We should investigate."

Baloch set off with Chodary in tow. McCarter shot Hawkins a look that said, essentially, "I don't know; let's look." The two Phoenix Force commandos followed the village elder and his lieutenant.

Baloch led them between two of the stone buildings to a structure facing an open field. Immediately, Hawkins could smell the distinctive odor of discharged firearms. The field, he realized, was dotted with wooden posts set in the ground. To these, targets of wood and paper had been nailed. Each of the targets bore the holes of many passing bullets.

Behind a makeshift firing line set up at the rear of the nearest building, several bearded villagers were arguing with a pair of men wearing expensive hiking clothes. Hawkins recognized the two immediately as stereotypical "ugly Americans." He recognized the brand logo on their clothes but, more important, he recognized their attitude.

"He said I could have six shots," the first one complained. An embroidered name on his jacket proclaimed him Alan. His partner wore no such label. "I paid for six shots."

"But the gun is broken," said one of the bearded villagers.

Hawkins realized what was going on, then, when he caught a glimpse through the back door of the shop. Supported on pegs on the walls were countless rifles and handguns, all of them very clearly patterned after recognizable weapons. Hawkins saw what looked like a German WWII MP-40, a Thompson submachine gun with a drum magazine and countless bolt-action rifles that resembled Enfields. But every one of the weapons had a bare steel finish, and each was slightly…off…in some way.

Hawkins noted the stone chimney jutting from the shop, which was likely connected to an oversize furnace within. This was a weapons forge. He had read about the gun trade in remote parts of the world, Pakistan in particular, where smiths with moderate skill cobbled together handmade look-alikes of the world's most famous guns. They sold these both to locals and to what visitors passed through such terribly remote regions of the world. The weapons were completely unlicensed. Some worked and some didn't. Some would go on working; others would fail quickly. It was luck of the draw in a place where that was no law—and no one to enforce it should laws to be enacted.

"Bloody gun-tourists," McCarter said under his breath.

"That's what I figure," Hawkins whispered "Probably figure the 'extreme' way to spend their vacations is to visit remote Pakistan and rent unlicensed guns."

Hawkins had read that some of these shops even boasted rocket launchers and other heavy weapons, but that was not the case here. Had it been, the people of Baloch's village might have had some way to fight back against the forces of Jamali and Gera.

The man apparently named Alan was holding what might have been a Magnum-caliber revolver. It had a heavy cylinder and a tremendous nine-inch barrel. It was also split along the length of its frame.

"I want my money back or I want to take the shots I was promised," Alan demanded. He was red in the face and shaking his finger at the villagers. "You think you can rip me off? Do I look like I'm fresh off the turnip truck, you mountain hillbillies?"

"That is enough," Baloch said. "You are guests here.

Return to wherever you came from if our terms do not meet your liking."

Hawkins edged closer to the rear door of the shop. His goal was to place himself between the angry tourists and a large supply of firearms. As he looked inside, he saw several rifles of the type he'd seen earlier, with ornately carved wooden stocks and receivers he did not recognize. That's what Manning had been hinting at before: The village was a source of locally made firearms, built by hand right here. The craftsmanship was a bizarre mixture of delicate skilled work and rough-hewn, hand-tooled expedience.

"You're the same the world over," Alan said. "Money-grubbing con artists playing the poverty card in a search for pity, then cleaning out the pockets of honest men with your games!"

"Take care," Chodary warned. Baloch's face darkened. The elder reached into his outer wrap for something at his waist.

McCarter, who probably could read the situation as well as Hawkins, stepped between the elder and the florid American. "Say, mate," he barked through a broad smile. "I wonder if you've got any bleeding idea what you're into here."

"Excuse me?" Alan said.

"Your friend there," McCarter said, pointing to Alan's unidentified companion, "looks terrified. Have you picked up on that? He's got good reason to be afraid, too." McCarter looked the man up and down. "So what is it?" he asked. "Stocks or some kind of internet search engine thing?"

"Excuse me?"

"You're obviously wealthy," McCarter said. "At your age there are only a few ways that would happen. A few years back I'd say the stock market. Used to be any idiot could make a fortune and drive a BMW with a few junk bonds in his wallet. These days it's all high-tech stuff. So what is it?"

"I'll have you know I work for—"

"Sod off, mate," McCarter interrupted, holding up a hand. "I don't care. Here's what I do know. You're so full of yourself and what you think you're owed that you've come to one of the most remote parts of the world on bleeding vacation. And it's never once occurred to you that there is no law here. None whatsoever. You've had good luck so far. You've dodged the war that's going on here. You've probably got a digital camera full of pictures of your rugged adventure. And your buddy there strikes me as the bookish type. He's writing a travelogue or something, right?" The Briton stared hard at Alan's friend. The man turned bright red.

"Are you some sort of law enforcement?" Alan said, more quietly.

"No," McCarter said. "That's my point. There is no law enforcement here. And you've come very close to calling their village elder a liar. These people have almost nothing. Do you understand what they'll do to someone who's called them liars and thieves?" He pointed in Baloch's general direction, careful not to gesture straight at the old man. "He's about to gut you, mate. He's about to put a knife in your belly and let you bleed out on the floor of this shop. And if you think that rust color on these floorboards is paint, you're wrong. You won't be the first."

By this point in McCarter's little speech, Alan was pale. His companion, whether journalist or just "extreme" travel companion, looked even worse. Baloch, for his part, wore a smile. His hand was still inside his cloak.

"He speaks the truth," the old man said. "Listen to the lion."

Alan opened his expensive coat. He had what looked like a brand-new, American-made. fixed-blade knife on his belt. It looked very expensive. His hand dropped to the hilt of the knife.

"I've trained with some of the world's most famous knife-fighting experts," Alan said. "I fear no man. Step aside, little man, or I'll show you why your country lost its empire—"

McCarter punched him in the stomach.

Alan doubled at the waist, making choking noises as he gasped for air he suddenly could not draw. McCarter dropped an elbow on his back, although the blow was a gentle one as far as Hawkins could tell. The assault drove the American to his knees.

Hawkins saw Alan's friend shift position. If the other tourist was thinking of pulling a knife of his own, it was time to neutralize any ideas the fool might have about standing up for his buddy. The Phoenix Force commando took a step forward, whipped his Tavor up to his shoulder and let the barrel of the futuristic-looking weapon speak for him.

Alan's partner froze, staring into the 5.56 mm death that was the Israeli weapon.

"That's right, fella," Hawkins drawled. "You just stand there and don't make any sudden moves. You'll have a hell of a story to tell folks when you get back to the States."

McCarter began very methodically, very professionally, working Alan over. He kicked the man, dragged him to his feet and punched him again. Then he repeated the process.

Hawkins could see the restraint that McCarter was using. The beating looked fierce but, honestly, the Briton was doing no serious damage to his "victim." The attack was a show of force for the villagers. Hawkins was the only man close enough to overhear when McCarter leaned close to Alan—now struggling to get to all fours—and whispered to the man.

"You idiot," McCarter snarled. "I want you to know I've saved your stupid life. If these people thought you hadn't paid for your show of disrespect, they'd have killed you. Do you get me, Alan What's-Your-Name? They'd have killed you, and I can't guarantee they wouldn't have tortured you first."

Once more, McCarter dragged the American to his feet. He held him in place until Alan, swaying, managed to stay upright on his own. "Now get out of here," the Phoenix Force leader said. "Go home. Don't stop anywhere. Don't visit some other exotic land. Just get the hell home where you belong."

Alan, bleeding from the nose, exchanged glances with his unnamed friend. Then the American very quietly bent, picked up the borrowed, damaged weapon he had paid to rent and handed it respectfully to the shopkeeper. Without another word, the two tourists hurried out.

Baloch began laughing. It was a deep, belly-shaking laugh. The old man was practically crying with amusement by the time McCarter signaled Hawkins that it was time for them, too, to leave.

CHAPTER NINE

Elmore, Ohio

"Here it comes," Schwarz said.

The roar of the Osprey shook the building, rattling the full-length panes. From their vantage behind the freezer, Blancanales could just make out the twin-rotor craft descending into the view of the floor-to-ceiling glass. Gunfire raked their position as their attackers continued to move up through the cafeteria, using the emplaced tables for cover, seemingly oblivious to the monstrous airborne threat that had just dropped into their midst.

"Stay on the floor and to my right, gents," Grimaldi directed through their transceivers.

The whine of the Osprey's cannon again filled their ears. Glass shattered. Tables were ripped in two. Steel and plastic and fiberglass shards became flying wreckage, cutting through the attackers, adding damage to the annihilating power of the multibarrel cannon's rounds. Screaming again filled the air.

Blancanales closed his eyes briefly, in silent respect for the lives they were taking. He had no pity for hired guns, for mercenaries, for enemy soldiers...whatever these would-be murderers were. But a man would have to be inhuman not to acknowledge the weight of snuffing out so many living, breathing men in so short a time. Understanding that was one of the things that made Blancanales so good with people—a skill that had resulted in his nickname, "Politician."

Of course, there were some who considered "Politician" an insult and not a compliment. Blancanales understood the spirit in which the appellation was meant.

"Clearing your way in three," Grimaldi stated. "Two. One. Good hunting, gentlemen. I'll be on standby if you need me." The Osprey, as quickly as it had appeared, disappeared once more, ascending beyond the roofline and rattling the building as it soared past.

Having that kind of destructive power at the other end of a radio was a heady feeling, indeed, Blancanales thought. He checked his M-4, took three quick breaths and broke cover.

"Go, go, go," Lyons shouted.

The three men of Able Team charged the cafeteria, their weapons at their shoulders, gliding in a combat crouch that gave each of them a stable firing platform. Their weapons barked now and again; there were a few men still left mobile after the Osprey's attack. Most of the men in the cafeteria now, however, were dead or dying. A few still moaned. Lyons paused long enough to put a mercy round through one with his shotgun. Schwarz did the same with his 93-R.

The floor of the cafeteria was awash in blood.

"Clear," Lyons said.

"Clear," Schwarz said. He turned to Blancanales and his eyes widened. "Pol! Your six!"

Blancanales whirled on one foot, dropping low to the opposite knee, trying to get himself out of the firing line. The man drawing down on him held an AR-15 and was dressed in "Blackwater chic"—commercial BDUs and a load-bearing MOLLE vest, with plenty of accessories. Blancanales snapped off a shot that punched through the man's thigh, toppling him, causing him to lose his grip on his weapon. The wounded man cried out.

"Secure that man!" Lyons ordered.

Blancanales was already on the move. He dashed to the wounded shooter, kicked the man's AR-15 away and put the barrel of his own M-4 under the man's chin.

"Do not move!" he ordered. "Do not attempt to take any hostile action or I will blow your brains all over this floor."

The shooter froze. He looked up at the Able Team warrior, his face creased in pain, and nodded once. Lyons and Schwarz joined Blancanales with the wounded man before Lyons took a look around and gestured.

"We need to secure a perimeter," he said. "It looks like we've broken the resistance offered, but if there are pockets of more guards, we want to be ready for them." He knelt and picked up the shooter's fallen AR-15. He ejected the magazine, racked the bolt and looked inside, inspecting the chamber. The weapon had a considerable set of optics mounted to it, as well as a flashlight and laser. He handed the rifle to Schwarz.

"It's like Christmas morning," the electronics expert said. "I always wanted one of these with all the bells, whistles and gad—"

"Knock it off," Lyons growled. "Find yourself roof access, get somewhere high and keep an eye on the building. Especially if the local cops start to show, I don't want any interference from somebody more interested about jurisdiction and his pride than in finding out what the hell is going on here."

"Got it," Schwarz said. He knelt, patted down the wounded man and took the shooter's extra magazines for the AR-15. The gunman looked irate but did not try to stop Schwarz from taking the gear.

"Pol," said Lyons, "I'm going to post over there by the

door to the cafeteria. I think maybe you should have a heart-to-heart talk with our friend here."

"Understood," Blancanales said. He grabbed the man by the collar and dragged him toward one of the few tables that had escaped the Osprey's wrath. Then he pushed the wounded operator onto a bench and broke out his first-aid kit. Lyons watched long enough to make sure the prisoner didn't try anything hostile before he took up position by the door.

"Ironman," Schwarz said through the transceiver link, "something fishy is happening out here. I've got figures moving through the tank field behind the main building. I think they're outer perimeter security."

"Trying to regroup and stage an incursion on our location?" Lyons asked.

"Looks like it," Schwarz said. "I'm going to play sniper up here, keep as many off for as long as I can. But you're going to have company before we're done."

"Understood," Lyons said. "Pol?"

"We're on the clock," Blancanales said. "Got it."

With his first-aid kit, Blancanales bandaged the wound in the shooter's leg. The shot was a through-and-through, fortunately for the gunman. With pressure and a dressing on the wound, Blancanales was able to get the bleeding under control. He distracted the shooter during the procedure by talking to him. "What's your name?" he asked.

"Carlisle," the operator said. "Doug Carlisle."

"Well, Doug Carlisle," Blancanales said, finishing with the man's leg and patting him down for weapons, "I think you should tell me everything you know."

"Carlisle," repeated the operator. "Doug Carlisle."

Blancanales sighed. "The name, rank and serial number jazz won't take us very far," he said. "Let me break this down for you. You are now in custody of the Federal Justice Department."

"Since when does the Justice Department have field operators?" Carlisle asked.

Blancanales sighed again. "Do you understand what happens when we take you back to the rest of the world?" he asked. "Somewhere that isn't this factory. *Anywhere* that isn't this factory. You'll be judged, de facto, a terrorist operating on United States soil. You'll have no rights. You'll have no privileges."

"That hardline fascist crap doesn't scare me," Carlisle said. "I served in Iraq. I've seen people killed. I've seen people blown to pieces. Nothing you got to say to can frighten me."

"Not even Guantanamo?" Blancanales asked. When that caught Carlisle's attention, the Able Team operative said, "Because I know someplace worse. Someplace so secret the press and the protesters would get shot before they got within fifty miles of the place. The kind of black hole where the worst enemies of the United States, the ones dumb enough or unlucky enough to survive their black-ops, under-the-books attacks on United States' interests, go to live out their natural lives until they die."

Carlisle swallowed. "You're full of shit," he said.

"Look at me," Blancanales said. "Do I seem serious? Do you know how many operations like this never make the news? How many private armies get taken down off the books?"

Carlisle looked at Lyons, standing in the doorway to the cafeteria. He looked back at Blancanales and said, "I want a deal. I want to cut a deal."

"That's right," Blancanales said. "Look at him. Do you have any idea how many men just like you that guy has taken down? No, you don't. And long after you're rotting in the deepest secret dungeon our government manages to keep hidden from the world, he and the rest of our team will still be sending more prisoners to keep you company."

Carlisle seemed to be considering that, but at the last minute, his pride got the better of him. He shook his head. "I won't. I won't do it."

"All right," Blancanales said. He toed his M-4 out of the way with one foot, making sure it was beyond reach, and withdrew the Glock in his waistband.

Carlisle looked at him in horror when Blancanales racked the slide and put the barrel of the gun in his face.

"It's nothing personal, Carlisle," he said. "But all that business about a secret prison? I lied. We're a government death squad. And I'm sorry, but it's your turn." He stood off with his palm held above the Glock, as if he were concerned about getting splattered with blood at close range.

"Wait! Wait! Wait!" Carlisle begged. "I'm just a mercenary! Just a mercenary! I work for a company called Cudgel Security. I was just hired to do security here. I didn't ask more questions than that."

"What's with all the Asian backup?" Blancanales demanded. "They're fielding different equipment and they're obviously not from around here."

"Those are the Chinese," Carlisle said. "I was told to stay out of their way and to defer to them if there were any operational disputes. It was clear that the Chinese were in charge."

"And who are you both working for?" Blancanales asked.

"EarthGard," Carlisle answered.

"Who in EarthGard?" Blancanales demanded. "We know the company is involved in what's going on here somehow. Who are the key figures? Who's calling the shots?"

"Cudgel only ever dealt with middle-men, cut-outs," Carlisle said. "And even if someone at the company knows, there is no reason they'd tell me. I'm nobody."

"You're nobody?"

"That's what I said."

"Hey, Pol?" Schwarz said. "Ironman? I have contact at the rear of the building." The sound of rifle fire from Schwarz's AR-15 was audible from outside, even though their transceivers did not relay it. Schwarz was taking his time, picking his shots. "I have nine—no, ten incoming. Looks like… Wait. I've got what looks like… Chinese special forces? That's a camouflage pattern used by ChiCom special operations."

Blancanales looked at Carlisle. "They yours?"

"All our operators were in Cudgel uniform," said Carlisle, shrugging. "I don't know what that's all about."

"Contact, contact, contact," Schwarz warned. "Approaching shooters are entering the building, repeat, entering the building. I got three of them."

"Left or right?" Lyons asked. "Left or right? Give me a vector here, Gadgets."

"Both," Schwarz said. "They're swarming the rear of the building. Now I've got more of them. Reinforcements. They're coming through the tank field."

"Which means we can't put Jack on them," Lyons said.

"Not unless you want to create a beryllium dust cloud that will travel who knows how far," Schwarz said.

"That's what I thought," Lyons commented. "Pick off the ones you can. We'll stay on them over here. I'm falling back to the freezer. Pol, you're coming with me."

"We've got to secure the prisoner," Blancanales said.

"Then let's secure the hell out of him and get a move on," Lyons urged. He put an arm under one of Carlisle's. Blancanales did the same. Then the two Able Team members worked to drag the wounded man back to the relative safety of the freezer that had previously afforded Able Team shelter.

The rattle of full-automatic fire now emanated from the roof. Schwarz was doing his best to keep the enemy off their position, but they were outnumbered. This tactic was a holding method at best.

A trio of men in the new camouflage pattern Schwarz had identified burst into the ravaged cafeteria. One of them actually slipped on the floor, slick with blood as it was. He recovered and, as he did, fired his weapon from the hip.

Carlisle's head exploded.

Lyons and Blancanales dropped the corpse and threw themselves behind the freezer barrier. The men in the Chinese camouflage came storming through the cafeteria in pursuit, firing their Kalashnikovs, spraying down the already bullet-riddled space. More troops brought up the rear. The tide of battle, the momentum and initiative of the conflict, had turned against Able Team just that quickly.

It felt all wrong. Blancanales had been in enough firefights to sense something had changed, some new variable. It felt for all the world as if the enemy had been resupplied, as though they had been reinforced from the outside. But how and why would the security forces here have known to call for reinforcements? Able Team's attack had been sudden and swift.

"Pol," Lyons said. "I'm going to take it to them."

"Another grand Ironman play?" Blancanales asked. "You don't want to end up like our buddy Carlisle. We could call Jack down again."

"We could," Lyons said, "but if the targets drift back out toward Gadgets's tanks, we're back to our cloud of death dust again."

"How are they *my* tanks?" Schwarz protested. He was

still shooting on the roof; there were still more soldiers moving in from the tank field. "Just because I explain the things that can kill us doesn't mean they belong to me somehow."

"Complain, complain, complain," Lyons said. He reloaded his automatic shotgun and waited while Blancanales reloaded his M-4. Then he handed the big shotgun to Blancanales. "Cover me," he said. He secured the Colt Python and jacked the hammer back for a single-action first shot.

"Don't get killed, Ironman," Blancanales warned.

"No promises," Lyons said. He charged.

Carl Lyons was a big man. When he barreled at the smaller shooters who were piling into the cafeteria, he took them by surprise. Before they could bring their guns to bear on him, Blancanales was up behind the freezer, the triggers held back on both automatic weapons. He braced the guns on top of the freezer, pulled them back against his shoulders and rode out the punishing recoil of the USAS-12 as the shotgun churned out its incredible volume of firepower. The recoil of the M-4 was less extreme, but no less lethal, as he walked the weapons from side to side as if operating an emplaced machine gun.

The hardest part was letting up on the triggers to miss Lyons. For his part, the big ex-cop had turned berserker on the approaching gunmen, running, ducking, dodging and rolling as if he were bulletproof.

Lyons aimed and fired. The big Magnum round from his revolver punched a hole through the throat of the closest enemy. The blood spray coated the face of the next man, and Lyons smashed the revolver against that man's face.

Blancanales resumed firing, washing down the cafeteria deck with flying lead. Lyons kept up his attack. He shot another man, then a third. He smashed his inseam into the ankle of yet another, toppling him, and shot the man through the head while he lay on the floor. As the Able Team leader reached the cafeteria doors, however, they opened again, and this time there were half a dozen new gunners waiting.

"Carl!" Schwarz shouted. "Floor!"

Lyons went prone. Schwarz, who had climbed down from the roof and was now behind the enemy shooters, sprayed out the 30-round magazine in his AR-15.

Blancanales was actually forced to take cover as some of the stray rounds that didn't stay in the knot of shooters found their way to the back of the cafeteria—and the much-abused steel hide of the freezer.

The building shook once more.

"G-Force, this is Able," said Lyons. "G-Force, this is Able. Check your fire, Jack. Check your fire. Those tanks are off limits."

"Absolutely, Able," said Grimaldi. "But I thought you'd like to know that the last of your hostile forces has exited the tank field and is now converging on your position. So I thought I'd lose a little altitude and even out the odds for you. Permission to proceed?"

"Granted," Lyons said. "Knock 'em down, Jack."

The Osprey cut through the yard of the processing plant. Grimaldi was one of the foremost combat pilots in the world; he had no trouble deftly maneuvering between the building and the processing equipment on the grounds of the beryllium plant. The enemy soldiers were caught in the open between the equipment and the main building. Grimaldi fired the Osprey's cannon and tore them apart.

"Clean-up detail," Lyons ordered. "Let's split up. Hunt the grounds. Find any of them still mobile and neutralize them. Pol, I'll take my shotgun back. You secure the cafeteria. Gadgets and I will see to the rest."

"On it," Blancanales said. He handed Lyons the USAS-12 as the bigger man passed him.

"Way ahead of you," Schwarz said.

"G-Force," Lyons said to Grimaldi, "get over to the main entrance. The gate we took down coming in. Block any locals that try to get in. We've been at this long enough that I'm surprised we're not already knee deep in cops. Pull whatever government authority cards you have to keep them off us, but make sure we're left alone."

"Understood," said Grimaldi.

Blancanales found himself standing alone in the torn-up cafeteria. He took a breath, reloaded his M-4 and slung it. Then he pulled a spare magazine from his pocket and reloaded his Glock. The empty magazine clattered on the bloody cafeteria floor.

He hated this part of the job.

Securing the Glock, Blancanales moved from body to body with his sat phone. He took a digital photograph of each man. Some didn't have faces for him to photograph; he left these, except where identifying tattoos on other parts of the body might help. When he had finished with all the men in the cafeteria, he moved out into the hallway.

The smell of death, the coppery tang of blood and the unmistakable aroma of discharged cartridges, filled his nostrils.

"This is G-Force," Grimaldi said through the transceivers. "Ironman, you were right. I've got multiple local police units inbound. I took the liberty of getting the Farm on the line."

"Good call, Jack," said Lyons through the transceiver link.

"This is Price," said the Farm's mission controller, her voice transmitting to all the members of Able Team.

"Carl, we're running interference with the Ohio State

Police, but they're not happy about it," she said. "I've also dispatched a federal clean-up team to you. Estimated time of arrival is one half hour. You need to hold that location until then. We think we can delay the cops by about that much, maybe a little more. Anything beyond that and they'll start agitating for entry. There's only so much I can do."

"Much appreciated," Lyons returned. "Barb…it's a slaughterhouse here. If the locals see this scene before we have a chance to assert governmental control over it, they'll throw us in jail no matter what identification we've got on us. And I can't have Jack blowing up any police cars from on high. Besides, we need to refuel and re-arm our transportation. We've made heavy use of it, this outing."

"Understood, Carl," said Price. "This data dump I'm getting from Able's phones is part of the problem, I presume?"

"It's weird," said Lyons. "We've got one, possibly two, contingents of private security working here, one of them through something called 'Cudgel.' Can you run that?"

"The name rings a bell," said Price. "One of the less reputable outfits. They make most contractors look warm and fuzzy by comparison."

"I have a name for you, too," said Lyons. "Doug Carlisle. Private contractor working for Cudgel. He clued us in to the presence of the Chinese special operators before another group killed him. It may have been an accident or it may have been deliberate. That's not really clear. And it adds to the confusion."

"I'll say it does," said Price. "It doesn't come together neatly, that's for sure. What other support do you need from us?"

"Just that clean-up crew," said Lyons. "Fuel and ammo for Jack's ride. And we could do with a resupply and a new vehicle ourselves, once we finish in and around Elmore," he admitted. "We've, uh, taken more than a few scratches and dents in our truck."

"No worries, Able," said Price. "Let us crunch the data on this end and run facial recognition on your deceased. I'll be in touch when we've given Bear a chance to run identifications to see if he can find any connections."

"We'll have to work quickly," Blancanales said. "I think I hear sirens."

"He's right," Grimaldi said. "I'm looking at what I think are flashing red-and-blue lights to the west and east. If the perimeter has auxiliary entrances, they're going to waste no time breaching those and coming to you."

"Roger," Lyons said. "We'll be prepared. But stay handy, Jack. If they won't listen to reason, we're going to count on you to bust us out."

"Will do," Grimaldi said. "Let's hope it doesn't come to that."

"Yeah," Lyons said. "Here's to hope."

As he listened to Lyons's sign-off with the Farm, Blancanales took out his Glock, ejected the magazine and placed it on top of one of the cafeteria tables. He locked the pistol open and placed it next to the mag. Then he unloaded his M-4, put that on the tabletop and took off his jacket.

The sound of men shouting echoed from the corridor beyond his position. That would be the police, entering and establishing control.

Patiently, Blancanales put his hands on the tabletop, assuming the stop-and-frisk position.

Might as well make the locals' jobs as easy as possible. He waited.

CHAPTER TEN

Doru Shahabad

"Step on it," McCarter ordered James. "Let's see if we can make it to the end of the village before they drop the hammer on us."

"I'm giving her all she's got, man," James said.

"Rafe, get ready on the turret," McCarter said. "They're lying for us and I don't want to find out they've got heavy artillery hidden somewhere." He looked back over his shoulder. "T.J., you ready?"

"Ready," Hawkins said. "We get to the next opening in the dwellings, we cut right, take it back around the outskirts and take up station with Gary on the automatic grenade launcher. Once our friends make their presence known, we drive them up the main road from both sides of the village and squeeze them together. This will neutralize the surprise they think they have waiting for us."

"Right, then," McCarter said. "Let's show them how we do it. This is where I get off, lads." He opened his door and climbed down from the MRAP, hurrying to take shelter between two of the stone structures.

The contingent of Pakistani gunmen that now held Doru Shahabad most likely thought they were very clever. If they were up against low-tech soldiers, such as those of General Gera, they would have had the makings of a bloody ambush that would deal a terrible blow to the other side.

Pakistani forces belonging to General Jamali had been imaged from the satellites overhead, based on the intelligence the Farm had received through Phoenix Force.

Thermal analysis had been used to determine that the Jamali soldiers were distributing themselves throughout the village, in the buildings along the main road leading through it, where they would doubtless try to catch any forces who came through subsequently in an ambush. From the real-time stamps on the images, it was also clear they had taken their time getting into position. That meant Jamali's people weren't expecting any force specifically. Rather, they were setting up shop to fish for Gera's men when the latter finally came through the village.

No doubt they were passing the time brutalizing the villagers, too.

McCarter had spent the trip from Banihal examining closely the satellite images transmitted by the Farm. They showed some traffic in and out of the village shortly after the Jamali forces showed up. The vehicles used were Toyota pickups, as best as the Farm could identify. They had carried quite a few thermal signatures. Jamali might have been planting backup forces, reserves of some kind, in an adjacent location. The trail connected this site to a neighboring village, Anantnag.

Bloody hell, thought McCarter. Anantnag. Say that five times fast.

Phoenix Force approached the village, then, forewarned. The desire was to hit Jamali and make him pay. This attrition, this constant harassment by the light, mobile strike team that was Phoenix Force, served two purposes. One, it would eventually drive out Jamali and Gera, make one or both of the generals overcommit in reaction to the repeated damage done to their forces. Two, it would neutralize the operations of Jamali and Gera as such.

It reminded McCarter of the "winning hearts and minds" mission that had been so much a part of Vietnam. Here, though, the villagers were not responding to Phoenix Force as an invading army. They were already invaded and arguably occupied, watching both Indian and Pakistani forces strike at each other again and again, abusing any of the locals unfortunate enough to be caught in the middle. This was happening on both sides of the border, because where the border was disputed, there was no delineation at all among the factions. There were only people, and many of those people were suffering because of animals like Jamali and Gera.

From what they had seen so far, Jamali was the more bloodthirsty of the two rogue commanders. That did not absolve Gera of any blame for his crimes, but it was a relative gauge of the threat potential each man faced. Then, too, the less excitable a man of war was prone to be, the more methodical you were likely to find him. You really could not afford to assume anything on the battlefield.

McCarter pressed himself against the stones of the house or shop—he was not sure which it was—and waited. He had already loaded a grenade into the launcher of his Tavor. He did not need to check his Browning to know that a round was in the chamber, ready to go. He was as deadly a shot with the weapon as any on Earth. It was one of the reasons he always insisted on the venerable old Hi-Power, instead of accepting whatever flavor-of-the-month Kissinger wanted to equip the team with. Although he had nothing against modern weaponry, he did believe that it was better to be deadly with one than conversant in all.

There was that old saying, "Beware the man who owns only one gun." The best operators he had met did not spend their money on collections of weapons. They spent their money on ammunition and training time, and ran that ammunition through the same well-worn, well-maintained, high-mileage firearms. Only the nature of McCarter's job kept him from hanging on to the same Hi-Power from mission to mission. He had to make some concessions to the covert requirements of his time with the Special Operations Group.

There were people who, McCarter supposed, did not know the origin of the term "eavesdropping." It referred to the practice of listening for voices under the overhang of a roof. There was a time when simple homes were constructed in a way that made it possible to glean useful information in this manner.

McCarter was eavesdropping now.

He could hear the men shifting around inside the stone house. There were at least two women inside, no more than girls, really, and he could hear the Jamali soldiers shouting and treating them roughly. As he listened, his blood boiled. It was a long, slow boil, and when it reached its peak, that was when he was going to take action.

The soldiers were also arguing with each other. He didn't need to speak the language to know what was up. The lead MRAP had rolled through town with its accelerator floored, then stopped at the perimeter on the far end. The second was still at the opposite end of the village. With nobody to attack and no idea what these tactics might mean, the Jamali men were watching what they thought of as a clean, simple ambush turn into a mystery assault. Right now it was dawning on them that they could be the hunted as well as the hunters. No one who spent time as a predator enjoyed the notion of being on the opposite line in life's ledger.

The stone house had only one door, in the front. McCarter was going to have to move quickly. As soon as he left the narrow alley of sorts between the neighboring structures, he would draw fire from any Jamali men watching the crude road leading through town.

Glass was a rarity here, in villages as poor as these. There were one or two more modern structures that had glass windows, but most were stone houses and hovels that had painted wooden shutters. The shutters were closed facing the main road of the village. This was to conceal the gunmen behind them. He would therefore have a moment's warning, a moment in which to act, before those shutters were thrown open to let the gunmen inside open fire.

If the operation went as it should, it would happen too quickly for the enemy to save themselves, despite superior numbers and the superior firepower that came with them.

Inside the house, a woman screamed. McCarter felt his face grow hot. He checked the Tavor, brought it to his shoulder and left the comforting dimness of the shadow between buildings. He did not break his stride once he was circling around to the house's front door. He simply kicked in the wooden barrier as hard as he could.

The lock was a strong metal bar. He felt the jolt up his leg, but the door gave, and he pushed on through behind it. The flash picture in his mind told him there were four Jamali men in residence, plus three hostages. One was an old woman. The other two were younger women, one of whom was being stripped on the floor by two of the Jamali soldiers.

McCarter shot the first man in the head.

The spray of blood was met by the thunder of countless gunshots outside along the street. The sound carried; the gunfire was the signal the Jamali forces had been waiting for. They were shooting all up and down the street, firing blindly, with no target in sight. McCarter did not have to eyeball them to know that was true, because with the MRAPs parked at either end of the little town, he was the only conceivable enemy game for the gunners to target. A few shots struck the stone building and one burned through the open doorway, but were too high and too wide to be of much concern.

McCarter shot the second man through the neck, stepped over his body and pumped a 3-round burst into a Jamali soldier attempting to draw a combat knife. The girl on the floor was screaming, over and over again, and another young woman—possibly her sister—was crying along with her. McCarter ignored them both except to gauge whether they held weapons. In scenarios such as these, you could not take for granted that a hostage would not try to kill you. People under pressure, citizens under occupation, often did strange, counterintuitive things.

He felt the fourth man trying to come up behind him, dropped to one knee, spun and let go of the Tavor. His combat dagger was in his hand as he sprang up and forward, ramming the knife blade into the man's gut, twisting the knife and then ramming it home again. The Jamali fighter folded against his shoulder, gasped and collapsed against him. McCarter felt thick, warm liquid on his knife hand.

He let the dead man fall, bent and cleaned his hand and knife on the dead man's fatigues. The blood left a glaring blotch against the mottled white of the man's snow camouflage.

The girls were still screaming.

McCarter turned to the old woman, who simply leveled her gaze at him, nodded and crossed her arms. Whether mother, grandmother or aunt, this old lady knew the score. She knew not to interfere and she knew that the enemy of her enemies was still not necessarily her friend. She was waiting for McCarter to declare himself, to indicate what he was here to do.

McCarter gestured for her to get on the floor, to get

down with the other two women. She did so, slowly and carefully. The Phoenix Force leader offered her a nod and went to the only window. There he threw open the shutters.

The response was immediate. Bullets began striking the stone around the window. McCarter ducked, making sure he did not get tagged. The Jamali men thought they had the advantage. They had seen one man; they had lost no one that they knew of, unless they understood that McCarter's presence in that house meant that, obviously, the soldiers stationed there had been killed. Now was the time to surprise them. Now was the time to teach them the lesson that Phoenix Force had taught dictators and predators around the world.

"One," said McCarter. "Start your run. Up and back. Make them earn it."

"Acknowledged," James said. "Starting run. Repeat, starting run."

The rumble of the MRAP was audible from McCarter's position. The big armored vehicle picked up speed as it began to make its way down the street. Gunfire from the open shutters along the dirt road intensified, making every humble dwelling appear to be spitting flame.

The turret on the MRAP opened up with Encizo behind it. Heavy 7.62 mm rounds blew apart shutters and tore stone from the buildings. Where the concentrations of enemy fire were greatest, the turret's return fire was most intense. Encizo worked the turret like a virtuoso on the instrument of his choice, moving left and right, never too heavy on the trigger, never allowing the enemy a moment's respite.

"Two," McCarter said. "Now. Keep it near the road."

The second MRAP roared. This time it was Manning on the automatic grenade launcher, picking up the harmony to the tune Encizo had played. With Hawkins behind the wheel of the armored vehicle, Manning punched grenade after grenade into the road near the fronts of the houses.

There was no way to know how many civilians might be trapped inside the dwellings, prisoner to the Jamali men. Simply blowing the houses apart was out of the question. But the overwhelming power of a fully automatic grenade launcher was that it was more than a physical weapon. It was a psychological weapon, one that could terrify and unman the enemy.

That was how Phoenix Force was using it now.

The grenade rounds made the entire village reverberate. Plumes of dirt, dug by trenches created in the explosions, showered the fronts of the stone houses and pelted the open windows with debris. The enemy soldiers were driven to take cover. No human being could stand in the face of explosive power like that. Phoenix was using it simply as a diversion. The two MRAPs crossed each other near the center of town.

Now it was McCarter's turn again.

"One, Two, continue your runs," he said. "Make sure you steer clear of me as I go. I am executing. Repeat, I am executing."

"One, roger."

"Two, affirmative."

McCarter ran. He dodged across the street, using the passing MRAP as cover, and kicked in the door of the house across the road. There was only one soldier here who was not already dead, taken down by Encizo's expert machine gun work. McCarter shot him in the face with the Tavor. Then, from the open shutters, he took a visual assessment of the village and gauged the most intense pockets of return fire.

The plumes of muzzle-flash were sporadic now. Jamali's men were finding out that they weren't the predators, but the prey. They had spent enough time under superior fire to know true fear; to wonder when a bullet would come for them; to ask themselves who it was that was fighting them. Clearly it was not the forces of General Gera, who were in no way capable of dealing so decisive a defeat.

The fear, the lack of knowledge of their foe, would be the worst part. Uncertainty was always a greater tool of leverage than simple threat. A man who did not know what he faced exactly, would supply his own fears, fill in the gaps with his own worst case scenarios. These were always far more effective than any threats an enemy could pose for him.

McCarter shifted to the next house. When he kicked in the door, there was no one to be seen. He immediately dove into a roll. The two men who had been holding themselves in the rafters dropped down but missed him. They had knives in their hands. Evidently they had fired out their weapons out of fear. From his back, McCarter swiveled and punched two shots through each of them. They collapsed and were still.

Where were all the people?

McCarter had seen only the three women whom he had freed from their Jamali tormenters. There should be more villagers, more hostages. There should be more local activity. Where were the civilians? His thoughts turned to some of the horrors he had seen in the course of his counterterrorist work and, before that, his time in the SAS. Would they find a mass grave behind the village, full of the recently executed? Had Jamali turned from whatever this dispute was with Gera over the disputed territory of the region, to some kind of genocide, some agenda-driven pogrom? If that was the case, the Farm would need to know, and quickly. It would be necessary to implement an even more decisive response if what they were dealing with was genocide, regional slaughter, and not simply a socio-politically driven military conflict.

Simply, McCarter thought. The word used in this context was absurd. But skirmishes, opposing military forces, were one thing. Vengeful, genocidal mass movements were another.

There was another scream.

McCarter was almost relieved. Screams meant civilians, and where civilians still lived, there was hope. The noise had come from a structure two houses away. With one between him and it, he could either bypass that home or he could hit it before he hit the second. But time was of the essence.

He decided to risk himself rather than the lives of innocents. He took a grenade from his web gear, popped the pin and held the bomb tightly in his hand. Creeping up along the front of the neighboring house, he shoved himself in front of the open window.

The gunmen inside actually started at the sudden presence of the Briton in their window. Before they could recover and train their AKs on the Phoenix Force leader, he had let the spoon of his grenade fly free. Ducking down to avoid the enemy's shots, he dumped the grenade inside the house and scrambled from the danger zone.

The grenade exploded, pulping the men inside, scattering chunks of stone across the street.

Weak gunfire followed him now. As soon as a pocket of the enemy identified themselves, the two MRAPs were on them like robotic killers, shedding the gunfire that struck their armor, belching retribution from their turrets. Manning was content to dig trenches in front of the homes with his automatic launcher, filling the air with dirt and chaos. It was Encizo who did the targeted damage, pounding away with his machine gun, leaving long lines of death and destruction as he went.

Jamali's forces were being ground to hamburger under the gears of the righteous war machine that was Phoenix Force.

The house where the scream had been uttered was next on McCarter's list. The door was already ajar. He rolled through it and found a dead Jamali soldier on the floor. The man's combat knife was missing from the scabbard on his belt. A middle-aged woman, half-undressed, was sitting next to him, breathing heavily. She held up the bloody knife she had obviously used to kill the man.

"I'm not going to hurt you," McCarter said.

"American?" the woman asked him, eyes wide in shock. "Are you American?"

"You speak English?" McCarter asked.

"Yes," she said. "I have... I attended university. One year."

"I don't have time to explain, miss," he said. He knelt to check the pulse of the dead soldier, just on principle. "I'm with a peacekeeping force. We're here to help you, to fight for you against Jamali and his thugs, and against General Gera, too. But I need you to help me. I need to know what's happening here."

"They took many away," the girl said. "Many of the villagers. Women and men. It was the women they wanted. They left some of us...to entertain them. They took the men to make them work, digging trenches and other things. I worry we will not see them again."

"Do you know where they've gone?" McCarter asked. "Do you have any idea where they've been sent?"

"Jamali wants it known that he controls this area," the woman told him. "That he commands all. That is why he is so brutal. Our people have been taken to Anantnag. He enjoys making Anantnag suffer. No one knows why. It is said he picked it in a coin toss. Others say dice. Still others say he amuses himself by throwing lots to determine which of our settlements he will hurt next. With one such as him, there is no saying."

"All right," McCarter said. "I'm going to go to Anantnag. I'm going to set your people free. You have my word."

"Thank you, American."

"I'm British, actually," McCarter said. "But your meaning is taken all the same, miss. I have to go now."

"You will really save them?"

"You have my word on it," McCarter said.

He ducked out of the house. The next few dwellings were occupied by only dead men. The onslaught of the MRAPs had done its work, eliminating the Jamali resistance. When McCarter got to the end of the road, there was just one more stone dwelling with enemy personnel inside. He did not try to charge the door, however. A glance through the open shutters showed him that the men inside had already been hit. The big, ragged wounds were those of the 7.62 machine gun in MRAP One.

McCarter stepped inside. One man was almost dead. His eyes had rolled into the back of his head and he was trying to hold his guts in. McCarter ignored him. The other man had a sucking chest wound and had gone almost completely pale. His blue lips told McCarter he, too, was going to die, but he might linger for some time yet.

"Can you understand me?" McCarter asked. "Do you know what I'm saying to you?"

The wounded man looked up defiantly. He bared his teeth, which were bloody, and motioned with the knife in his hand, the only weapon he had managed to retain. He gestured cutting his own throat and then laughed, once. The pain of the laugh cost him badly. He began coughing.

"You lot," McCarter said. "You're scum. You prey on the weak. You brutalize the innocent. These people are pawns to you. Just pieces in a game that your warlord is playing. And that's what Jamali is. A warlord. He's not a man. He's not a legitimate military commander. He's just a strong-arm bandit, a bully. And that's why he's going to lose. That's why my people and I are going to teach you all a lesson."

The soldier spit on the floor. He reached out as if he would put the knife in his hand into McCarter's guts.

McCarter stepped back, withdrew his Hi-Power and put a single mercy round through the dying man's head.

It was time to move on to Anantnag. And pity save any of Jamali's thugs who got in Phoenix Force's way.

CHAPTER ELEVEN

"Roger that, Barb," Lyons said, sitting in the driver's seat of the rental Suburban. He and the rest of Able Team were outside Elmore, Ohio, at the corporate headquarters of EarthGard. In theory, it was at this very building that all of EarthGard's American operations were based. Lyons held his satellite phone to his ear. "I have you five by five. What did you find out?"

Lyons's working theory was that any entity capable of hiring so many mercenaries had to be a monied corporate interest. An EarthGard employee had been found in the disputed area between India and Pakistan. EarthGard domestically was using firepower on a phenomenal scale to secure its interests. Able Team had seen it countless times before here in the United States, as had Phoenix Force. A rogue CEO or other company interest using military means and political brinksmanship to line his own pockets. It wasn't too far a leap. They just had to figure out who, behind all this, had the deep wallet that was paying for it.

The Farm had called in as Able Team was approaching the facility outside Elmore. Something about the proximity to the beryllium plant struck Lyons as funny, but he couldn't decide what it was. He generally mistrusted anything that was too easy on its face. Maybe that's all that was at play here.

"We have preliminary identifications on many of the men you've encountered so far," Price said. "At least the ones that came through intact enough for facial recognition."

"Don't remind me," Lyons said. "Go."

"What we've got is very interesting. Several of your Chinese operators are current special forces for the Communist government there. Quite a few *more* are former special ops for China, disclaimed as dead or deserters. What's odd is that there are essentially two groups of special forces operators all tracing back to the ChiComs, but with different layers of security attached. One is still active and linkable to the Chinese government, the other is clad in plausible deniability."

"The way a mercenary team would be."

"In the case of the disavowed operators, yes," Price said. "We're used to seeing this kind of thing when one of their military commanders decides to go into business for himself. Typically he seeds his unit with those loyal to him, the soldiers in question miss their ride back home and the next thing you know, the local warlord in residence has a fine new complement of well-trained, well-paid muscle."

"But not in the case of the current operators."

"No," Price agreed. "Those are the dossiers of men I would expect China to negotiate for if they were…you know, captured. So why the inconsistency? If it is Chinese special operations, I would expect them to be a lot less sloppy. And if it isn't, where do these currently viable operators fit into the mix? Something's really wrong."

"But EarthGard hired them?"

"EarthGard's corporate finances are…complex," Price said. "Bear and his team have been digging through them all morning. Given the number of empty-shell holding corporations, there's definitely something illegal taking place. We're trying to run it down now. We have verified that a company owned by another company that is in turn majority-owned by EarthGard has done extensive business with Cudgel Security."

"Well, at least that much adds up," Lyons said. "I'm really not liking all these loose ends and complications."

"I have one more complication for you that you'll like even less," Price told him. "We are transmitting to your phones the dossier of one Lao Wei. We have reason to believe that Lao is in the United States right now. He's nominally a general assigned to the Chinese government's special operations branch. In reality he's a midlevel military shot-caller with a considerable amount of real authority. Our sources say that Lao entered the country just two days ago, and if that's the case, he can't have been in position to entrench his forces here before now."

"So the Chinese are sending military operatives directly to us now?" Lyons asked. "How's that not an act of war?"

"We don't have confirmation that Lao is even *here,* much less working with the groups who've shot at you," Price explained. "He's rumored to have come in via the Canadian border, but it could as easily be misinformation to throw us off. Official inquiries have been made to the Chinese, but they're stonewalling us. That's normal for them, both when things are all right and when things are bad, so it doesn't tell us anything."

"We both know the Chinese have run terrorist operations on United States soil, and in recent memory," Lyons said. "If Lao is here—"

"General Lao is in the country without benefit of diplomatic aegis," Price said. "If he is eliminated, it's doubtful the Chinese will ever admit he was here."

"But that also means the ChiComs are mixed up in EarthGard somehow," Lyons speculated. "This wouldn't be the first time we've seen foreign military interests tie up with corrupt corporate management, either."

"It looks likely," Price said.

Lyons looked at his phone, where a digital photograph of Lao Wei, as well as a flashing icon indicating a data download, was displayed.

"What do we know about Lao?" Lyons asked.

"Details are in the report," Price told him, "but I can give you the short version. Lao Wei is forty-five. He's a hardline Communist and known for both his loyalty and his ferocity. No family that we know of, no particular vices on record, no blots on his record that we've been able to find. He's the poster child for a true believer in the Communist system, whose only life is his service to the Chinese military. Also has something of a reputation as a 'fixer,' the sort of person you send in when you want something cleaned up."

"Great. So in other words, the human personification of everything that could make our lives most difficult in the field."

"Yes," said Price.

"What I love, Barb, is how you always know how to cheer me up," Lyons said. More seriously, he said, "I'll look through the mission data. We're starting here at EarthGard headquarters and working our way back through the priority list from there. At least, that's the plan now. You know how fluid it is out here."

"I do. Bear says he's close to having more on EarthGard and their Ohio headquarters. We'll get in touch with you as soon as he's ready. And the satellite will be overhead soon. That will give us a chance to run a thermal scan for you, give you an idea what you're up against."

"Okay. Send scrambled text to all of our phones when

you get the thermal imaging back," Lyons said. "Time for us to go shoot people and break things."

"That sounds familiar," Price said. "Good hunting, Ironman."

"Thanks. Able Team out," Lyons said.

"So what's the play this time?" Schwarz asked. "Do we ram the front gate and immediately lose our security deposit, or do we wait until we park, get out and ask nicely, then lose our security deposit when they start shooting at us?"

"Anybody'd think you pay that out of your pocket," Lyons said.

"I'm just thinking of the Farm's budget," Schwarz said.

"Our secret black-bag special ops budget that gets skimmed from a thousand different line items like three-hundred-dollar toilet seats? That budget?" Blancanales put in.

"You guys are no fun anymore," Schwarz said.

Lyons drove the Suburban to the gate in the fence surrounding the EarthGard office building. There was an intercom on a metal post. "To answer your question," he told Schwarz, "we'll knock this time."

"Just so long as there's some variety to all the shooting-at-us that keeps happening," Schwarz said.

"You'd rather sit behind a desk?" Blancanales asked.

"I'd probably get shot at behind a desk, too," Schwarz said.

"If I had to sit in an office and listen to your jokes all day, I'd say that's true," Lyons said. He pushed the intercom button. "Justice Department," he said. "We have a warrant for the search of this property." He released the button.

"We don't have a warrant," Blancanales pointed out.

"They don't know that," Lyons retorted.

They waited a moment and, when no response was forthcoming, Lyons stabbed at the button again. It popped out of its housing and fell to the pavement. "What the hell?" Lyons said.

"They don't call him 'Ironman' for nothing," Schwarz said.

"Wait," Lyons said. "This isn't right." He grabbed hold of the intercom housing, shook it back and forth and succeeded in loosening it in the ground below. Eventually the whole intercom simply came loose. The post that had been set in the ground ended in a metal cylinder that was solid, with no room to run wires. There were no trailing cables.

"It's a fake," Blancanales said. "A prop."

Lyons allowed the Suburban to roll forward. When its front bumper touched the locked gate of the fence, he very slowly applied the accelerator. The heavy SUV leaned on the fence until the lock securing the gate popped free. The gate came loose and fell forward onto the roadway. Lyons pushed his foot down and the Suburban rolled over the fence, headed toward the visitor's parking lot.

"Break out the long guns," Lyons said. "We're headed in there fully loaded. Gadgets, hand me a couple of grenades." The Able Team leader took the grenades and put them in the pockets of his jacket. Blancanales, meanwhile, was checking his M-4 and Lyons's Daewoo. When it came to their weaponry, the men of Able Team trusted each other completely. They had shed blood on enough square miles to know where they stood with each other.

Lyons put the Suburban up the drive to the office building. This was not a processing facility. On paper, per the Farm's cyber sleuthing, this was the location from which EarthGard conducted all of the coordination of its various mining and processing activities, both in the United States and around the world. The facility was supposed to house a staff of close to one hundred people. The Suburban crossed a parking lot that could have held three times that many automobiles easily. Able Team drove across row after empty row of yellow painted lines. The parking lot was utterly deserted.

"Not a single vehicle," Lyons noted. "Not so much as a stray Hyundai. Is this a national holiday?"

"No," Blancanales said. "This place should be as busy as it ever gets. Where is everyone?"

Schwarz sent a text message to Stony Man Farm as they neared the building itself. EarthGard deserted, it said. Response from telephone inquiry? He was essentially asking the folks at the Farm to impersonate an external caller, which the cybernetics team was more than equipped to do. It was one of the most basic tactics used by everyone from private investigators to detectives. When in doubt, call the target to see who answers.

Lyons parked the Suburban in a parking slot marked Reserved: CEO. The men of Able Team climbed out, weapons at the ready. Schwarz's secure sat phone vibrated in his hand.

Female receptionist answers when called, Price wrote back. Not a recording. Traces to your geo-loc.

"Well, that settles that," Schwarz said. "Barb says they get a human being when they phone the site and that the transmission can be traced to this specific physical location. Not a recording, she says. I'm guessing Bear would be able to spot an algorithm mimicking human responses."

"He'd kick our butts if we expected less of him," Blancanales said.

"Well," Lyons said. "Nothing to do but to knock on the door."

Despite their otherwise casual attitudes, however, the men of Able Team approached the entrance to the office by the book, covering each other, expecting a massive assault at any moment. Given its small size, Able Team was essentially a three-man fire team, flexible and maneuverable. The three commandos had long forgotten how many times they had marched into overwhelming odds, striking up the middle to come out, bloody and victorious, on the other side. This was the attitude with which they approached the EarthGard headquarters. This was the keep of the enemy, was it not?

The reception desk bore a laminated sign: Welcome Visitors. Please Use the Company Directory and Dial Your Party's Extension. There was what looked for all the world like a late 1980s vintage office telephone sitting on the desktop.

Lyons walked up to the front desk, picked up the receiver and dialed a four-digit extension at random. He paused and then said, "Why, good morning to you too, Sheila in Accounting. My name is Carl. I'm with the Justice Department.... Yes, that Justice Department. I was hoping we could pop in and have a look at your books. You see, we think your company is up to its neck in an illegal mining operation and has ties to extra-legal private mercenary concerns."

"Five bucks she puts him on hold," Schwarz whispered.

"You're on," Blancanales said.

"Yes, I'll hold," Lyons said. Blancanales winced. Schwarz grinned. Lyons pulled the receiver from his ear, his expression odd.

"Is that what I think it is?" Blancanales asked.

"Why is the hold music always so loud?" Lyons grumbled.

"'Soul Finger,'" Schwarz said, his smile broadening. "By the Bar-Kays."

"Come on, guys," said Lyons. "You can get nostalgic later. Let's go find the accounting department."

"You always pick on the number-crunchers," Schwarz said.

"Wouldn't you?" Lyons said.

The hallway leading from the reception desk bore offices on either side. Each one was a carbon copy of the one next to it: An outdated steel desk, an antiquated office telephone, a paper blotter with a few supplies. Schwarz ducked into one office and stared at the motivational poster on the wall. It was of a kitten hanging from a tree branch by its forelegs. The slogan Hang In There was written in large white script below the kitten.

Lyons followed Schwarz's sudden frenzied dash from one office to the next. "Gadgets?" he said. "Where are you going? What have you got there?"

Schwarz held up another framed poster. It was the same one: a kitten with the words Hang In There.

"Does it seem odd to anyone," Schwarz said, holding up a second poster next to the first, "that every one of these offices has the same silly decoration hanging in it?"

"Over there," Lyons said, pointing to a "bull pen" suite of desks at the end of the corridor. "Pick one of those workstations and hack into their network or something."

"'Ironman," Schwarz said, rolling his eyes. "You really need to update your lingo with the…" He stopped, pointing. "Is that a twenty-year-old photocopier?"

Blancanales went to the cluster of printers and copiers at the end of the bull pen. He opened the lid of the copier.

"There's no glass," he said. "This is just the plastic shell of what was once a copy machine. There's nothing in the guts but a metal frame and some loose screws."

"Problem," Schwarz announced. He was sitting at one

of the desks. He gestured toward the old CRT monitor in front of him.

"Too old?" Blancanales asked. "Can't you get in? What do you need, a floppy disk or something?"

"More like a magic marker," Schwarz said. He picked up the monitor far too easily and tossed it over the desk. It hit the floor and rolled to Lyons's feet. The Able Team leader picked it up.

"Cardboard," he said. "Nothing here is real."

"So we go on a scavenger hunt," Lyons said. "Somebody's gone to a lot of trouble to make this place look like a real business. The only reason to do that is to hide the actual seat of EarthGard's operations. Somewhere in this building must be at least one person, maybe more. I want whoever's on the other end of the phone here. Maybe she's locked up in some spider hole or safe room somewhere in the building. Maybe there's a room full of EarthGard mercenaries from Cudgel or China or what all just hoping we'll knock down the wrong door. Well, I want that door. Let's find it, trip the trap and put anyone on the ground who's pointing a gun."

They searched the EarthGard facility thoroughly. The longer the search went on, the more frustrated Lyons became. He began taking real pleasure in kicking in any locked doors they found. But each room revealed only more fake equipment, more mocked-up workstations, more file boxes and file cabinets full of sheets of newsprint and even blank reams of paper. Finally, the three Able Team commandos regrouped. Lyons was thoroughly sick of the ersatz offices by then.

"All of this stuff is well used," Schwarz observed finally. "Probably purchased at an auction or something. Clearance for a corporation that closed its offices. The only real books in this place are computer books that are three decades out of date. The rest is props."

The three commandos' phones vibrated. Lyons sighed and ripped open the glass door labeled Server Room. There were a series of metal housings there, but there were no computers inside the server racks. Lyons jerked his chin at Schwarz. "What's the latest?"

Schwarz checked his phone. He stared at it for a moment. "Uh…the thermal analysis is in. Nobody here but us."

"But that's not possible," Blancanales said. "There has to be at least one more heat signature."

The triple vibrations of Able Team's phone signified another text message coming in. This one was lengthier. Lyons opened his own phone and eyed it suspiciously.

Employment records for EarthGard facility outside Elmore, Ohio, analyzed. All persons listed do not exist, repeat, do not exist. Identities faked. Company roster is fiction.

"Fiction," said Lyons. "What does it mean? Is there just the one person here? One person left to helm a completely fictitious company?"

"Our girl could be in an insulated chamber of some kind," Schwarz offered. "But…it doesn't seem likely. Why go to that level of effort? There's another explanation."

"Which is?"

"The Farm said the physical location of the land line transmission traces back to here," Schwarz said. "Somewhere in this building there must be a digital trunk. A means of routing all the business EarthGard does through this location, like forwarding a land line to a mobile phone on a massive scale. Data spoofing writ large. A means of masking an entire corporation's physical location, to draw

FREE Merchandise is 'in the Cards' for you!

Dear Reader,

We're giving away FREE MERCHANDISE!

Seriously, we'd like to reward you for reading this novel by giving you **FREE MERCHANDISE** worth over $20. And no purchase is necessary!

You see the Jack of Hearts sticker above? Paste that sticker in the box on the Free Merchandise Voucher inside. Return the Voucher promptly...and we'll send you valuable Free Merchandise!

Thanks again for reading one of our novels—and enjoy your Free Merchandise with our compliments!

Pam Powers

Pam Powers

P.S. Look inside to see what Free Merchandise is **"in the cards"** for you!

YOUR FREE MERCHANDISE INCLUDES...
2 FREE Books **AND** 2 FREE Mystery Gifts

FREE MERCHANDISE VOUCHER

**2 FREE
BOOKS**
and
**2 FREE
GIFTS**

Please send my Free Merchandise, consisting of
2 Free Books and **2 Free Mystery Gifts**.
I understand that I am under no obligation to buy
anything, as explained on the back of this card.

166/366 ADL GECK

Please Print

FIRST NAME

LAST NAME

ADDRESS

APT.#   CITY

STATE/PROV.   ZIP/POSTAL CODE

NO PURCHASE NECESSARY!

GE_314_FM13

heat should the Feds come a knocking. It's like using a fake address on your driver's license. The cops come to arrest you and they end up at Wrigley Field instead."

"Can we use it to find the real center of operations?" Lyons asked. "Trace it back to wherever the forwarded data starts?"

"We can if we can find it," Schwarz said. "It's got to be on the grounds somewhere for the physical spoof to work."

"Then let's do that," Lyons said.

"G-Force to Able," said Grimaldi through their transceivers. "G-Force to Able. Come in, Able."

"Able, go," Lyons said.

"Gents, I have what looks like choppers inbound, judging from their speed and the lazy way they're circling you. I checked with local air control. They're not registered. You've got multiple hostiles about to drop in. We're at the center of a tightening perimeter. I think I see at least one four-wheel drive. Not so much in the way of ground troops, but there's at least some ground presence."

"Can you keep the choppers off us, Jack?" Lyons asked.

"I'm going to try," Grimaldi said. "But I'll be honest with you, Able. If they're lighter than me and they've got air-to-air armament, I'm going to have a hard time dogfighting in this albatross. We've got straight-line speed, we've got vertical takeoff and landing, we've got cargo capacity, and we've got firepower. Maneuverability against a lighter chopper, not so much."

"Then put it down," Lyons said. "Drop yourself into the dirt. Stay out of their way. Maybe we can pull the G-card again when we have a better idea what we're dealing with, spring you on them when they're occupied with us."

"Understood. Don't get killed."

"People keep telling me that," Lyons said. "Get lost, Jack."

"Getting lost. G-Force out."

Lyons took a look around. Everything surrounding them in this sham office was insubstantial. None of it would stop a rifle bullet, much less the type of hardware an armed chopper might sport. He supposed they would have to make the best of what was available.

"Help me turn over these metal desks," he said to his partners. "Drag those others over here. We'll layer them, hopefully put some barrier between us and the outer wall. Those windows are going to shatter like prop sugarglass. Let's see if we can't find something to tape them up. Maybe there's some 1980s packing tape in one of the desks."

"You inside," called an electronically amplified voice from outside the building. It was so loud that they heard the rhythmic beat of the choppers' rotors only after they heard the first call from without. "We know you are in there. Place all weapons on the ground."

"A trap, you think?" Blancanales asked.

"Doesn't make sense," Lyons said. "Something is off about all of it."

"I repeat," said the voice from the chopper. "Put your hands on your head. Exit the building. You are now the prisoners of General Lao Wei of the People's Republic of China."

CHAPTER TWELVE

Anantnag, Kashmir

Anantnag was one of the more wealthy villages Phoenix Force had seen in the remote Kashmiri landscape. Some village elder or local wealthy person, at least by the standards of this place, had built an elaborate stone home on a hillock at one end of town. While it was a single story, it had multiple segments, as if three homes had been joined by smaller hallways at the sides and in the back. Here in Kashmir, the dwelling was the equivalent of a mansion.

Several of the shops on the dirt road running through the center of town boasted glass windows. Merchandise was somewhat spare, but again, here in remote Kashmir, the village verged on opulence by relative measure. Such a place would attract Jamali's thugs, McCarter thought, because it would afford them more opportunities for theft and abuse. It was always more fun to misuse a rich fellow and his lady than it was a poor man's family. That was human nature.

Jamali probably knew full well what went on when his troops quartered here. He probably encouraged it, both for the intimidation factor and because it gave his troops a chance to let off steam. Warlords were like that; they generally knew their fighters well and encouraged their baser instincts, as long as those instincts served the overall cause.

The Briton wished for a Coke. The MRAPs were supplied with enough rations to get them through the mission, but something like a good can of sugary soda was considered a nonessential. Bloody hell. Sometimes it was as if the folks in charge had never been in the field.

"Are my satellites overhead, Barb?" McCarter asked, talking into his sat phone. "I'm going to need full heat signature analysis. You've got the data we sent so far?"

"Yes," Price said. "And we're cross-referencing against what little international census data there is. There's just one satellite, David, but it's in position. Between you and Able we've been kept hopping."

"Stay on the eyepiece or whatever it is," McCarter said. "When I need you I'll text the letter Q."

"Why Q?" Price asked.

"Because God save the Queen," McCarter quipped. "Phoenix out." He closed the phone.

The two armored vehicles were parked well back from the village, hidden in the lee of a hill that overlooked Anantnag. The village was too well guarded for the type of high-speed, high-profile play Phoenix Force had run before. There was a pair of T-55 tanks down there, as well as several armored personnel carriers. Armed Jamali fighters dotted the streets—some moving from house to house, some drinking and carousing, others clearly posted as guards.

Through his field glasses, McCarter noted the positions of the guards, but he was looking for something more significant. He found it when the door of one of the adjacent stone homes opened. Three Jamali men emerged, pushing a pair of women ahead of them. The women, either locals from Anantnang or some of the hostages taken from Doru Shahabad, were herded to the big house at the end of the street.

That was where he'd hold court if he was the commanding officer of this group of thugs, the Briton thought. That, too, was human nature: Pick the nicest digs for yourself and then sit back and enjoy the spoils you've just taken. Women from Doru Shahabad would probably be there in larger numbers, although they might also be scattered throughout Anantnang. That was another reason a bum's rush through the center of the little town was out of the question. It had been difficult enough not knocking down the entire affair with Manning on the big automatic grenade launcher. There, they had only expected there could be civilian casualties. Here, it was virtually assured.

The viciousness of the plan, as well as its cunning, struck him. The hostages weren't merely for the Jamali soldiers' amusement. They were also human shields. If any of Gera's men showed up and the two sides did battle, it also seemed likely that any Pakistani casualties among the civilians would be blamed on the Indians, further enflaming the international tensions that Gera and Jamali were stoking with their private war.

Funny, how purposeful that seemed, when he thought about it along those terms. It was one more element of all this that just didn't seem to add up quite right. McCarter had to admit to himself that he was deeply suspicious of *everything* happening here.

The operation to free Anantnang was therefore the very definition of "the hard way." Hawkins was to post up here, on the rise overlooking the village, playing the role of sniper with his Tavor. The short bullpup weapon was not a true sniper's rifle, of course, but the distance was not that great, and if any member of Phoenix was not capable of making shots with a 5.56 mm NATO weapon from that distance, McCarter would count his leadership of the team a failure. What was critical was having an eye up above the battle, someone who could take in the sum total of the movements in the village below. The members of Phoenix Force would be in constant contact with each other, which should enable them to get in, infiltrate the village, eliminate hostiles in a house-to-house search and free any hostages.

Attention to detail, it was sometimes called: when you had to get in close, room to room, rifle to rifle, and get the job done at close quarters.

"Ready, lads?" McCarter asked. Flanking him were Calvin James and Rafael Encizo. The two Phoenix Force commandos nodded. "Let's move, then," said the Briton.

The path from the rise was long and low, relatively shallow in terms of degree. The elevation at which Hawkins lay prone behind his Tavor was sufficient to give him a commanding view of both ends of the little village. Behind Encizo, the MRAPs sat, with Manning in MRAP Two parked closest to his teammate. The MK-19 was Phoenix Force's final play. Should something horrible go wrong, Manning could break the sky and bring it crashing down upon them all. But that was not the plan.

The three Phoenix Force members moved quickly to get into position. They were vulnerable while descending to the level of the village road. McCarter did not allow himself to think about the tempting target silhouette they must present while transitioning from above to below. But nobody in the village was paying them any real attention, despite the fact that Jamali's men had posted guards. To a man, the guards were drunk. Several of them swayed visibly in place where they stood their posts, dark brown bottles clutched in their hands.

The ever-present cold had something to do with that, to be sure. The false warmth of a belly full of liquor was tempting indeed to a man who was feeling the ache of the endless snow and ice. To say nothing of what it must have been like for those poor devils in the glacier region....

For his part, McCarter expected to stay warm with the help of vigorous exercise. Vigorous exercise and gunfire, that was. He allowed himself a tight smile.

They reached the edge of the village without incident. McCarter signaled for Encizo to take the left while he and James took the right. The three men took up cover as best they could against the stone houses on their respective sides of the street.

It was time to light the candle.

McCarter took aim at the nearest sentry, who was squatting against the wall of the house across and down one from his position. Each Phoenix Force commando would target men on the opposite side of the street. It would make their shots easier to take while also confusing the Jamali men, at least initially.

In the crosshairs of his Tavor's optics, McCarter watched his man pause and look up. He had finally noticed the interlopers in the village. He grabbed for the AKM slung on his shoulder while taking a deep breath to shout an alarm.

McCarter put a bullet through his open mouth.

The shot echoed up and down the street. It took them a moment, but the other posted guards finally reacted, dragging the barrels of their weapons into something like target alignment, pulling back their triggers as they sprayed the street and the neighboring homes.

Steel shell casings fell into the dirt and snow. Phoenix Force held their ground. The trained commandos were much better shots than their Jamali-sponsored counterparts. The sentries fell, staining the snow red with their blood. The road in the center of the village would not stay clear for long, however. In moments, the men in the houses would be exiting with weapons in hand. Phoenix Force would need to use the element of surprise while they could, clearing the first of the dwellings while they had the initiative.

McCarter kicked in the nearest wooden door. Across the street, Encizo did the same. McCarter and James entered their target dwelling, acquired a single Jamali soldier lying in a drunken stupor on the floor, and put a pair of bullets in the man's head when he stirred and tried to draw a pistol.

Across the street, Encizo stumbled into a nest of Jamali men. A half-naked woman ran screaming from the house, holding her hands across her chest. The exchange of gunfire turned the interior of the house into a strobe light. Encizo managed to stay clear of the worst of it, shooting from just beyond the doorway, but it was finally necessary for him to discharge his Tavor's grenade launcher at close range. The Phoenix Force fighter threw himself into the dirt of the street and fired from his back, letting the concussion wash over him and crack stones from the building.

"Calvin," McCarter said. "Back up Rafe. Make sure he's not injured."

"Got it," James said. The black man hurried to back up his teammate.

McCarter carried on. The thought brought a grim smile to his lips. "Keep calm and carry on." It was an old English war slogan, one intended to inspire the usual stiff-upper-lip response in his countrymen. That was supposed to be the ideal reaction to, say, having your country bombed day and night by a hostile enemy force. You kept calm and you carried on.

Well, thought McCarter, he was calm, all right. Deadly calm. And he wasn't going to stop until the village was pacified and the innocent people held hostage here were freed.

It was to be house to house, then. Gunfire headed his way was picking up now, as the enemy figured out that there were intruders close at hand. The face of one of the stone houses exploded, raining down fragments of mortar and rock. That was a grenade explosion; one of the drunken Jamali men had fumbled his—

"Grenade!" McCarter exclaimed. He had time to bend, scoop up the bomb and whip it back from where it had come. It exploded in the middle of the street, doing little damage. The Briton fired off several bursts from his Tavor.

McCarter caught movement in his peripheral vision. He turned, and as he did, he realized it would not be fast enough. The Jamali killer drawing down on him was already aiming, already taking up slack on his trigger. He was standing at the edge of the road, the door behind him hanging open, more Jamali men boiling out of the house from behind. As time slowed and McCarter saw his death, the shooters behind David McCarter's murderer were jacking back the bolts on their own weapons.

The killer's throat opened up. McCarter dropped to one knee and the dying man's shot went wide. Through the sound of automatic weapons, the Briton could not hear the telltale report of T. J. Hawkins's sniper fire. It could only have been Hawkins who'd saved him, however.

"You're welcome," Hawkins said in his earbud.

"I'll buy you a steak when we get back, mate," McCarter said. With the Tavor leveled, he pumped 3-round burst after 3-round burst into the oncoming Jamali fighters, knocking them down, folding them in two.

It was time for the next house.

Encizo crossed the street, followed by James. Together the three men worked their way back and forth, from house to house, crossing and recrossing the dirt road, leaving muddy, bloody footprints in the snow.

"Go," McCarter would order.

"Moving," his two teammates would respond. McCarter would cover them as they took up a new position farther down the road. Together they would breach the next house with McCarter on point or watching their backs, depending on the alternation. Then the process would repeat, this time with James or Encizo covering as the other two men took the next leg of their rapid-fire, methodical journey from one end of the village to the other. Several times, Hawkins made his presence known, shooting down soldiers the other teammates either could not see well or whose positions made effective counterattack difficult.

Several times they rescued hostages. In most cases, when Phoenix Force shot down the invaders, the people of Anantnag were content to shelter where they were, to wait for the firestorm of combat and wrath to pass them by. A few had been tortured; a few had been badly misused. Several were dead, and there was nothing more at all that could be done for them...except to avenge them.

"Calvin," McCarter said. "Did you have a chance to plant the charges?"

"Caught them both," James said. "Unless there's one hiding in a barn I don't know about."

"Good," McCarter said. "Let's close the loop on this plan, lads."

For the Jamali men it was an object lesson in small-unit tactics. In less time than it would take for one of the Phoenix Force commandos to describe the details of the operation, the three operatives had made their way to the big house at the end of the road, where shooters had barricaded themselves inside. As the three commandos used the nearest adjacent houses for cover, muzzle-flashes bloomed at the windows on either branch of the structure. It quickly became what, to the Jamali men, would appear to be a stalemate. They were trapped in the house defending their positions, while Phoenix Force could hammer away with their rifles but could do little else. Grenades would endanger the hostages who were surely held inside. There was only one thing McCarter could instruct his men to do.

"Cease fire," said McCarter, much more loudly than he needed to. His words were already being transmitted to the other members of the team. What was important, however, was that the armed men inside the house hear him. "Cease fire. I repeat, cease fire."

A few more shots cracked from the "rich" village home. These trailed off. McCarter was counting on it. It was all part of the plan to extricate the hostages with a minimum of bloodshed.

Well. Bloodshed on the side of Phoenix Force and the villagers.

Someone shouted from within the house. McCarter found himself smiling. It was going to work. He shouted back, "English!"

There was a pause. Then the voice from inside the house shouted back. "I speak. You leave. You leave this place."

"We will, mate," McCarter shouted from his vantage. He was using a corner of the nearest stone house for cover, just as were his teammates. This was not exactly the strongest fortification known to man. If his ruse didn't work, the men inside could chip away at his defensives with their assault rifles. It would be incredibly easy. His life, and the lives of Encizo and James, would be worth nothing. Taking a bullet quickly in an exchange like that would be a mercy. Jamali's men would be the sort who thought of torture and mutilation as an amusing way to spend their idle hours.

"Go!" came the emphatic reply.

"I want to speak to your commanding officer," McCarter said. "Whoever's in charge here."

There was some kind of argument from within, portions of which were audible as voices were raised. Another voice, deeper and with more gravel, shouted back. The man's accent was much worse. "I am in charge. I am Harwan. You and your men will leave the village. We will let you. We will not shoot."

"It's not safe passage we're looking for," McCarter countered. "You've lost a lot of men. We killed them easily. We could have killed more. Right now, there are hundreds of United Nations forces surrounding our position, just waiting for my call to come in here. Armored vehicles. Helicopters. We have everything we need to level this place."

"Man, David," James whispered through his transceiver, "you might be overselling it."

"Bugger off, mate," McCarter whispered back. More loudly, he shouted, "You send out the hostages. *All* the hostages. We have thermal satellite imaging overhead. We'll know if you hold anybody back. You send the hostages out. You stay here. We'll take the villagers of Anantnag and anyone you took with you from Doru Shahabad. Send them out now and we won't kill everyone here."

"If you attack, you kill them anyway," shouted Harwan. "All the villagers. Not just my soldiers."

"I don't think you understand," McCarter said. "There are only two possible outcomes. Either I kill everyone here and completely destroy this village, or you let the hostages walk out of Anantnag with me, into the hills. You have ten seconds before I signal for the launch of the cruise missiles!"

"Cruise missiles," Hawkins drawled from his hilltop. "Now that's rich, David. Cruise missiles, he says."

McCarter ignored that. "What's it going to be?"

"You are a liar," Harwan said. "You do not have the power you say."

"I have the power of death in my little finger," McCarter said. "Don't believe me? Send a man out here to fight me, hand to hand. You chaps can even watch the show, get a little entertainment in."

Harwan said nothing. After a few moments the front door of the big house opened and a gigantic Pakistani soldier came out. He made a show of taking off his heavy outer coat and throwing it into the snow. His breath left ice crystals in his beard as he advanced toward where McCarter was crouched.

McCarter stood and walked brazenly into the street.

The big man cracked his knuckles. He pointed to McCarter and then slashed an index finger across his throat. The meaning was clear enough. But David McCarter had been counting on the need for a show of force.

McCarter extended the little finger of his right hand and traced it slowly across his neck. Then he pointed at the big Pakistani.

The crack of Hawkins's single gunshot, from the hilltop above the village, echoed for what seemed like a long time. The big Pakistani collapsed in the snow without a sound. There was an entry wound directly above his right eye. It was not a large hole. It had been just big enough to end the Pakistani's life.

Walking calmly back to cover as if he hadn't a care in the world was one of the harder things McCarter had done in recent memory. It was important, however, that the image of all-powerful disdain for the enemy be carried through. It was the only way his little fiction would get them to where he needed it to go.

He breathed a short, sharp sigh of relief when he once

more had a stone wall corner between himself and the target house, however.

"All right!" Harwan shouted.. "You can have them! Take them and go!"

That's right, thought McCarter. That's what I imagined you would say. Aloud, he shouted back, "Make sure you send all of them out. Every last one! You hold anyone back, our thermal imaging will tell us so, and I'll have that house blown out from under you from a mile away!"

"We are sending them," Harwan shouted sullenly.

McCarter took out his phone and texted the letter Q, using a hot key programmed for the Farm. The response took a few seconds to trigger, but when it came through, he was not disappointed. The image on his phone turned into a real-time thermal pattern of the topography around him. He watched the configuration of red-orange blobs that indicated human beings.

It looked as though the Jamali men were complying. That was good. They were only pretending to do as he ordered, of course; that. too, was good. Or at least it was not bad. It was just what he had counted on them to do.

The ragtag parade of villagers soon swelled to include those who had been hiding in the other structures. First they congregated on the main road. Then, as James and Encizo guided them with hand motions and reassuring words, they began to follow the two soldiers out of town. It would be slow going, on foot and in the snow. Many of the villagers lacked proper outer clothing. What they really needed to do was to circle back, reenter the homes of Anantnag, and take whatever the villagers would need to travel to their neighbors in Doru Shahabad.

And they would. But something very important had to happen first.

McCarter watched the screen of his phone. He spoke

to it as if he could will the little heat blobs to move, to follow, to cluster on the road. Slowly but surely, they began to do just that.

Just give me the space I need, he thought. He was at the rear of the procession of refugees, of rescued hostages. That was important to him. He needed to verify that they were at a safe distance.

"David," Hawkins said through his earbud, "they're mounting up. Armored vehicles and the two tanks. They're getting ready to follow."

"Men on foot?"

"Yes," Hawkins said.

"How many?"

"I'd say all of them."

"Good," McCarter said. "Let me know when the tanks are abreast of the infantry."

McCarter kept walking. He could practically hear the numbers falling in his head, could picture the sights of enemy rifles lining up on his back. He checked his phone one last time and was satisfied with the target distribution.

"Calvin," he said. "Hit them."

At that command, James would be pressing the activate button on the portable detonator he carried—

The tanks exploded.

Among the supplies carried by Phoenix Force for just such occasions were small, light satchel charges filled with plastic explosives. James had brought two such charges from the MRAP for the purpose of taking out the T-55 tanks. During the raid on the village, James had broken away long enough to plant charges on both of the parked T-55 tanks.

The explosions tore apart the ranks of the soldiers nearest the tanks. One the armored personnel carriers was rocked onto its side by the blast. When it flipped, it killed still more of the pursuing Jamali fighters. But the pain and destruction, for Jamali's men, wasn't over yet.

It had been necessary to make the Jamali thugs believe that they could win, that they could allow the hostages to leave the village, then pursue en masse and take down the relatively small number of rescuers. There was no doubt in McCarter's mind that Harwan had not believed the story about UN troops just waiting to descend. But Harwan had also understood that he had to at least pretend to release his hostages to get free of what he thought was a stalemate. McCarter had gone to great pains to make the Jamali men believe they were evenly matched with their foes.

These were long-chain, almost grandstand plays, and McCarter generally disliked them. He preferred much simpler, much more direct military plans. But this had gone as he had intended. He had gotten the hostages clear, had goaded the Jamali forces into pursuing and now he had a clear field of fire.

Well, not McCarter specifically. Technically, it was Manning who had a clear field of fire.

"Gary," McCarter said, "hit the MK-19."

Manning did not respond verbally. There was no need for him to do so. The automatic grenade launcher opened up from the hilltop overlooking the village, pumping its deadly rounds into the center of the village, straight into the bloody, flaming, screaming, scattered clump of Jamali soldiers. The damage done by the tank bombs had put them in complete disarray. The damage done by the automatic grenade onslaught buried them in the mud and snow, churning them to pieces and sending the lot of them to whatever punishment awaited them in the great beyond.

McCarter turned away from the destruction. "Bloody hell," he whispered.

CHAPTER THIRTEEN

Elmore, Ohio

"This is not good," Schwarz said. "This is not good at all."

Through the window of the sham office building outside Elmore, Ohio, the members of Able Team watched the helicopters glide in and out of view. They were sleek, black, predatory-looking things, with enclosed fenestron tail rotors and tandem seats.

"What are they?" Lyons asked.

"Those are Chinese Black Whirlwinds," Schwarz said. "Harbin WZ-19s. They're a lightly armored scout chopper, basically their Z-9 helicopter with guns on it, ripped off from the Eurocopter Dauphin. Sort of a scaled-down version of the Apache. Well, actually, it's a scaled-down version of the WZ-10. When the Chinese couldn't seal the deal for Hind or Kamov attack helicopters built by the Russians, they decided to develop their own. They're very modern. Composite construction, forward-looking infrared, shielded exhaust to prevent heat-seeking surprises. They're nothing to sneeze at. These have 23 mm gun pods, from the look of it. The other options would be air-to-air or air-to-ground missiles, but I don't see any."

"Probably because the gun pods can be covered up," Blancanales said. "Harder to disguise missiles when you're already running over airspace you ought not to be."

"Those cannons," Lyons said, "are bad enough."

"The Osprey's outnumbered and much heavier."

"In other words," Lyons said, "you stay out of this, G-Force."

"What's that?" Grimaldi's voice came over the link. "I didn't quite make that out."

"I said you stay out of this!" Lyons bellowed. "Jack, do not put yourself in the air with those sharks. Getting yourself shot down won't—"

"You're breaking up really badly, Able," Grimaldi said. "Possibly more local jamming in place. I'll just have to play this by ear."

"Jack!" Lyons roared. "Damn it, Jack!"

"We've got a live one out here," Blancanales said, checking the window again. "One man. Chinese, wearing black battle dress utilities."

Lyons and Schwarz traded glances and then went back to the glass, careful not to expose too much of themselves above the sill. There was indeed a single man approaching the building. If he was backed up by others, they weren't visible. He seemed to know precisely where to find them and walked straight up to their position. When he was close enough to communicate without shouting too loudly, he spread his hands wide to show he was carrying nothing. A pistol was holstered at his hip.

Lyons, with the butt of his shotgun, smashed a hole in the pane of glass in front of him. The Chinese man in the black BDUs smiled at that. He hooked his hands in his belt.

"Thank you," he said. "I am General Lao Wei of the People's Republic of China. I have no doubt that you know that. I have no doubt that my presence here will have certain…repercussions…for international relations between our two countries. But my presence is necessary and, if you cooperate with me, I will see to it that a minimum of damage is done to American personnel and property."

"Well, at least he speaks English really well," Blanca-nales said.

"Maybe he does high school graduations," Schwarz said.

"You're making an awful lot of assumptions," Lyons commented. "You're a known special forces operative. You're illegally operating on American soil. There isn't enough diplomatic immunity in the world to save your bacon, pal."

"I think you misunderstand the nature of the relationship between our two countries," Lao replied. "You are—how shall I term it?—a debtor nation, are you not? I know at one time your people used to worry that it was the Japanese buying all of your assets. Well, times change. And the People's Republic of China now holds a substantial portion of your nation's debt. As we proved when we hosted the Olympics, we are a superpower now. We will finally have the respect we deserve. And with that respect comes a certain amount of…flexibility…when it comes to breaking the rules."

"I could just shoot you right now," Lyons said. "That would make you real flexible."

"You could," Lao admitted. "I am standing here quite within range. My men have been held back well beyond effective range; I cannot call them in time to save my life, not ten times over. I have only four small helicopters."

"Four armed attack choppers operating illegally in United States airspace," Lyons said.

"Oh, yes," Lao agreed. "We have committed egregious sins against the mighty nation of America, have we not? And tell me, American, how many times have you, or men just like you, mounted secret attacks on foreign soil to secure your own interests, or to prosecute what you claim are 'counterterrorist' goals?"

"He's got a point there," Schwarz said quietly.

"Shaddap, Gadgets," Lyons whispered back.

"Gentlemen," Lao said. "Please allow me the concession that I am not stupid. I will offer you the same. We both know—although I will deny it should anyone ever ask me—that many operations have been conducted by Chinese operatives on American soil. Quite a few of these were the responsibility of men I would consider less than honorable. Men who had their own reasons, their personal motivations, for attempting to damage your country. But I represent a new China. A superpower China. We do things differently now. I will ask you to forget the many operatives from my nation who have met what we know are less than glorious ends here. I will ask you to forgive these as…missteps. They should not have occurred. Had I been in charge, I know they would not have occurred."

"You talk like a man who thinks he knows something," Lyons said.

"I know that your nation has access to special operations personnel of its own," Lao said. "I've made a study of the previous operations here in the United States. A study of our many failures, you could say. And I know that it was not simply American law enforcement or the American military that was responsible. I strongly suspect that I am now in the company of men who have the specialized training needed to face men such as mine. Are you not?"

"Stand still while I shoot you in the face," Lyons said. "Then you'll know for sure."

"But I *am* standing still," Lao argued. His voice was mocking now. "Come now, gentlemen, you understand. If my methods seem brazen it is because I know your nation is now weak. Your budgets collapse under their own weight. Your debt looms larger every day. Your military is exhausted from fighting wars on multiple fronts. Crime, drugs, shootings, sexual perversions and barbarity of every kind are destroying you from within. If China and China's economy were not propping you up, you would be drowning already."

"Bored now," Lyons said. "Make your point."

"My point is that your government will look the other way," Lao said. "Just as I will pretend to forget about those among my men you have already killed."

"Current Chinese special forces," Blancanales said quietly. "They were *his*."

"And if we take you down?" Lyons asked.

"Unlikely," Lao said. "My forces have tested you, but it was only that. Only a test. You are few. We are many, and my equipment is superior. You see the evidence of it in the sky above you, yes? But let us say you did 'take me down,' as you put it. Should you capture me, your government will be only too quick to negotiate for my release. And then I will return to the work that I do. And if I wish once more to enter your nation and do the work I am tasked to do by my government, I shall. And there will be nothing you can do to stop me."

"I guess you've got it all figured out, then," Lyons said. He eased the Colt Python from his shoulder holster, holding it low against his body, careful to do this beneath the edge of the window so that Lao could not see. "Now that you've got us over a barrel, I guess you better tell us what you want."

"I have already told you," Lao said. "You are my prisoners. I intend to take you into custody. You will surrender yourselves and allow my men to search this facility."

"You want to…search…EarthGard."

"Yes," Lao said.

"What are you after, Lao?" Lyons queried. "What do

you know about former Chinese special ops personnel working on American soil?

"I am not at liberty to tell you anything," Lao answered. His smile seemed a bit forced now. "Nor am I going to indulge any more prattle. You men are prisoners. Resist and I will have you killed. Only out of respect for the diplomatic pressures that could be brought to bear do I offer you the option of being taken into my custody for the duration of my work here. When I have concluded my interrogation of all of you, when I am satisfied that I know everything that you know about the work of this EarthGard, then I will arrange for you to be shipped to the People's Republic of China. There you may await a prisoner exchange. An...eventual...prisoner exchange. This is the best deal you will receive. I advise you to take it."

"No deals, Lao," Lyons said. "Shove it up your—"

"The alternative is death," Lao interrupted. "That death will not be long in coming."

The Black Whirlwinds began to fly lower. They were starting to move into attack formation. Lao looked up, clearly about to walk out of the way. He was going to clear a fire lane so that his choppers could dump their 23 mm cannon pods' payload directly into Able Team's position. A few stainless-steel desks from an office products auction weren't going to stop those rounds. Hell, Lao could be loading depleted uranium, explosive rounds or any kind of nasty ammo.

It was time to play the only card Lyons had left. He'd be kidding himself if he said it didn't burn him just a little, but he'd deal with that in person later.

"You know, Ironman," Schwarz said, "just once we could tell the bad guy 'yes' and *then* tell him to shove it up his you-know-what. After we aren't about to get killed."

Lyons glared at him. To Lao, he said, "Hey, Lao?"

"Yes, American?"

"I'll bet you'd kill a man who didn't immediately follow your every order. A man who didn't obey you the second you told him to jump."

"At the very least," Lao said, "an insubordinate soldier would find himself very uncomfortable in his future assignments."

"Yeah," Lyons said. "You Chinese Communists, you do tend to put anybody who thinks for himself in prison."

"We prefer the term 'reeducation facility,'" Lao countered.

"I'm sure you do," Lyons said. "But here's *my* point. Here in the States, occasionally, one of my men makes a call after I tell him not to. That's rare, but it does happen. And when it does, I can forgive it if it's the right call. Oh, there will be hell to pay. But that'll be between me and the other guy. Because my teammates are my *teammates*. They're not my slaves. They're not my robots."

"Now I am the one who is bored," Lao announced. "And it is time for you to die."

"Wait for it," Lyons said. "Wait for it…wait for it…"

"Until when?" Schwarz asked.

Lyons paused, listening. It might have been his imagination, but he could swear he felt the air pressure change, felt his ears pop ever so slightly. The noise of the mammoth rotor wash was so loud it dwarfed even the sound of the four enemy choppers overhead.

"Until now," Lyons said.

The massive twin-rotor Osprey flew in so low that its belly gun nearly scraped the pavement of the empty parking lot. Compared to the two-man Harbin choppers, it was impossibly large; dwarfing the smaller machines in what was, for a moment, a display of ominous military superiority.

The nose of the Osprey rammed the tail of the closest low-flying Harbin, snapping the smaller chopper up into the air faster than the pilot could compensate. The Harbin's rotors dug into the asphalt of the deserted parking lot and the chopper tore itself to pieces, spinning the fuselage up and over the lot to smash on the grounds beyond. The chopper erupted in a fireball.

"Surprise, assholes!" Lyons shouted.

The Osprey shot up, its twin rotors pointed skyward and churning out power at more than their maximum rated capacity. Grimaldi had the engines pushed all the way to their limits. The heavy Osprey rocketed upward, and as it did, the automatic cannon in its belly came to life.

Grimaldi strafed the parking lot, narrowly missing the fleeing Lao, before he walked the cannon's rounds across the tail rotor of a second Harbin. The enemy craft broke in two. The pilots were able to eject before the chopper crashed. Lyons could not see the chutes of the pilot and his gunner.

The third Harbin was maneuvering for a shot as the Osprey, its belly gun still whirring away, cut across its path. The rounds from the belly gun sliced through the tandem canopy and pulped the men inside. The chopper sat down heavily before spinning off and crashing, rolling end over end.

Grimaldi was still climbing skyward, obviously aware of the Chinese choppers' superior maneuverability. As the last Harbin struggled to get position, Grimaldi used his superior altitude to walk the Osprey over the enemy helicopter. The wash of the twin rotors smashed into the small Black Whirlwind like the hand of a giant, rocking the chopper and putting it beyond the pilot's ability to compensate.

"Fun fact," Grimaldi said. "The maximum rotor down-wash from these twin props is more than 80 knots. That's more powerful than a 'weak' hurricane."

The Chinese pilot was struggling for control now. Grimaldi let off the rotors, making the other man think he was getting things under control. Then he dropped the nose of the Osprey on the tail of the chopper and banked, shoving the Harbin left, and throwing the chopper into a spin that ended with it shattering all over the grounds of the sham office building. Once more a blaze of flame rose up.

"Did that just happen?" Schwarz asked. "That just happened."

"Jack," Lyons said. "I am not happy with you. But also I am very happy with you."

"I figured," Grimaldi said. More seriously, he continued, "I've filed a report with the Farm already. If you need to sign off on a disciplinary—"

"No, Jack," Lyons said. "That's not going to be necessary. But the next time we get away long enough for a decent steak, *you're* buying."

"That's gratitude for you," Grimaldi said. "G-Force flying overwatch. I think your buddy Lao is beating a retreat for an SUV in the tree line. You want me to light him up?"

"My sense of patriotism says yes," Lyons said, "but my gut says no. Lao knows something. He's involved somehow. And he was clearly here to check out EarthGard, just as we were. Let him go. And have Barb send in a clean-up crew. We need to document the fact that the Chinese are running gunships over our soil."

"Will do," Grimaldi affirmed.

"I'd give a lot to see the look on Lao's face right now," Blancanales said.

"I can probably patch him in," Grimaldi said. "I see a radio whip on his truck."

"Why the hell not," Lyons said. "Might as well taunt him back."

There was a pause. Grimaldi came on again. "Go for it. You're live."

"Oh, Lao? Lao, buddy," Lyons said. "You there?"

The icy silence that greeted them in return was not radio silence. It was Lao at the other end of a keyed mike, obviously furious. "What do you want, American?" he demanded.

"Just so we have an understanding, Lao," the Able Team leader said. "You and what's left of your team had better get out of the country. But you should probably tell us what you were doing here. You know, so we can tie up any loose ends."

"My business is China's business, American," Lao said. "It is not for you."

"You try to get in our way again, Lao," Lyons warned, "and I'll make sure you get the .357 Magnum round I've already got specially picked out for you."

"Yes," Lao said. "An understanding. We have one."

"Don't come back, Lao," Lyons said. "I mean it. It's going to get ugly if you do."

"I agree," Lao said. "It will, as you say, get ugly." The line went dead, full of nothing but static.

"Well, I'm glad you made a new friend today, Ironman," Schwarz said. "You realize you just guaranteed that he's going to come after us again."

"I'm counting on it," Lyons said. "So far, Lao is the only one around here who might know just what exactly is going on."

CHAPTER FOURTEEN

Shopian, Kashmir

"I swear," Calvin James stated, "I just saw General Gera walking past the fruit market with an entourage."

The town of Shopian was much more built up than the spare villages the team had encountered so far. Here there were paved streets, shops on top of shops, multistory dwellings and commercial buildings, and the narrow alleyways and side streets that went hand in hand with so many people living in so small and fetid an area.

There was also plenty of militarization here. Armed soldiers patrolled the streets with AKM and RPK rifles, while armored personnel carriers and other heavy equipment rolled through the alleys and formed barricades at strategic locations. Troop presence was high, but the villagers seemed accustomed to it.

What wasn't normal was the presence of both Pakistani and Indian military insignia in the same town.

On foot, with their weapons slung over their backs, the men of Phoenix Force walked through Shopian as if they were invisible. They simply weren't notably different in appearance from the other uniformed, armed men walking the streets.

"Mercenaries must pass through here," Encizo said. "They must be used to seeing armed, nonaffiliated contingents."

"That doesn't explain how Gera's and Jamali's people are occupying the same ground without going to war with each other," McCarter argued. "Calvin, stay on Gera. Follow him to wherever he's going."

"Guys," Hawkins said, "you're not going to believe this. Jamali and a force of bodyguards are crossing the iron bridge on the Rambiara River, west of the old bus station. They're heading in Gera's direction."

"Follow him," McCarter instructed. "I want eyes and ears on that meeting."

"Can you get close enough?" Encizo asked.

"I think so," James said. "It's pretty dense there, lots of traffic, lots of visual obstacles. Benches, kiosks, that sort of thing. Gera is definitely taking up a position in the old Shopian bus station."

"Calvin, T.J., move in," McCarter directed. "But watch your hind ends."

Leaving Manning and Encizo with the MRAPs on overwatch outside Shopian, McCarter had taken James and Hawkins on foot into the town. Stony Man's satellite sweeps had indicated a large force moving toward Shopian that Kurtzman and his team had initially identified as a possible Jamali strike force. The idea, on the ground, had been to infiltrate Shopian, take up positions to fight the Jamali invaders and call in heavy support from the MRAPs once the nature of the threat was more fully known.

What had instead occurred was the bizarre set of circumstances that had met them in Shopian. The streets were teeming with soldiers and civilians. The civilians had the wide-eyed, rattled look familiar in the faces of occupied and abused peoples the world over. The soldiers, by contrast, seemed remarkably relaxed, even amused. It was if they all shared some secret joke together. There were groups of infantry wearing Jamali's logo and a roughly equal number of troops wearing Gera's flag. They seemed to be taking more or less equal duty among the barricades and security checkpoints, too.

What the hell was going on here?

The "strike force" the Farm had been tracking was likely a motorcade belonging to one or the other of the generals. Apparently either Gera or Jamali had been on site previously, moving into place during one of the windows of opportunity the satellites couldn't cover. It didn't matter now. What mattered was that no attack was coming…and both Gera and Jamali were in the same place at the same time.

A decisive strike now could end the conflict here once and for all. But both generals had multiple bodyguards and, given the nature of the meeting they seemed about to have, it stood to reason that they would both be on guard. That meant hitting them here and now, with no advanced planning and with only the firepower Phoenix could bring to bear as a mobile strike team, was a difficult proposition indeed.

McCarter hated to admit it, but what they really needed was more information. That meant listening in on this meeting, if that's really what was happening, and basing their plans on the outcome. Hell, it was possible the two generals had reached some sort of peace agreement, and that was why their men were cooperating here in town. Stranger things had happened.

War and strange bedfellows, McCarter thought.

McCarter waited, tense and irritated, as James and Hawkins moved into position. It was not them that he was annoyed with; it was the situation, the scenario in which they now found themselves. But he was satisfied that each of them had a good vantage from which to listen in on the meeting. Gera and Jamali were right there, in the center of the bus station, sitting on a set of benches surrounded by their guards. They obviously thought their power was unchecked, that nothing could touch them. Otherwise they wouldn't be so blithe about meeting here, out in the open, where any daring sod could listen in.

The Briton watched as the two men made their greetings. They seemed unusually chummy for two men determined to wipe each other off the map...and to provoke a nuclear confrontation between their respective nations in the process. Around the men, and screening Phoenix Force from notice, a surprisingly large throng of people moved here and there, or sat on benches and at rickety tables, presumably waiting for buses. Some of them, McCarter supposed, might not be waiting for transportation at all. In a town like this, a central point of activity, a place to "hang out," as the Yanks put it, would attract people who simply wanted to be where the activity was.

Still, McCarter was astonished at how comfortable Gera and Jamali seemed to be. So confident were both men in the power of their respective forces that they seemed to be neglecting even basic operational security. How else could the men of Phoenix Force have gotten close enough to listen in to some sort of summit meeting between the two?

To the Briton's surprise, Jamali and Gera took a table near the center of the old bus station courtyard, smiling and shaking each other's hand as they took their seats. One of their bodyguards brought a silver tea service and began pouring. The strong Turkish blend was powerful enough that McCarter could smell it from where he sat among the benches.

The bus station was essentially an open courtyard flanked by various commercial stands, some shuttered, as well as a ticket counter. There were lots of armed guards milling around, but even more civilians. The civilians seemed not to notice the soldiers in their midst. He had seen that kind of apathy before. These were a beaten-down people. If Gera and Jamali had declared Shopian a neutral way station, that would bode ill for any group of locals caught in the middle.

Gera and Jamali apparently shared English between them, which was logical given the prevalence of English as a second language for both commerce and convenience in this part of the world. Gera took a moment to sample his tea, nod to one of his men and indicate to Jamali that he should do the same. Jamali was all toothy grins as he drank from his own silver teacup.

"You look thinner, Ibrahim," Gera said.

"Bah," said Jamali. "As always you waste time with dishonest flattery." He sipped his own tea. "But I will gladly accept your lies. And I shall repeat them to the pretty young girls my men select for me."

"But is that not the benefit of having those young girls selected for you?" Gera said, leaning in conspiratorially. "You don't have to lie to them. You merely tell them what to do."

Jamali snorted. More seriously, he said, "I have a packet of the latest casualty figures." He removed the folded sheaves of paper and slid them across the table to Gera. "We are leaning too heavily in your disfavor. Again."

Gera sighed and sipped more of his tea. "My men simply cannot meet the ferocity of yours," he said. "They are well trained and equipped. They are given every opportunity. But time and again, even outnumbered, your men are more effective."

"We shall have to coordinate a few skirmishes," Jamali declared. "You can hand-pick a few detachments and I'll funnel some of my more expendable troops into areas where my men are hopelessly outnumbered. That should even things out a bit. It's important that neither side appear to be gaining the upper hand, or we'll lose the indifferent attitude we've enjoyed so far from the rest of the world. As long as the dispute over the region is seen as an unwinnable, unending…what is the term the media adore? 'Quagmire.' Yes. An unwinnable quagmire. As long as we maintain that stalemate, the world's various powers will see no benefit in meddling. If they cannot ride in and achieve a fast victory, they will have no interest in spending their blood and treasure on what they see as a pointless local matter."

"A fine balance indeed," Gera said, "given that my nation and yours are at each other's throats. It will not be long before the nuclear threats become more overt."

"This was always our plan," Jamali said. "From the first overtures I made to you, from the moment I suggested that there was a way that you and I could profit from our nations' posturing, we have known that ultimately there will be war. The nuclear option is far too horrible for either India or Pakistan to do more than drop a strategic tactical nuke or two. Or three. And there is nothing about the remote region that you and I will control that is in any way strategic."

"Or tactical," Gera put in.

"Precisely. The very thing that makes it difficult for either your nation or mine to mount an effective assault on our positions, on our entrenched militaries, is the remote nature of the disputed territory between the two. Once we have driven the two nations to war, nuclear or otherwise, they will be too busy prosecuting that war to worry about the small fiefdom we will carve for ourselves. Thus shall we become masters of the region."

"There have been problems."

"'Problems'?" Jamali repeated. "Oh. Yes. You speak of

the losses both our forces have experienced at the hands of a foreign power."

"Precisely," Gera said. "If an external power has taken an interest in us, does it not mean that India and Pakistan will refuse to go to war?"

"Why ever would you think so?" Jamali asked.

The question confused Gera. "Why…because our two governments surely know by now that you and I, the forces we control, are behind the unrest. They have divined that we are sacrificing our more…ignorant troops, troops in the more remote regions, such as the Siachen. The ones that are, as you say, 'expendable.' They know we are deceiving them."

Jamali put his cup down. His thick face split into a wide, toothy grin and he began to laugh heartily. "My dear General Gera," he said through his laughter. "Have you been under the impression that our skirmishes were for the primary benefit of the governments we serve?"

Gera again looked bewildered. "But if not for them… who?"

Jamali steepled his fingers and leaned across the table. "General Gera, we put on our little show for all the other nations of the world. The nations of the world who will look on Pakistan and India and see not two powerful nations, but two weak, bickering neighbors."

Gera nodded. "I think I understand."

"Of course you do," Jamali said. "Our display of force, our continued stalemate, makes it appear to other nations that Pakistan and India have fought each other to a standstill. The governments, our governments, look as if they have no control. And in lacking control they lack power. They lack honor. They rattle their sabers now in the name of saving face. They cannot be made to look weak in the eyes of the world. They will not tolerate such an insult.

They dare not consider what it will do to their political stature if they do nothing. And so they will go to war, knowing that it is us who brought them to its brink…and perhaps not caring, for the hatred between my people and yours runs deep."

"Have you asked yourself," Gera said, his tone tentative, "if perhaps what we are doing is too big? Too much? You seek to redraw the map of the world."

"I?" Jamali asked. "We, you mean. We seek to redraw the map, and not of the world. Only of India and Pakistan and the territory in between. This is not so great a thing. Men like us have been drawing and redrawing the map of the world for centuries. Should we decide that nothing can change in the modern world? All that makes the ancient world is the passage of time. And dead or alive, time will pass us, my friend."

"There is rumbling among the men," Gera said.

"About what? Are they uncomfortable with the arrangement we have here in Shopian? Are they so eager to fight each other that they would overlook the riches that can accrue to us all if we pursue our plans to their completion?"

"No," Gera said. "The problem is the invaders."

"Oh, yes," Jamali said. He withdrew from his belt a long, wicked-looking combat knife with a double-edged blade. This he began using to clean his fingernails. McCarter thought the act looked deliberate, a calculated air of menace. He could not decide if Jamali looked dangerous or comical, picking his fingers with a tapered, six-inch blade.

"Even if the presence of foreign operatives does not hinder our plan to send Pakistan and India to war," Gera said, "it—"

"*Nuclear* war," Jamali corrected. "Hopefully."

"You have a curious definition of 'hope,'" Gera said. "But regardless. Even if our plan to pit our nations against each other proceeds as it should, what are we to do about these men? We have both lost troops to them."

"Do you see any nation eagerly taking credit for their attacks?" Jamali asked.

McCarter, watching him, began to get an uneasy feeling in the pit of his stomach. This Jamali seemed just a little too smug. He acted like a man with a secret. He acted, in fact, like a man who was just bursting at the seams to tell someone what that secret was.

"What difference would credit or blame make?" Gera asked. "Whether United Nations or Americans, whether the French or the British or some other group of meddlers, if they have taken an interest in our war, they could seek to stop it. Perhaps even to assassinate us, if our roles are known to them."

"Oh, rest assured, our identities are known to them," Jamali said. He grinned more broadly than ever. "Every detail of our plan, in fact, is something of which they are only too aware. But don't you see? All reports to date are of one or two armored vehicles and a handful of men. Hardly an invading army. Surely you are skilled enough in world military operations to understand what that implies?"

"Why do you not explain it to me?" Gera said.

"A small force is sent when a larger one cannot be," Jamali explained, as if it were the simplest thing in the world. "What is a small attack force of men? It is one that can be denied. One that can be…lost. The nations of the world will not take a stand because their interests will not be met. They dare not involve themselves in the costly stalemate we make them believe is occurring. And when India and Pakistan finally go to war, they will find reasons not to involve themselves in what results. 'Too expensive,' they will say. 'The affairs of sovereign nations,' they will protest. But really it will be the money and the risk they seem so eager to avoid."

"So our foreign invaders are a small group of covert operations specialists."

"Clearly," Jamali said. "Obviously they are very well trained—otherwise they would not have prevailed against such larger numbers. And they have done so repeatedly. This is nothing new of them. Study your world affairs, General. You will see that this sort of thing happens more often than you or any of us realize. Usually the activities of such clandestine groups are hidden under the cover of 'accidents' and 'coincidences.' But whenever world affairs miraculously resolve themselves in favor of the West, one must at least suspect that their covert agents are responsible. Or that they *could* be."

"You do not seem concerned."

Jamali placed his knife beside his empty teacup on the table and ran one thick finger around the rim of the cup. "No," he said. "I am not. For the man of daring, the man who plans, the man who understands how to execute his plans, there is no need for concern."

"I don't understand," Gera said.

"No," Jamali said. "But you will. You see, General, I gave my men, and yours, explicit instructions not to interfere with these foreign invaders the moment I received word they were here in Shopian."

Bloody hell, thought McCarter. We're blown! He reached into his pocket, grabbed his satellite phone and texted the digits 9-1-1 to the operational channel. This would cause the emergency abort code to display on all of Phoenix Force's phones.

"Here?" Gera asked. He began looking around. "How can they be here?"

"Because they think we are stupid," Jamali explained.

"They think we are poor, backward fools, barely capable of running our respective militaries. And so they have underestimated us." Jamali stood suddenly and raised one arm.

McCarter shot to his feet, whipped his Tavor up and aimed it directly at the two generals. His finger tightened on the grenade launcher's trigger.

Chaos erupted.

Before he could fire, McCarter found his rifle being knocked upward by a Jamali soldier's Kalashnikov. The grenade round flew into the air.

"That's coming back down!" James shouted.

"Run!" McCarter roared. He pulled back the trigger of his Tavor and began spraying 5.56 mm NATO rounds in every direction. He did, however, make sure there were uniforms on the other end of his shots and not civilians.

He needn't have worried, however. The hardy people of Shopian were well used to being misused by their government's military forces. They melted into the background, disappearing from the bus station and the surrounding neighborhood as if someone had thrown a switch. In fact, someone had. The war switch, the death switch, the switch signaling open battle in their streets, had been thrown by Jamali the moment he'd made his intentions clear.

He was lying for us the whole time, thought McCarter. Probably couldn't resist the feeling of jawing Gera's ear off while he knew we were nearby. Arrogant bastard.

Running at full speed now, shooting his Tavor as he went, McCarter made for Soura Road, west of the bus station and leading to the iron bridge. There were too many soldiers behind him and on all sides of him. There were simply too many enemies. They were converging on his position. He was going to die.

Or he would be close to death, if it weren't for the

text code he had sent to the two MRAPs waiting outside of town.

MRAP One, with Encizo behind the wheel, picked him up as it roared over the iron bridge. Two was close behind, and the moment Hawkins was on board, the second armored vehicle began spitting grenade rounds at the enemy soldiers. Shopian became a ground-level fireworks display as enemy soldiers, their armored personnel carriers and the cover behind which they were hiding exploded into millions of splinters.

The MRAPs smashed aside smaller utility trucks and enemy soldiers alike, flattening some of the latter under their heavy wheels. McCarter took the machine gun of MRAP One and began pouring automatic fire into the legions of uniformed opponents, Pakistani and Indian alike, who now pursued the armored trucks like so many enraged hornets. Round after round ricocheted off the armor of the MRAPs, shaking the trucks and causing McCarter to duck and dodge behind the shield of the MRAP turret. Soon both vehicles were roaring over the Rambiara River.

"Gary!" McCarter shouted. "Target the bridge over the Shopian Srinigar Road!"

There were two bridges connecting the halves of Shopian to each other. The Rambiara River raged through the center of town, with only the iron bridge and an unnamed structure along the Srinigar Road to allow vehicle and foot traffic to pass from side to side. Most of Jamali's and Gera's forces were concentrated on the other side of the river, in the vicinity of the meeting point. They were now actively pursuing, but if deprived of the bridges, they would not be able to bring their vehicles across.

"Where the bloody hell is Calvin!" McCarter shouted. "Calvin! Report! David to Calvin, report!"

MRAP Two's grenade launcher unleashed a howling

fury of airborne destruction on the neighboring bridge, blowing it to shrapnel. The two vehicles were just clearing the iron bridge farther down the Rambiara. Enemy troops were in hot pursuit, including a pair of APCs mounting machine guns.

"Have we lost Calvin?" Hawkins asked through his transceiver.

"David," Manning said, "if we don't blow the bridge, Gera and Jamali are going to come down on us with the full weight of their forces. I don't think we're in a position to fight them off."

"Wait, what about Calvin?" Hawkins demanded.

"T.J.!" McCarter shouted. "Clear the bloody channel!"

"David?" Manning asked again.

"Blow the bridge!" McCarter concluded. "Blow the bridge now!"

Behind the two MRAPs, Manning's grenade launcher annihilated the iron bridge that was now the only span across the Rambiara River. The explosion was deafening.

"Get us out of here, Rafe," said McCarter.

Behind them, the wreckage left by the MK-19 produced a great black plume of smoke.

Shopian was burning.

CHAPTER FIFTEEN

Detroit

"Underground?" Lyons asked from the driver's seat of the Suburban. "Well, I guess that makes sense. Not that it does us a whole lot of good."

"That's where I would run the data trunk if I wanted to keep it hidden," Schwarz said from the passenger seat. "But I think we can put even money on the fact that this facility will be hardened in some way. They've gone to extremes to hide it. You don't build an entire fake property, right down to the cardboard computers on the surplus desks, complete with a data-forwarding operation to cloak it all…and then just leave your real operation wide open."

"This message has been brought to you by Captain Obvious," Blancanales intoned behind them.

"Now don't you start," Lyons said. "One budding comic on the team is enough."

"You used to be fun, Ironman," Schwarz said.

"I was never fun," Lyons denied.

Kurtzman and the cybernetics team at Stony Man Farm had, with Schwarz's help on-site at the fake EarthGard office, traced the data trunk from the phony facility. The data equipment itself had been concealed in the floor of the reception area. They had found it simply by tearing the place apart, although Schwarz had also applied some educated guesses as to the size of the needed hardware and where it was most likely to be tucked away.

Eventually, the Farm had traced the trunk line out of the facility. It was through this line, according to the Farm's computers, that EarthGard simulated its official presence. The trunk line also afforded them a domestic IP address, which, although encrypted, was finally hacked by Kurtzman after an all-night, coffee-fueled session in front of a keyboard and a room full of screens.

It had been, in Kurtzman's words, a "tough nut to crack," even for him.

The IP address, and therefore the forwarded data trail, had led them to a crumbling neighborhood in Detroit, Michigan—although, in Schwarz's opinion, anyone would be hard-pressed to identify a neighborhood in Detroit that *wasn't* crumbling. Still, the area in which they were about to walk was particularly bad. There were bars on the windows of the shops, which was never a good sign. They had also passed a series of gunshot detectors, which had been erected in hopes of alerting police to gunfire in the murder-ravaged metropolitan area.

While Gadgets pitied whatever poor mugger decided to make the life-altering decision to try to take Carl "Ironman" Lyons's wallet at gunpoint, stranger and stupider things had happened to Able Team in the field. He kept his eyes open and his head on a swivel as they left the truck, leaving Blancanales to guard the vehicle and keep watch outside.

The trail led them to an ostensibly abandoned tenement. Abandoned dwellings, in a city where nearly eighty thousand homes stood empty, were not hard to find. Many of the empty dwellings had been ravaged by scrappers, pulling out copper wire and other valuables, and infested by rats and other wild animals. Squatting abounded, but there were many more homes than there were homeless to occupy them. At least in certain neighborhoods, which lay across the map of Detroit like swatches of leprosy, the city was dying.

It was in one of these charming areas, therefore, that the data trunk IP address was traced, which seemed only appropriate to Schwarz. Law-enforcement presence in such an area would be far less than it would be in an affluent neighborhood, or even a less run-down but still poverty-stricken area. Criminals, terrorists and other people operating outside the normal confines of law and civilization always gravitated to no-man's lands such as these.

As they walked from the Suburban, which was parked at the curb in front of the tenement building, Lyons grumbled about the fact that he would rather not be poking around inside some grimy basement.

Schwarz did not have the heart to tell the Able Team leader that their problems would likely run deeper than that. The Farm had established a basic elevation for the trunk's IP address. It was a set of figures relative to sea level, the kind of thing that Schwarz wouldn't normally annoy Lyons with. But the end result was that they were going to have to descend by a few floors to get where they were going. That meant that, unless this building had an extensive subbasement system, they were going to be navigating tunnels before their visit to Detroit was through.

Lyons hated tunnels, Schwarz well knew. The Able Team electronics whiz wasn't overly fond of them, either. Narrow corridors were choke points, and choke points were places where bad things happened.

The Able Team leader wore his USAS-12 shotgun slung over his back. He had his Colt Python out and in his hand the moment they'd exited the vehicle. Schwarz had done the same with his 93-R. He snapped open the forward grip and took a two-handed hold on the weapon, ready to unleash the contents of its 20-round box.

The door to the tenement was sealed and boarded. Schwarz checked their six o'clock, stowed his Beretta and took a mini pry bar from his pocket. He carried a multitool and a variety of other small items that were helpful for situations such as this. The pry bar was no bigger than the palm of his hand, but it would give him enough leverage to pop the board on the door. In minutes he had the barrier free and was opening the door itself.

Lyons took out a combat flashlight with a tail cap switch and, holding it together with his Python, shone the bright white LED light into the inky blackness that Schwarz's opened door revealed.

"Ready to get down?" Schwarz asked.

"Let's just get this taken care of," Lyons rumbled.

The dank basement smelled of urine and other things Schwarz didn't want to think about. The entire area was filled with stacks of old newspapers, sodden cardboard boxes coated with mold, piles of desiccated garbage, and what must have been, to Schwarz's eye, about three full thrift stores' worth of discarded clothing in black plastic trash bags.

Lyons played the bright white beam of his flashlight around the basement. "Garbage," he said. "Rotten garbage. Stuff that should be garbage. Boxes of garbage. And one sneaker. Not two sneakers. Just one."

"I always kind of wonder about that," Schwarz said. "It's like, who loses just one shoe? Wouldn't you find two shoes, if somebody threw away their shoes? Or if they forgot to take them with them when they left?"

"Gadgets," Lyons said, "let me ask you something. If you *had* both shoes, wouldn't you be wearing them?"

Schwarz honestly had nothing to say to that.

"Any ideas?" Lyons asked. "We've checked the whole basement but I don't see anything. We need to know how to proceed."

"The data trunk is here," Schwarz said. "Access to it must be here. We just need to find where the entrance is hidden. Remember, this is something that the boys and girls from EarthGard would want to access, at least from time to time if not regularly. So it can't be impossible to uncover. Your cop's mind has to be perfect for finding—"

"Got it," Lyons said, interrupting.

"That's more like it," Schwarz said. "Uh…got what?"

"What do you see?" Lyons moved his flashlight beam toward the center of the room.

"Besides the aforementioned garbage?"

"I see a wooden pallet," Lyons said. "The only wooden pallet in this entire basement. Pallets are worth money, Gadgets. Anything of value has been taken out of this basement except that pallet. And while they've tried to darken it with paint, it looks brand-new compared to the other crap in here."

The two Able Team members went to the pallet. Lyons cleared it of the bags of trash that had been piled on it to cover it. When he was done moving the trash, his light showed the distinctive square outline of a seam in the middle of the pallet.

"Hello, trapdoor," Schwarz said. He stomped it experimentally, as he saw no handles or other protrusions. The magnetic lock reacted to his push and the door popped up and open.

"Like a medicine cabinet," Lyons commented. "Tricky." He opened the door and shined his light down inside, pointing the barrel of his Colt Python. A stainless-steel metal ladder practically glittered in the beam of the combat light. "Let's see what's down there. Pol? Comm check."

"Still reading you," Blancanales said, "but your signal is weak."

"The RF transceivers won't work much deeper," Schwarz warned. "And if our satellite phones aren't already having difficulty, they'll get no signal down there. We're going to be on our own for the duration of this little jaunt."

"You copy, Pol?" Lyons asked.

"I copy," Blancanales said. "When do you want me to call in the cavalry?"

"We can't have Jack overfly this location unless we want to put the entire city in a panic," Lyons said. "The airspace is layer on layer of controlled. That's why we left him at the airport. If you don't hear from Gadgets or me within the next hour, notify the Farm and come in after us…but not before Jack shows up to pour firepower down their throats. And air traffic regulations be damned."

"Hal's gonna love you," Blancanales said.

"Tell me about it," Lyons said. "Stand by. We'll be in touch."

Lyons put his phone away. He nodded to his partner. "Age before beauty."

"Doesn't that mean you go first?" Schwarz said.

"Yes," Lyons replied. "Yes, it does." He slid down, gripping the ladder with the edges of his boots and using his hands to slow his descent. At the bottom, he deployed his Python and light again, shining it down the tunnel.

Schwarz joined him, feeling the walls close in. The tunnel was lined in concrete and braced with steel X-frames throughout. It looked to be of relatively recent construction. It extended on into the darkness beyond the throw of Lyons's flashlight. There were work lights strung to heavy industrial extension cords and hooked along the ceiling of the tunnel. Schwarz could not see any way to switch them on. He assumed that must be at the other end of the—

Schwarz's train of thought stopped abruptly as his shin brushed something taut.

"Carl!" he shouted. "Freeze!"

Lyons obeyed immediately. He looked back at Schwarz, then played his light down at their feet. The big former LAPD cop had apparently stepped right over the line, but Schwarz had blundered into it. The electronics expert's leg pushed up against a tripwire.

"Gadgets," Lyons said, "don't you move. And don't crack any jokes. Let me see what this is connected to." Very carefully, Lyons knelt down and used his light to track the tripwire. He found it plugged into a metal cylinder on the opposite wall. The curse he uttered under his breath was a particularly rare and vivid one.

"How screwed am I?" Schwarz asked.

"I think this is a Bouncing Betty," Lyons reported. "The pin is half in and half out of the housing. Another inch and you'd have set this off. Judging from the barrel here, the charge will pop up at more or less a right angle. If I was setting it I'd want it to go off right in the middle of the tunnel. This thing will juice us both, Gadgets."

"Good thing I'm an expert at defusing bombs and improvised explosives," Schwarz said.

"You stay right the hell where you are," Lyons ordered. "You so much as bend and you'll shift against the wire."

"The best part," Schwarz said, "is that depending on how sophisticated this is, if I let off the pressure suddenly, it might still go off."

"You're going to walk me through this," Lyons said. "Just stand as still as you can and tell me what to do."

"All right," Schwarz said. "You've got to ease the charge up through the canister while holding the pin at the degree it's sitting now. Once you get both clear of the cylinder, you should be able to just pull the wires. The cylinder is a conductor. Once you're outside of that, you've just got the direct wire connection to worry about. Don't touch the outer walls of the cylinder."

"So this whole thing is like that kid's game, with the electric buzzer," Lyons said, easing the Bouncing Betty from its housing.

"Except if you do it wrong we blow up," Schwarz said.

"I blow up, I'm going to be really upset with you, Gadgets. Come on. Let's keep going. Try not to step on any more explosives."

Their forward travel was much slower going. It was necessary to sweep the floor, the ceiling and the walls with each step they took. They weren't just looking for tripwires, either. Schwarz suggested they look out for pressure plates in the floor. There was the possibility of lasers or infrared at any height that could, quite invisibly, trigger an explosive device or a booby trap. Presumably anyone from EarthGard, or whoever was running EarthGard, who happened to come down here would also know where the traps were, or have some means of circumventing anything they could not avoid.

They encountered two more explosive surprises. One was indeed a pressure plate in the floor. The second was an infrared or other invisible beam that served the same purpose as a tripwire. They simply avoided both of these, stepping over them and noting their locations.

Finally they found themselves in front of a sealed steel door with a keypad.

"This is all you, Gadgets," Lyons said. "Unless you think smashing the keypad itself is going to get us in."

"Probably not that," Schwarz said. He removed the multitool he kept in his pocket, snapped open one of the flats screwdriver blades and pried up the housing of the keypad. He stopped abruptly.

"What is it?" Lyons demanded. "Can't you do it?"

"Shine your light over here, Ironman," Schwarz ordered. "I need to get the angle just right... Yes, that's it. See this pattern?"

Lyons grunted. Four of the buttons on the keypad showed extreme wear. The others looked almost brand-new.

"Amateur night," Schwarz said. "After everything they've gone through...the key to the kingdom is a greasy four-digit keypad combination."

"How do you know it is four digits?" Lyons asked. "Couldn't it be any combination of those four numbers for any length?"

"It could," Schwarz said. "But as sloppy as this keypad is, I doubt it."

"So, what, do you know some fancy algorithm or prime number thingy to get you in there?"

"No," Schwarz answered. "I'm just going to tap in four-digit sequences at random until the door opens." He tapped in half a dozen number patterns.

The door opened on hydraulic hinges.

The room beyond was full of Asian men wearing the uniform of EarthGard's private security force.

Schwarz was behind Carl Lyons at the keypad. In the moment that he had available to him, he reached into the inner pocket of his jacket and then deposited the item he found there in Carl Lyons's back pocket. The tail of Lyons's jacket covered the telltale bulge. Schwarz did his best to look inconspicuous as a voice from inside the chamber called, "Come in. Or we shoot you out there."

The electronics expert followed his team leader through the chamber door. The pair found themselves in a large octagonal room that boasted multiple workstations and computers. Judging from the machinery and the cabling running in all directions, Schwarz concluded that they were standing in a data "boiler room" of sorts. This had to be where EarthGard's processing power was funneled. From here it was forwarded to the fake facility they had already raided.

It was sometimes very difficult to determine an exact nation of origin for a specific Asian person, but Schwarz had to guess these men were more Chinese mercenaries. What still didn't add up was that there seemed to be a division between Lao Wei and his special forces, and the Chinese working with EarthGard. Just what that distinction was, given that Able Team had faced both in battle already, Schwarz couldn't guess.

A variety of pistols and a couple of micro-Uzis were pointing in their direction. Schwarz put his hands up.

"Fire department," he said. "We're just here to check your fire extinguishers."

"Kill him," one of the Asian men snapped.

"Whoops," Lyons said, dropping into their midst the grenade that his partner had slipped into his pocket. The metal canister bounced off the floor with a musical clink.

For the briefest of moments, every pair of eyes in the room looked down at the grenade.

"Boom," Carl Lyons said.

When the grenade went off, the otherwise harmless smoke canister spewed thick purple smoke from both ends. The first volley of gunfire that answered it came from the micro-Uzis of two of the guards. In their zeal to attack, however, they neglected to verify their targets. Lyons and Schwarz were untouched as automatic gunfire spread blood and brain matter all over the computer stations.

Into that chaos, Lyons introduced the deafening roar of

his .357 Magnum Colt Python. Schwarz unlimbered his weapon, too, and soon the Beretta 93-R was spitting flame. Schwarz felt himself being lifted up and he began to panic. Then he realized the big man nearly crushing his biceps was Lyons. The Able Team leader threw Schwarz bodily past one of the computer desks, causing the smaller man to fall behind it. Bullets hammered away at the desk and the equipment on it, but did not penetrate.

And then Schwarz understood why Lyons had moved him out of the way.

He heard the big bolt of the USAS-12 being racked back. Lyons threw himself onto the floor of the data boiler room, held the shotgun up above his chest and, with superb effort of both will and muscle, pulled the trigger back on full automatic while not bracing the weapon against his body. Then he kicked his legs as if he were riding a bicycle, walking the weapon in a circle at waist height, emptying the drum magazine of its 12-gauge slugs in a death-dealing spiral of eviscerating firepower.

The noise was unbelievable. Schwarz's ears rang so badly that he could hear the blood pumping in his head. Moments later he felt blood against his knees as he sheltered behind the computer desk. The pool was spreading from the pile of dead enemy shooters on the floor. More were falling. Lyons finally exhausted his weapon's ammunition.

The rhythmic thump-thump, thump-thump of his own pulse was all Schwarz could hear. He looked at Lyons through the smoke and the emergency lighting now illuminating the data boiler room. Lyons's mouth was moving, but Schwarz couldn't make out any of the words. Slowly he realized he should be trying to read Lyons's lips. He looked up as the big former cop loomed over him and did his best to make out what Lyons was saying.

"No," Schwarz said. "I'm not thirsty."

"I said," Lyons screamed at him, "are you okay?"

The electronics genius shook his head. He had heard that. "Wait," he said. "Wait. I think it's clearing. I can hear you. And I have the world's worst headache."

Lyons leaned against one of the bullet-riddle computer tables and wiped his forehead with his hand. "My arms hurt," he said simply.

"You're lucky you didn't dislocate something with that stunt," Schwarz said. He looked around once more. "Wait," he said. "Where's the smoke going?"

"Automatic ventilators," Lyons answered. He pointed to grilles in the ceiling. "They're sucking it right out. This is a pretty slick setup."

"Did we leave anything intact?" Schwarz asked. "Or is everything smashed?"

"We're running out of time," Lyons noted. He checked the chronograph on his wrist. "Can you get a signal to the outside world? Or is Pol about to crash this party?"

"Find me a terminal," Schwarz said. "Something that isn't blown up. I may be able to figure out how to get to something on the other side of their firewall. Assuming there is one."

"Do what you can," Lyons said.

There were several computers, one with obvious network access, that were still intact. Schwarz managed to get into the network relatively quickly, but routing communications to the outside world was a little more difficult. By the time the message reached Blancanales, the Able Team member was getting ready to call in both Grimaldi and a small army from the Farm. Schwarz reassured him that all was as well as could be expected down below, and to please stand by for further details.

"So now what, Gadgets?" Lyons asked.

"Now I start poking around inside these machines," Schwarz replied, "to get us some real answers to what's going on. This is the jackpot, Ironman. Whatever Earth-Gard is doing, it's buried in here somewhere."

"Can we somehow funnel all this crap to the Farm?" Lyons wondered aloud. "March the electrons outta here and over there?"

"Something like that," Schwarz said. "Just…let me handle the tech stuff."

"Says the guy who nearly tripped over a Bouncing Betty," Lyons said.

Schwarz called up a schematic of the data boiler room. He glanced left, then right. "There are two other entrances to this place," he said. "That means two other routes. I'm going to see if I can seal the tunnel where we came in and isolate the one of these others that gives us the fastest shot out of this dungeon. That way we don't have to walk past the traps and what-all."

"That would be great," Lyons commented.

"Uh-oh," Schwarz said.

"Uh-oh?" Lyons echoed. "What is 'uh-oh'? That's never good when you do that."

"I've got surveillance up on the other two access corridors," Schwarz explained. "One of the hallways has company." The electronics expert tapped a few buttons on his console. The black-and-white image showed a man in Chinese-pattern BDUs staring up at the very camera that had him under surveillance.

Lao Wei, looking annoyed and with plenty of armed backup, stared back at them from the monitor.

CHAPTER SIXTEEN

Guirat, Pakistan

The Pakistani fortress resembled a medieval keep more than a modern military facility. A barbed-wire perimeter, dotted with antitank barriers, extended for several hundred yards around the reinforced concrete structure itself. There was a helipad on the eastern side and several prefab wooden buildings with corrugated metal roofs on the western end. The main entrance to the fortress was a massive steel door that appeared to rise and lower like a drawbridge, judging from the outline in the gravel-pocked soil in front of it.

Night had fallen over Guirat. The men of Phoenix Force, using the darkness for cover, gathered on a ridge overlooking the fortress. McCarter was examining the foreboding military base through a pair of compact field glasses. Encizo, meanwhile, was reading through several dispatches from the Farm on his satellite phone. The brightness of the phone's screen had been dialed back to the point it would be unreadable—not to mention all but invisible—to anyone not positioned mere inches from the unit.

"Barb verifies that these are the coordinates," Encizo said quietly. "Calvin is there, in that fortress. Or at least his satellite phone is."

"Here's the plan, then," McCarter began. "Gary, I want

you and your RPG up on this ridge for close support. Rafe, T.J., take the turrets in MRAP One and Two."

Hawkins and Encizo nodded. The armored vehicles were parked on opposite sides of the ridge, where they faced the corners of the fortress. This was an extremely strategic layout and one they could use to control traffic flow from and to the fortress quite effectively.

"I'm going to lone-wolf it," McCarter continued, "and sneak into the fortress under cover of your assault. On my mark, you're going to strike the fortress with the full might of everything we can bring to bear. That will be the cover I need to slip inside, find Calvin and free him. And along the way we'll be neutralizing a good portion of Jamali's forces in the area. According to the Farm's dossier files, Jamali has half of his reserve troops staged here and the other half staged at his joint facility with Gera on the India-Pakistan border. We make trouble for Jamali here, we go a long way toward neutralizing the rogue operation in Kashmir. Let's make it happen, lads."

The other team members agreed quietly. McCarter checked his Tavor, his supply of 40 mm grenades and the spare magazines for his rifle and his Hi-Power. Then he finished blackening his face with paint from his camo kit, nodded to the men of Phoenix Force and started his jog down the hill. Behind him, Hawkins and Encizo made their way to the MRAPs, while Manning and his RPG dug in on top of the ridge.

Nothing like having a big Canadian guardian angel watching your back with rocket-propelled explosives, McCarter thought.

The fox-faced Briton jogged as far as he dared. When he was within sight of the sentries marching patterns around the fortress, he flattened himself on the ground and positioned his rifle in front of him.

"Go, lads," he said quietly into his transceiver.

The first of Manning's rocket-propelled grenades streaked through the night and struck a guard shack on McCarter's left. The shack and the man standing inside it were blown to pieces.

The MRAP's automatic grenade launcher began chugging away. Explosions dotted the front of the fortress, laying waste to the men guarding the battlements. Chunks of stone were blown free to become whirling shrapnel. More of Jamali's men were ground to meat in the fiery blasts.

McCarter pushed himself up and ran for the fortress.

Phoenix Force was the ultimate small unit. Their tactics were flexible and mobile, based on fire-team strategies and proven guerilla methods. When taking on an overwhelmingly large force such as this one, their victory was found in hitting so quickly and so ferociously that the enemy did not have time to process his greater numbers. A man who believed his force was strong enough to win would generally find a way to make that happen. If he thought his enemies were insignificant, he would fight longer and with more confidence. That confidence was a self-fulfilling prophecy, just as defeat could be.

McCarter intended to fill Jamali's men with defeat. He would pour it over their minds and hearts. He would make them believe it.

Grenades tended to do that.

The pyrotechnics at the front of the fort intensified. Now McCarter could hear the rattle of the machine gun on MRAP One. Still more rocket-propelled grenades from Manning's launcher began to descend, ripping apart whatever they touched. McCarter threw caution to the wind and simply started running at full speed, heading for the nearest entrance, firing his Tavor as he went.

The entrance he had chosen was guarded by a trio of

sentries. They tried to hunker down behind a concrete barrier that formed a balcony of sorts around the steps leading to their doorway. Two of the three started shooting blindly, holding their rifles above the barrier while keeping their bodies below it.

Bloody cowards, McCarter swore to himself as he paused long enough to drop to one knee, brace the Tavor and trigger his grenade launcher.

The 40 mm projectile blew a hole through the barrier and shredded the men on the other side. He leaped the smoking wall and rammed the door, which was not otherwise barred. On the other side, he collided with the wall.

There were men on either side of him, about to shoot him with AKs.

He dropped to the floor. The shooters fired. One of the men was actually hit by friendly fire from his counterpart. McCarter yanked the Hi-Power from his belt and shot the other man through the face.

He was in the fortress.

"Pour it on, lads," he said into his transceiver. "Keep them jumping. I've penetrated the facility and am looking for Calvin. Prepare to roll out in the MRAPs with Two covering One until we're out of range."

"Understood," Manning acknowledged from the ridge.

"Roger," Encizo said.

"Affirmative," Hawkins added.

"And a partridge in a pear tree," McCarter muttered to himself.

The building began to shake.

They had taken him at his word. The Phoenix Force commandos were raining down death and destruction using everything they had available. If McCarter was doing the math correctly, they would have enough heavy firepower to take on the joint Gera-Jamali headquarters on the Kashmir-India border…barely. But he was getting ahead of himself.

For a moment he stopped to consider what he would do if James was dead. McCarter had volunteered for the most dangerous component of the assignment, which was sneaking into the fortress and finding the missing Phoenix Force man. It was not simply leadership that dictated this. The Briton took his responsibilities very seriously, for all that he was given to sarcastic commentary the rest of the time.

McCarter stopped in a doorway. There were footfalls ahead in the corridor. He waited with the Tavor braced against his shoulder. When the first of the Jamali soldiers rounded the bend, he shot the man in the chest. He took down the second, and the third, and dropped the fourth on the growing pile of corpses before the others realized what was happening and started shouting to each other.

He didn't speak the language, but he knew what they would be saying: "We need to find another way." The corridor made a loop before connecting with the next hallway, and they would likely try to circle around to take him from behind. With his Tavor still pointing ahead, he withdrew the Hi-Power and leveled it in the opposite direction. He felt mildly silly, standing there with his bullpup assault rifle in one hand and a handgun in the other, as if he were a character in an adventure film.

Gadgets Schwarz would know just what film to suggest, too, McCarter thought. Trust a Yank to know the fine details of something like that.

The enemy was as predictable as he'd thought they would be. He emptied the Browning's magazine when they tried to come up from behind, killing two more soldiers in the process. The corridor was a ready-made fatal funnel. As long as they stood within it, he was hard-pressed to miss them. His doorway protected him from the worst of it, although ricochets were starting to scatter stone dust into his eyes, making it hard to see and to breathe.

He needed to change the paradigm, as the saying went, and find his way to the connecting corridor. He let his Tavor fall to the end of its sling and shoved his Hi-Power in his belt. Then he primed a pair of HE grenades and threw them in opposite directions. As a sop to his beleaguered hearing, he put his hands over his ears and dropped into a low crouch with his back against the wall.

The explosions sprayed men and pieces of equipment up and down the corridor. He stood, threaded his way through the wreckage and took the connecting corridor, mindful of armed men hiding in wait. There was no one.

Eventually he came to what was Jamali's mess hall. Whatever had been cooking on the stove was not at all pleasant, and if the standards by which Jamali's cooks operated were at all analogous to the West's militaries, whatever was on the stove must be thrice as bad. The idea made his stomach churn just a bit.

He smiled. Squeamishness like that would have earned him the boots of his superiors back in the SAS. They'd have kicked in his ribs and reminded him that a man was lucky, in the field, to eat at all—and luckier still to eat something that was not still alive.

Beyond the mess hall were dormitories and shower facilities. He was about to pass these by when a thought occurred to him. There was always at least one blighter hiding under the bed. As irrational as it sounded, it happened more often than one might think.

The hallways were lighted by bare bulbs hanging from electrical cables stapled into the concrete. As the fortress shook even more, as the pounding of grenades and gunfire grew more intense, the lights began to flicker. Something

Phoenix Force was doing must be straining the generators running this place.

He smelled smoke in the air. That was as likely an explanation for the flickering lights as anything else. A fire had started within the fortress. The concrete structure would not itself burn; it would take a bunker-busting thermal charge to wick the interior clean with flame. But the contents of the fortress itself would burn, and there was no better way to start such a fire than to start throwing grenades at the place.

He took a quick run through the dormitory. The beds here had been made with reasonable military precision, although the entire camp was sloppier than a regular military facility probably would be. Jamali was essentially a warlord. He valued loyalty. His men would be permitted to get away with minor things, to adhere to a lower overall standard of military discipline when it came to the niceties.

And damn if there wasn't, in fact, a single bloke hiding under a bed.

"You there," said McCarter. He kicked the man's boot with his own. "Come on out of there, lad. I don't want to shoot you while you're hiding, but I will if you make me."

The soldier crawled out from his hiding spot. His eyes were wide with terror.

"I need information," McCarter said.

The lights flickered again. The entire building was shaking and rattling under the firepower outside. The young Jamali fighter looked up at the lights and then back to McCarter. If it were possible, he grew even paler than he'd been.

"The American," McCarter prompted. "Tall black fellow. Can't miss him. You tell me where he is, I don't shoot you in the face. That sound fair, mate?"

The Jamali fighter looked at him without comprehension.

"Bloody hell," McCarter said. "You don't speak English, do you? English?"

The Jamali man shook his head. He said something in his native tongue, but McCarter couldn't follow it.

The sound of a foot scraping on the concrete caught McCarter's attention. He snapped his Hi-Power up and fired a single round that took the oncoming enemy soldier in the throat. The dead man fell at the entrance to the dormitory, his Kalashnikov still clutched in dead fingers.

McCarter swung the Hi-Power back to the pale young man. The soldier hadn't moved. He seemed truly paralyzed by fear.

McCarter realized that he was carrying his smartphone. He took it out of his pocket and accessed its secure memory. There were photographs and cover identities for each of the Phoenix Force members, for use when it was necessary to confuse an enemy. He called up James's file, enlarged the photo and showed the photo to his temporary prisoner.

"This man," McCarter said. "I want to find this man."

The Jamali soldier's eyes widened. He nodded and pointed. McCarter followed his gaze—

The knife appeared as if from nowhere. McCarter turned back to the man he had presumed to be a scared, compliant prisoner, and nearly took the blade of a combat knife through the neck. He reared back just in time and, on instinct, slapped the knife away with the barrel of his Hi-Power.

The Briton scrambled backward, putting distance between himself and the knife. The Jamali fighter, who had apparently been shamming, leaped to his feet and advanced, waving the knife back and forth in elaborate patterns in the air.

"Bloody hell, mate," McCarter said. "I'm still holding this gun."

The Jamali fighter charged.

McCarter shot him three times. He landed in a crumpled heap at the Briton's feet and did not move again.

Disgusted, McCarter left the dormitory area. He headed for the exit that the dead man had indicated, stepping over the corpse closer to the entrance. What he found when he rounded the last corner of the concrete hallway was a set of stairs leading down.

Concrete dust filtered down from above. The lights went out for a full five seconds. McCarter kept his Tavor slung and took out his combat light, holding it with the Hi-Power to search the darkness below. He descended the steps, knowing that he might well be running out of time. He did not know if the fortress was strong enough to remain structurally sound while Phoenix Force pounded it. The plan was built on the assumption that he could get to James, and get him out, fast enough that destroying the fortress would not also kill James.

He continued down the stairs.

The lowest level of the fortress was cold and dank. Mold clung to the walls, making the air hard to breathe. McCarter resisted the urge to release the bile rising to his throat. Somewhere down here, he would bet, was a garbage dump for the fortress, probably adjacent to an incinerator of some kind. That made the most sense for a remote location in this climate. Waste heat from the incinerator would be used to help keep the fortress less frigid.

He came to a metal door that was sealed from outside with a bar. This was promising. A fortress would undoubtedly keep its dungeon on the lower level. There were traditions to be obeyed, were there not? A door barred from the outside indicated someone held within.

Carefully, mindful of booby traps and watchful for more soldiers, he eased the bar off the door and opened the steel barrier. Another, smaller hallway, this one not lighted at all, awaited him.

"David," Manning's voice said in his earbud. "The building is on fire in multiple spots. I'm not sure what's burning on the exterior, but it's going pretty good. There's going to be a lot of smoke buildup in there. You need to get out as fast as you can."

"I'm doing my best here, mate," McCarter said. "Get ready. When we come out we're going to be hot as they get. Our friends will be hoping to make us dead long before we reach the exit."

"Have you found Calvin?"

"I'm on the scent," McCarter said.

More dust fell from above. Back in the outer hallway, where the lightbulbs hung, one of the bulbs fell from its fixture and shattered on the floor.

A door opened somewhere far ahead. The bloom of a muzzle-blast showed orange-yellow in the shadows. McCarter took cover behind the doorway and fired back with his Hi-Power, trying to illuminate the threat. He blinked his light, then changed his position, then repeated the process, but the enemy was too far away and too well obscured by some kind of cover. That cover was not visible in the darkness.

McCarter decided it was time to lighten the mood down on the dungeon level. He took a flash-bang grenade, pulled the pin and tossed it into the darkness.

Here it comes, he thought.

When the grenade went off, actinic afterimages floated in front of his closed eyes. His ears rang despite the fact that he had covered them with his hands. But he could still hear plenty well enough to fight. And what he heard was screaming.

The Jamali soldier who staggered out of the corridor was holding his eyes and screaming. He had taken the full brunt of the flash-bang blast, and probably while his eyes were adjusting for the darkness. McCarter felt almost bad for the poor fellow when he put a mercy round into the man's chest.

The body hit the floor.

McCarter stepped over it. The guard had been down here for a reason. He felt along the wall and his palm found a light switch. It was connected to a jerry-rigged LED panel hung over the door, of the type used to service automobiles.

"Hello?" McCarter called out. "Calvin? Is anyone there?"

There was no response. McCarter reached out and tried the door. It was locked from the other side. That was no proof of anything in particular; there was no telling how many redundant security measures had been taken on the dungeon level. But as the vibrations he was feeling through the fortress clearly showed, he needed to get James and get him out of there.

Once more he had to stop to ask himself, What if James was dead? What if he had been tortured and maimed in the process? But he could not face that reality, would not acknowledge it except on the theoretical level. Calvin James was one of the toughest soldiers he knew. The men of Phoenix Force were all experienced counterterrorists. That made them survivors.

Calvin James was a survivor. He would remain so. And he would be chagrined to have been found in this position, but in all honesty, any one of Phoenix Force might have been snagged in the chaos following the Shopian operation. If anything, responsibility fell on McCarter himself, for he had underestimated Jamali's cleverness and his tenacity.

McCarter considered the sealed door in front of him. He had sufficient explosives to blow it. But without knowing what was on the other side, he could be endangering James's life in the name of trying to save it.

Someone on the other side began rhythmically tapping on the steel barrier.

"Calvin?" McCarter called again. "Is that you?" He tapped back, banging out an SOS pattern. James would recognize that for what it was: simply an attempt to prompt recognition.

Whoever was on the other side of the door also banged out an SOS. McCarter tried the handle again, but still it would not budge. He thought, from the seams of the doorway, that the door opened inward. Perhaps he could use a small shaped charge to—

The door was suddenly released from within. McCarter fell forward.

He was staring into the barrel of a gun.

CHAPTER SEVENTEEN

Detroit

Schwarz's fingers flew over the keyboard as he sat at one of the few intact workstations of the EarthGard data boiler room. Lyons, watching the monitor where Lao Wei continued to gesticulate angrily, scratched his head and then held his chin in his hand.

"I'm going to go out on a limb here," he said, "and say that maybe we should do something about the Chinese special forces leader who wants to come in here and kill us."

"He's out there, Ironman," Schwarz said, "and we're in here."

"The problem," Lyons declared, "is that when he figures out how to get in here, we will be outnumbered and outgunned. I'd like to have a plan in place for dealing with that if at all possible."

"A plan like flooding an enclosed space with smoke while you shotgun everybody within range?"

"Yeah," Lyons said. "Like that." He looked at the monitor. Schwarz had brought up a dossier file. A Chinese man stared back at them from the monitor, but this man was not Lao Wei. He had a scar over one eye, which was milky and obviously useless.

"Carl," Schwarz said, "I'd like you to meet Dei Qiong."

"Dei Qiong," Barbara Price's voice said from the console. "We're on it. Keep going, Gadgets."

"You've got the Farm patched in?" Lyons asked. "When did that happen?"

"Keep up, Ironman," Schwarz said, making a show of cracking his knuckles. His fingers continued to fly over the keyboard, calling up supplemental files on Dei Qiong. "We are now looking at EarthGard's private, protected, firewalled-all-to-hell database," he announced. "The contents of which I am now transmitting to Stony Man Farm." A progress bar crawled along the bottom of his screen.

"It breaks down like this," Schwarz said, skimming through the files that he was also sending along to Stony Man Farm. "The Chinese operatives we're encountering are part of a false-flag operation originally set up here in the United States to protect EarthGard. That's what I can tell from the files we're into now. This Dei Qiong is a general just like Lao Wei. It seems Dei Qiong was in charge of the EarthGard mission here in the States. It was his job to front it and to coordinate it."

"Then what's Lao doing here?"

"Here's where it gets really interesting," Schwarz said. "Dei Qiong has been conducting regular transmissions of text, data and voice between here and both India and Pakistan, as well as the disputed zone between the two. A lot of these are encrypted or have been deleted by ordinary maintenance programs inside the network. But enough of them exist that I can keyword-search them." Schwarz tapped in a few search terms and opened another window.

Lyons leaned over the electronics expert's shoulder and stared at the screen. "Barb," he said quietly, "you getting all this?"

"We are," Price said, her voice echoing in Lyons's transceiver. "Everything's being logged. It looks like Hal is going to have to bring State and Homeland in on this."

"It gets juicier," Schwarz said. "From what I'm reading here, Dei Qiong cut ties with his government about six months ago. Whatever EarthGard and the Chinese were here to do in secret, Dei Qiong decided to take over the operation himself. He's cut some kind of deal with both Jamali and Gera. I have communications records here from both of them to Dei Qiong, and several in which it appears all three of them were conferenced in. There are travel records that cross check to it all."

"But what are they doing?" Lyons asked. "What is EarthGard's purpose here in the United States? It's a false flag operation, sure…but what is the op?"

"I can't tell," Schwarz said. "Whatever it is, they've gone to pains to eliminate any lingering records of it. Possibly as a safeguard against just what we're doing, should their data line or the trunk to the phony office ever be compromised."

"So Lao Wei is what?" Lyons asked. "Backup? Or a troubleshooter sent to clean up Dei Qiong's mistakes?"

"Given his background and reputation," Price said, speculating, "and knowing that this Dei Qiong cut off Communist China in a bid to take over the operation for himself, it's most likely that Lao is here to neutralize Dei Qiong. He'll either want to take him into custody or, more likely, he's probably here to kill Dei before any of this can blow back on the Chinese government."

"We've spoken to Lao," Lyons said. "Funny guy. Has some real definite opinions about his government, our government, and the places of the two relative to each other in the world. It's the sort of thing I'd love to discuss with him over coffee. You know, so I can drink coffee while I'm punching a hole through his face."

"Use Lao as an asset if you can," Price instructed. "Leverage his desire to make Dei Qiong go away while saving face for the Chinese. At the very least this clears up the confusion about the current and former Chinese special operators. The Chinese government must have disavowed those personnel who turned with Dei, siding with their field commander in whatever the EarthGard operation is supposed to be.

"Lao then shows up on U.S. soil with a fresh contingent of current special forces personnel, all of whom are tasked with taking out Dei and making all of this go away. Or perhaps their directive is to regain control of the operation. Either way, Dei is slated to be out of the picture if Lao and his government have anything to say about it. That seems most likely."

The sound of metal whining on metal brought Lyons's attention back to the sealed door. Lao and his contingent were using some kind of power saw to cut through the barrier. It would take them a while, but it would not take them nearly long enough to suit the Able Team leader.

"We need to get the hell out of here," he said. "Gadgets, have you finished transmitting everything?"

"The Farm now has the complete contents of the EarthGard database for analysis," Schwarz confirmed. He reached into his pocket and produced a USB memory stick. "And I'm going to leave a little something extra in their network for Lao's people to find."

"What have you got there?" Lyons asked.

"It's a computer virus of my own design," the electronics expert said. "It will sit idly and count down to itself like a logic bomb. Then, when network traffic picks up, it will start eating itself…and everything else connected to it."

"You just carry that around?" Lyons asked. "Like, just all the time, you've got a devastating computer virus ready to go?"

"Don't you?" Schwarz asked. "I also have duct tape."

"I worry about you, Gadgets. I worry about you."

"Let's see what's behind door number three," Schwarz said. He accessed the locks and released the third sealed panel. "If I'm reading this right," he said, "this corridor is free of booby traps."

"If?" Lyons said.

"Come on, Ironman," Schwarz said. The whine at the other door was louder now. Sparks began to filter into the chamber. "Lao's almost busted through."

"Can we lock that door behind us?"

"Not only that," Schwarz said, "but I can set that timer and then dump my virus."

"That," Lyons said. "Do that."

Lyons led the way with his Python and his combat light. The pair moved swiftly through the low-ceilinged corridor. There were no traps. As Schwarz had indicated; this was apparently meant only as an egress point. It rose rapidly but, judging from the distance they were covering by foot, the tunnel was going to put them well beyond the perimeter of the building. That made sense. An escape route would naturally put the escapees beyond the target building, such as in the case of a law enforcement or military raid. The only question in Lyons's mind was what they would find when they got to the other end.

The tunnel stopped.

Lyons played his flashlight beam around the ceiling and across the concrete cap.

"If this is a dead end," he said, "it's a literal one." He holstered his revolver and put his palm against the concrete, pressing experimentally. As he worked his way across the face of the barrier, Schwarz turned and looked back the way they'd come.

"Did you hear that?" he asked.

"No, and neither did you," Lyons said. "If they cut through from inside, we'll be fish in a barrel down here."

Lyons felt something give beneath his palm. He scraped away the plaster dust that had been painted to match the concrete. He reared back his fist.

"Are you going to punch your way out?" Schwarz asked.

Lyons punched the wall. His fist sank deeply into the plaster cover. When he removed it, he was holding a cord.

"Det cord," Lyons explained. He fished around in his pockets, looking for a lighter. Schwarz supplied one. He handed it to Lyons and then stared at the ceiling, pretending to whistle, as Lyons stared at the lighter in disbelief.

"Is this from that movie?" Lyons asked. "The one with the guys on the rocket-shooting motorbikes?"

"I had it made custom."

"You don't even smoke," Lyons pointed out.

"I like the movie that much."

"Fire in the hole," Lyons warned. He snapped the lighter open, flicked the wheel and watched as the flame caught. The distinctive smell of naphtha fuel reached his nose. He touched the flame to the detonation cord. "Go!" he said.

The two men hurried back the way they'd come until Lyons judged the distance was sufficient. As it was, the corridor would amplify the sound of the explosion. He wasn't looking forward to that. It was going to hurt.

It did.

The blast created a cloud of concrete dust. Lyons took a bandanna from his pocket and breathed through it, leading the way to the end of the tunnel. When he got there he could see light beyond it. These were the lights of a set of battery-powered emergency lamps built into the wall on the opposite side of the shattered barrier. A metal ladder led straight up.

There was a clatter at the opposite end of the tunnel.

"That's Lao," Lyons said. "Hurry, get up there. Go." He grabbed Schwarz and boosted the smaller man up the ladder. Then he took a grenade from his jacket, popped the pin and set the bomb very carefully against the base of the ladder, between the wall and the ladder strut. He made sure to step over it and grab high to pull himself along the ladder, in this way avoiding his own trap. Anyone who stepped on that first rung was going to get an explosive surprise. The toe of their shoe would dislodge the grenade, allowing the spoon to fly off.

A heavy, reinforced hatch waited at the top of the ladder. Schwarz put his shoulder to it and managed to force it open. The two Able Team commandos emerged in the back room of what had to be a neighboring block of shops. The heavy hatch slammed shut behind them.

"Maybe there's some ice cream left," Schwarz said when he discovered they were standing in an abandoned ice cream parlor. The franchise was part of a national chain, but while there were still logos on the wall, most of the equipment in the place had been stripped. An empty cooler sat in the middle of the scuffed linoleum floor, its compressor removed, its glass front grimy with layers of dust.

The floor shook beneath the two men. Flames and smoke shot up through the seams in the closed hatchway.

"Here they come," said Lyons. "Let's hit the street."

"Are you two all right?" Blancanales asked through their transceivers.

"We're a block to what I think is your west, Pol," Lyons answered. "Bring the truck, but watch yourself. Lao and his goons are about to bubble up from belowdecks right in our area of operation. We're looking for somewhere we can take cover and drive him back."

"You boys want me to break a few hundred regulations and get down there?" Grimaldi asked. His voice, through the transceiver, sounded eager. It nearly made Lyons smile.

"Negative, Jack," he said. "And this time I mean it.

Stand by. We'll put you in the thick of it if we have no other choice. But let's try not to give Hal a heart attack if we don't absolutely need to do so."

"How do you want to do this, Ironman?" Blancanales asked.

"We'll take this show on the road," Lyons said. "Gadgets and I will break left out the doorway here. Pol, swing around when you get to the end of the block, and make a right. You should come up right where we'll be."

"On my way," Blancanales said. The roar of the Suburban's big power plant was audible through the transceiver link.

The glass-paneled door had been shattered at some point and then sealed with a piece of plywood. Lyons unlimbered his USAS-12 and hit the plywood with the butt of the big weapon. It took several strikes, but he eventually succeeded in smashing it to pieces.

The area was deserted. There was no traffic on the street. The entire block was sealed up, blocked off and boarded up, reflecting the decay that was eating the heart of Detroit like a cancer. The only good thing about that was that there would be no innocent bystanders to get caught in the cross fire that was sure to come. Lao's people were going to make their way out of the shuttered ice cream store, and when they did, the shooting would start.

The Suburban burned rubber around the corner up ahead. Blancanales had his boot on the floorboard, pushing the big machine to its limits. As the GMC skidded to a stop near their position, the first shot echoed across the street. A rusted street sign next to the Suburban took the hit.

"Here they come!" Lyons shouted. "Go! Go!"

Schwarz piled into the Suburban. Back at the abandoned ice cream shop, Lao Wei's men were taking up positions on the sidewalk, shooting in Able Team's direction. Blancanales floored the truck as Lyons grabbed the running board and the side mirror. With his USAS-12 supported on his shoulder by its sling, he braced the stock under his arm and pointed the weapon ahead along the sidewalk.

Blancanales accelerated. Bullets flew past the truck, wreaking havoc as they struck the surrounding building façades. Lyons, undeterred, leaned into the Daewoo as he hung on to the truck with an iron grip.

He pulled the trigger and held it back.

The devastating twelve-gauge disgorged the full load of its magazine of rifled hollowpoint slugs. Knotted up as they were on the sidewalk, exiting the ice cream shop, Lao's men were sitting ducks. The slugs tore through them, shredding their bodies, blowing horrifying exit wounds. The front of the once brightly colored shop was now brightly colored again, this time in the astonishing crimson of freshly spilled blood.

Lyons heard the Chinese mercenaries screaming as the Suburban burned past them and then around the next corner. He motioned for Schwarz to roll down the window. Then he stuck his head through the opening to shout to Blancanales.

"Find us a good spot maybe half a block down the next street," he instructed. "Someplace we can dig in and wait. I'm not going to have Lao chasing us all over creation if we can help it. Things are going to change, here and now."

Blancanales nodded. Amazingly, the Suburban seemed to have sustained no major damage in the drive-by. Lyons marveled at this while Blancanales selected a spot, then slowed the big truck and pulled it back into a driveway. The driveway slanted down. It was the entrance to what had once been a parking garage. Well, Lyons thought, it still was a parking garage, but the place had a chain strung across the opening, with multiple signs proclaiming it Closed and Available. Yet another property left to turn fallow in a city falling down under the weight of its own crime and economic blight. It was sad to see.

Once they had backed down the ramp far enough to push the rear end of the Suburban up under the barrier chain, Blancanales put the GMC in park and switched off the engine. The men of Able Team piled out and took up positions behind the concrete retaining walls that both delineated the entrance to the parking garage and prevented pedestrians from falling into the drop-off. It was as tailor made a spot to take cover from Lao's soldiers as Lyons could have asked for.

When the Chinese special forces finally did appear again, Lyons had to give them credit for brains. They didn't just storm up the street in a throng, the way some untrained or poorly organized terrorists and gangs might have done. They covered each other in twos up the street, prepared to run and gun for the length of the block, he supposed. So far, they hadn't spotted Able's position, but that would change once the first shot was fired.

"Wait for it," Lyons urged his partners. "Let's get them in on top of us and then cut them down." He changed out the drum in his shotgun. Blancanales ran the plunger of his M-4 carbine, chambering the first round. Schwarz had apparently already checked his Beretta machine pistol.

They were ready.

The Chinese point men were almost close enough to reach out and touch when Lyons finally said, "Now!"

Able Team opened fire. From their carefully chosen cover, they eviscerated the first two soldiers, pausing only briefly to take out the second pair. The street became an open-air gun battle, closer to something Lyons would expect to see in Afghanistan or Libya than in any neighborhood in an American city. Part of Carl Lyons regretted that it was necessary to wage this battle here, to bring this type of carnage to the streets of Detroit…but even as he thought it, he knew how fundamentally ridiculous that idea was. This was Detroit. People died of gunfire here on a regular basis, like bloody clockwork. Only the scope, the scale, the stakes were different. This was violence for a purpose, violence that meant something. It was not simply civilian thugs wiping each other out in the name of petty grudges or gang disputes.

Two, then four of the Chinese special operators broke away from the main group and tried to cross the street. Blancanales took careful aim with his M-4 and began popping away. His 5.56 mm NATO rounds took the first man in the head, the second man in the neck and the third and fourth in the knees. The second two men were deliberate disabling shots. It was a ruthless tactic, but one that was necessary when facing overwhelming hostile odds. Wounding two of the Chinese soldiers was an attempt to preoccupy more of the enemy's numbers with saving the injured men.

Every wounded man took an armed enemy out of the fight while also occupying one or more of his fellow soldiers to care for him. This was small-unit tactics 101, unpleasant a reality as it might be.

The Chinese soldiers finished pulling their men to safety. Silence descended on the street. Somewhere far away, a police siren sounded, but as quickly as it began, it stopped. Lyons wondered if they were likely to see any local involvement from the authorities. He was a little surprised that they had seen nothing so far but, in a neighborhood this deserted, it was also possible the cops had declared it a no-go zone. Large-scale gunfire would be attributed to gang warfare and, honestly, why wouldn't the police let the gangs fight it out among themselves? There were no civilians to get mixed up in the battle here.

A single shot rang out. It came nowhere near them. Blancanales moved into position to fire back, but Lyons put up a fist. "Hold up," he said. "Cease fire. Something weird is going on."

Able Team waited. Another single shot met their ears. Lyons realized then that whoever was shooting was firing deliberately into the air. When one of the Chinese shouted from behind cover, there was no mistaking the fact that it was Lao Wei's voice.

"American," Lao shouted. "You have restraint. And you have mercy."

"I'm good at darts, too," Lyons shouted back. "Make your point, Lao."

"We need to talk."

"Then you put your guns down and surrender," Lyons said. "Problem solved."

"I am speaking earnestly," Lao stated. "I am about to approach you once again. You may shoot me, in which case my men will assault your position until you are overwhelmed and killed, or you may listen to what I have to say."

Lyons waited. When nothing happened he said, "Well? Come on if you're coming."

They waited a few moments more. Lao finally emerged from cover. Two men flanked him. At his signal, they slung their Kalashnikov-pattern assault rifles over their shoulders. Lao himself was unarmed and wore no weapon on his belt.

The three Chinese soldiers walked up the street. Their footfalls were the only sound.

"This is like something out of a Western movie,"

Schwarz commented. "Quick, somebody start whistling lonely theme music."

"Put a sock in it, Gadgets," Lyons directed, although his heart was barely in the banter. "Lao's got me curious. We know he's Mr. Communist Party Poster Boy. We know he's not looking to switch sides. So what does he want?"

"I guess we'll find out," Blancanales said.

Lyons cracked his knuckles. "Yeah," he said. "We will."

"Maybe I should talk to him, Carl," Blancanales suggested.

"Things are about to get better," Schwarz said, "or a whole lot worse."

CHAPTER EIGHTEEN

Guirat, Pakistan

Calvin James opened his eyes. He knew that he was in trouble; he knew that he had been captured by men belonging to the Pakistani general, Jamali. They'd scooped him up as he'd fled through the streets of Shopian and was cut off by the sheer crush of enemy soldiers. All things considered, James counted himself lucky that he wasn't simply killed on the spot. They had roughed him up a little getting him into one of their armored personnel carriers and then again transporting him here, but he didn't feel any injuries that were especially bad. Nothing he hadn't felt after an intense workout at the gym or following an extended battle in the field.

He supposed if he had a greater range of motion in his arms and legs, he might discover that something was broken or dislocated, but he didn't think so. There were no pains where there should not be when he pushed against his restraints. Oh, he hurt, yes. He felt it in his ribs, where they had kicked and punched him. He felt it in his jaw and his head, too. He was working on quite a headache, and somebody had elbowed him in the face more than once.

Man, he was never going to live this down.

The next time he saw Gadgets Schwarz, he could almost guarantee the dude was going to pick on him. Getting caught and then escaping after a harrowing brush with torture and interrogation. It was the kind of thing they put in movies, yeah.

He was putting the cart before the horse, as the old saying went, to be thinking already about what they'd do to him and how he'd get out of it, but what else did he have to do?

Every member of Stony Man Farm's counterterrorism units had specialized training, including Survival, Escape, Resistance and Evasion training. Most people not familiar with it thought of SERE as the kind of soldier games people played in the woods, where they lived off the land and tried not to get caught by enemy forces. That was certainly part of it, to oversimplify the mission. But a great deal of SERE was really mental training. Mental fortitude, mental toughness, was not necessarily something that could be taught in those lacking it. But men and women who already possessed mental toughness could be taught to access that fortitude when they most needed it, and to channel their thoughts more productively in times of crisis.

The worst thing a soldier could do, when captured by the enemy, was to lose his mental composure, to give in to fear. If he did that, he began the process of breaking himself down for his captors even before they came for him. This was, of course, the idea behind most of the procedures used for prisoner interrogation.

There were many ways his captors could try to break him down, try to make him more agreeable to telling them what they wanted to know. They could have stripped him naked before they'd tied him up. There was a visceral psychological reaction to being naked that had conquered many men who should have known better. You felt weak and vulnerable when you were naked. Almost no man liked to think of himself as on display that way. Depriving a man of his clothes, or a soldier of his uniform, was also a way of physically removing his identity. That breaking down of identity was the first step in the psychological warfare of an interrogation.

In James's case, the Jamali men had missed plenty of opportunities to dehumanize and degrade him. They had let him keep his clothes and most of his equipment, searching him only for weapons. Those weapons were replaceable. There were extra knives, rifles and pistols aboard the MRAPs. They had beat on him, sure, but not very much, and certainly not enough to do any lasting damage. James knew enough not to be cocky about that, though, because it probably meant they wanted him healthy for whatever interrogation they had dreamed up for him. You couldn't have your prisoner dying on you from the accumulated stress of your questioning and his previous mistreatment, after all.

Just what Jamali—or whatever commander or lieutenant was on hand for James's questioning—thought he could learn from questioning James wasn't clear to the Stony Man commando. He knew plenty that they would love to know, sure, but they had no way of understanding or even estimating the scope of covert knowledge he possessed. For all they knew he was just a contractor sent to do a job here in Pakistan, and he intended to play that role to the hilt.

He as lying on a board with his hands and feet wired in place. The wires were not barbed, but they would cut into his flesh if he struggled against them. Whoever had strapped him down hadn't been terribly thorough, though. The wire tie on his left hand was loose, and if he stretched his wrist just enough, he could reach the ends of the two strands with his fingers. He had been quietly unwinding those two wire ends since he woke up.

The board might have been an old door of some kind. He was propped up like Frankenstein in sort of a half-leaning, half-standing position, which he supposed would make it easier for his interrogators to speak with him when they got there. The room was otherwise empty except for a hard wooden chair and a cardboard box. The box was old and stained and had what he thought was an Arabic paper company's name on it. The idea of an Arabic paper company struck him as funny. Was there such a thing? Did they have enough trees in the Middle East for that to be a thing?

Your mind wandered to strange places when all you could do was hang around and wait to be tortured, he thought.

He had no idea what the layout might be outside his prison door. They could be half a mile up a mountain or in the deepest depths of a desert dungeon, for all he knew. He had scanned the walls for cameras, wondering if he was being observed from outside, but the stone walls were bare and blank. There were no two-way mirrors, no microphones that he could see—not that they couldn't be hidden—and really nothing on which to fixate or with which to concern himself.

Perhaps that was the idea; perhaps the mostly empty room was intended to engage a prisoner's imagination. It was a fact that if you let other people supply the details of some horrible or fearsome element, they always came up with something far more powerful than could be imagined for them. That was because when prompted to supply their own horrors, people were always their own best interrogators. It was a trick writers used when scripting horror, too: Whenever possible, you let the audience fill in the fear, so they wouldn't be disappointed when you tried to show them something.

Like all those television horror movies that had great build-ups but then collapsed after the "reveal" showed the big bad bugaboo everyone was so frightened of was a bad puppet or CGI monster.

The door scraped open. James did not try to pretend to be asleep. Frankly he was curious to see what would happen next. He made sure not to move his left hand, though. He did not want to call attention to the wires he had almost managed to undue.

"Hello," said the small Pakistani man who walked up to James. In the dim light of the single overhead lightbulb, he was hard to make out, but his features were unremarkable. His hair was unkempt and greasy, and his fingernails were long and very dirty. When he spoke he revealed half-rotten teeth. His spectacles were wire-rimmed and the glass lenses were heavily smudged. He did not seem to notice.

"Ahoy," James said.

"My name is Yousef ibn Asri," the man said. "I work for General Jamali."

"Kind of figured as much," James said.

"What is your name?"

"My name is Calvin, baby," James answered. "That's Calvin with one L. Make sure you spell it correctly."

Asri looked as if he hadn't heard. He went to the cardboard box and placed it on the chair so that it was close at hand. Then he turned back to James. "I am going to ask you questions," he said. His voice was flat, almost emotionless, but there was something behind it that made James's skin crawl. Asri was either a raging psychopath or simply mentally ill, but in either case, there was something seriously wrong with the man. James was suddenly much less curious about what was going to happen next.

"General Jamali wishes to know who you work for," Asri said. "I should make it clear to you before we start that there is a guard outside the door. He is waiting in a corridor that is locked from inside. There are more guards beyond. Even if you managed to escape and to get out of this room, you would be killed or, worse, returned to this room."

"Worse?"

"The things I do," said Asri, "are very unkind. I am good at them. There is something wrong with me, you see."

Uh-oh, thought James. I don't like where this is going.

"I'm happy to cooperate," said James.

"That is good," Asri said. "Did you know that there are born every year a certain percentage of people who cannot feel pain? They can feel the difference between heat and cold. Put one of them in an ice bath and he can tell you that the water is cold. Put him in boiling water and he can tell you that the water is hot. But in neither case does he feel the pain associated with the damage. The hot water could be scalding and blistering his skin, and he would not know this unless he watched for it. He cannot feel pain and thus does not know damage is occurring."

"You speak very good English," James said. "You a classically educated sociopath? You go to Psychotic State or something like that?"

"Oh," Asri said. "You are joking with me." His tone was completely flat. There was no way to know if he thought James's jokes were completely unexpected or as boring as dry toast. "I started to tell you. There is something wrong with me."

"You have nightmares that you come to work and you get somebody who can't feel pain?" James asked.

"No," Asri said. "I am the one who cannot feel pain."

"You'll pardon me if I drink in that irony for a while, man," James said.

"It is very dangerous when one such as I is growing up," Asri said. "A child with the condition cannot tell if, for example, his appendix is about to burst. I suffered many injuries as a child that I did not know were occurring. I lost most of my toes to frostbite. But I retained all my fingers because I can see them. There was no way to watch my toes, in my boots."

"I love that story," James said. "That is a hell of a story. Could you tell it to me again?"

"Because I can't feel pain," Asri continued, "it has always fascinated me. Even when I was conscripted, I asked if there was any way I could be used in the capacity I am now used. I just want to see it. To touch it. To understand it."

"See and touch what?"

"Pain, Calvin," Asri explained. "I have none myself. I enjoy so much inflicting it on others. It's the only way that I can learn what I am unable to sense."

"Let me tell you about this hangnail I had once," James said. "Real nasty sucker, too. It was so bad that—

From the cardboard box, Asri produced a stun gun. It was of the handheld transformer variety, basically just a nine-volt battery pumping out fifty thousand volts or more at very low amperage. Painful, but not even really debilitating to someone who knew what to expect. The stun guns were sold as self-defense items in the States, at least in those few areas where they were still legal. James had always thought they were silly. You could get a lot more done with a knife than you could one of those battery-powered gizmos. Most people just got annoyed when you shocked them.

Asri jammed the stun gun into James's gut and pressed the switch. James gritted his teeth but took the pain, letting it wash over him. Undeterred, Asri watched his face and then placed the stun gun against James's groin.

"Now that's just wrong, man," James said. Anything

he might have said after that was lost in an explosion of pain when the little Pakistani pressed the switch again.

Eventually, James started to lose consciousness as his interrogator worked him over. Finally, Asri apparently admitted to himself that he was not producing results, because he tossed the stun gun back into the box and then started rummaging around for something else.

James had been lucky so far. He knew that his tormentor could have used plenty of weapons that did serious damage. He had to conclude that this was still the "softening up" phase; that Asri didn't really expect to get results now. But the little man tried.

"Who do you work for?" said Asri. "Is it the United Nations? You are American. Are you part of an American invasion force? Was it you and your men who attacked General Jamali's troops in the disputed region? Was it you who killed Arthur Hughbright?"

"You're doing this all wrong," James said, still feeling the ache deep in his groin. "You're feeding me too much of what you want me to hear. You'll never know if what I tell you or what I agree to is really what's true, or if I just agreed with you to make the pain stop."

"Only the weakest men give in so soon," Asri said. "You do not seem weak to me. But I think you are making many jokes on me. I don't think I like that. I will probably try to hurt you more for it. I wish I knew what it felt like."

"Wow," James said. "You are just a dirty fish tank full of bad news, aren't you?"

"I do not know what that means."

"Where is Jamali now?" James asked. "Will he be sitting in on this little torture session?"

"General Jamali is at his headquarters on the border," Asri answered. "The one he shares with General Gera. I am asked to work there from time to time. There has been much work since Gera and Jamali started cooperating. I have enjoyed being so useful."

"Yeah," James said. "You're a useful engine, Toby."

"What?"

"Nothing," James said with a sigh. "Look, Igor, this has been fun and all, but I think I'm going to have to check out of here. You said there's one guard in the hall I need to kill, right?"

"He has a gun," Asri said.

"I'd imagine," James commented, "he would be pretty useless without one."

"I have a drill," Asri said. He took a power drill from the box and snapped a modular battery pack into place. The power drill whirred to life. "I will start by drilling a series of holes in your legs. I will miss the major arteries. I'm very good at not hitting them. I only make errors every once in a while. And I have a roll of tape I can use to seal any holes I make."

"I've got to be on one of those hidden-camera shows," James said. "Is Ashton Crasher or whatever his name is hiding behind one of these walls with a video crew?"

"I am starting to think you suffered a brain injury when they brought you in," Asri said. He gave his power drill an experimental press, smiling as if he enjoyed the sound it made "You could spare yourself the immediate pain and the long-term discomfort these holes will create. All you have to do is tell me what I wish to know. General Jamali will reward you with kindness if you cooperate. We want to know about your unit. We want to know who sent you. We want to know your mission."

"Okay, okay." James relented. "You got me. Don't drill any holes in me. My unit comprises a group of time-traveling, shape-changing robots from the future. For as long as I can remember, we've been searching the galaxy for the

EverSphere Cube, which is the only known power source that can jump-start our Hadron Collider in orbit around the moon. Once we do that, we can finally return home. And I promised myself I would stop at the duty free shop at the border of the solar system to get some maple candies."

"It is the drill, then," Asri said.

"Hey, little buddy?" James called.

"Yes?" Asri said.

James whispered something. Asri came closer, looking more curious than ever. James worked on making his expression as sad as possible. He whispered again. Asri walked over to stand directly in front of him. The little Pakistani put his ear up to James's face.

"I can't believe you fell for that," James whispered, and grabbed hold of Asri's throat with his teeth.

Another lesson of SERE was that sometimes you had to do things that were physically repugnant to save yourself and, possibly, to save the other members of your team. James did not have his transceiver—it was one of the few pieces of equipment they had noticed and thought to take when they'd captured him—so he had no way of knowing what Phoenix Force's status might be. As long as the sat phone he had also had taken was here in the fortress somewhere, which he believed it must be, his teammates would track him down. When they did, he was obligated to make their lives as easy as possible by effecting as much of his own escape as he could.

Calvin James bit deeply into Asri's throat. His mouth filled with warm blood. He jerked his face away from Asri's and felt the little man's throat tear away with the motion. The Pakistani tried to scream, but could produce only a wet, strangled noise as he collapsed onto the floor. A pool of blood began to spread around him. He thrashed and writhed, but was growing weaker with every second.

James watched, spitting blood that was not his own, as Asri's lips turned blue and his skin went pale. Eventually the torturer stopped moving.

James finished extracting his left hand from the loosened wires, then untied his right. Once he had both hands under control, it was easy to free his legs. He stepped over Asri's corpse and looked inside the cardboard box to see if there was anything inside he could use.

Amid the various torture implements, which included everything from a dental pick to a hack saw, he found a rusted hunting knife that looked to be local manufacture. The edge was razor-sharp and the point was a needle. He did not want to think about the uses to which that knife had probably been put, but it was what he needed right now.

It was time to find out just how loose Asri's lips were. The crazy little man had practically given James a blueprint to escape this chamber…probably because nobody left Asri's company alive. Or maybe because few people could still walk, talk and see when Asri was done cutting them apart.

He walked up to the door and rapped on it. There was a shout from beyond it. He shouted back, in a vague approximation of Asri's voice, a series of syllables that had no meaning. This guaranteed that the guard, frustrated he could not understand, would open the door.

The door opened.

When the guard took in the sight of Asri lying on the floor in a puddle of his own blood, he opened his mouth to call out an alarm. James was suddenly there, stabbing him through the eyeball and into the brain. The soldier fell forward and onto the haft of the knife with a sickening crunch. It was as if someone had found his off switch.

Well someone did, James thought. You can find anybody's off switch if you stab them in the brain.

The guard had a Skorpion machine pistol. James took it, checked it and made his way out into the corridor beyond the torture room. It was quite dark here. As he stood in front of the next closed door, pondering his next move, he realized that this door was barred from his side.

Someone on the other side tried the handle.

He thought he heard muffled shouting, but there was no way to tell through the thick steel barriers. He tried tapping on the door with the butt of the Skorpion.

Whoever was on the other side tapped back an SOS pattern.

James felt himself smiling. He thought there were only a handful of people he was likely to meet here in Pakistan who would answer a knock that way.

He removed the bar on the door. On the possibility that the other party was one of Jamali's men, he yanked the door open and brought up the Skorpion quickly, ready to fire.

"Oh, hi, David," he said.

"Bloody hell," McCarter said. "Sorry, am I interrupting?"

"No," James said. He looked up as he felt the building vibrate. "Is that what I think it is?"

"Yes," McCarter said. "Let's go. The boys have orders to cover us as we exfiltrate."

"I made a new friend," James said. "He told me that Gera and Jamali are likely at a headquarters on the border that they share. I thought that might be a nice place for us to wrap this all up in a nice, neat bow."

"Boy," McCarter said, "wouldn't that make Hal happy. Shall we?"

"Let's," James urged.

As they hurried through the fortress James asked, "David?"

"What?"

"The guys are never going to let me live down getting captured like that, are they?"

"Would you?"

"No," James admitted.

"Well, there you have it, lad," McCarter said.

Calvin James laughed all the way back to the MRAPs.

CHAPTER NINETEEN

Detroit

Lao Wei gestured to the boarded entrance of a chain coffee store. The shop, as all the others in the strip with it, stood abandoned and ostensibly for sale. Real estate was so cheap in neighborhoods such as this that homeowners could not give their properties away. Many who had fled Detroit had given up hope of selling and simply left their homes for the banks to repossess. The commercial properties had fared no better.

Lao snapped open a heavy automatic knife. Lyons did not recognize the model, but it told him the Chinese general was not so unarmed, after all. Lao pried open several inches of the plywood over the coffee shop's door. He stood back to allow his men to remove the barrier completely with their hands. Then, with a flourish, he gestured for Able Team to join him inside. He did not wait to see if they would follow. His men walked in after him.

"Seriously?" Schwarz asked. "We're doing this?"

"We're doing this," said Lyons. "Watch my back. And your own."

Blancanales waited at the doorway to keep an eye on the street and on what was left of the Chinese special forces unit. Schwarz entered behind Lyons. The interior of the coffee shop was a dust-covered disaster that had seen at least a small fire. The floor was charred and the tables and chairs were scattered around, broken, and overturned. Lao's men found a table and two chairs that were still serviceable. They placed these in the center of the room, arranged them, and then stepped back. The general pointed to the chair opposite the one on his side.

"Please," he said to Lyons. "Mister...?"

"Logan," Lyons said. "Carl Logan." He wasn't sure if that was the alias on his Justice Department identification or not. It didn't matter if it was. Lao would not make any assumptions, and Lyons was not about to give the man anything he could use against Able Team or the SOG.

"I remain General Lao Wei, of the People's Republic of China," said Lao.

"You've got a lot to answer for, Lao," Lyons reminded him.

"Perhaps so," said Lao. "But just now, you and I have a mutual problem." He looked back at his men, then to Blancanales in the doorway. "I brought two men with me because you also number three. This is acceptable?"

"Whatever," said Lyons. "Tell me, Lao, why are you making with the constructive conversation *now?* Not so long ago you were ready to make us all your prisoners on American soil. You've been trying pretty damned hard to murder three federal agents of the United States Justice Department. So why the change of heart?"

Schwarz stood behind Lyons with his arms crossed. Lyons was certain that the smaller man had his right hand on the butt of the Beretta 93-R in its shoulder holster. At a word from Lyons, Schwarz could clean the room of all three of their enemies, ending the threat Lao represented once and for all. But of course, Lao wasn't the primary problem...and it seemed the Chinese general knew it.

"Do you believe I am stupid?" Lao asked.

"Not especially," said Lyons.

"Then why would I insist on a stupid course of action?" said Lao. "I tried to take you prisoner. You refused. I tried to use force. You resisted me so effectively that you did serious damage to my operational capacity here in the United States. Those helicopters represented the sum total of my air power here. Without them I am at a significant disadvantage."

"I'm all kinds of broken up about that, Lao."

"In facing your men again here, while trying to pursue our own knowledge of Dei Qiong's operation, I have again been stalemated by your abilities. I refuse to lose more men to this. And when you did not fire as my soldiers retrieved our wounded, when you did not react with blind aggression when I fired a shot into the air, I knew then that you were men who could be reasonable."

"Reasonable about what?"

"You are aware of Dei Qiong?"

"We are," said Lyons. "Your man here, heading up the EarthGard operation." He was being deliberately vague. It usually paid to make the enemy believe you had more information than you did.

"Allow me to start from beginning," Lao said, "so that you will understand my intentions to be genuine. Understand, too, that I am not pleased to reveal to you business that is China's and China's alone. But if I am to accomplish my mission, if I am to neutralize Dei Qiong. I must have your cooperation. I see now that continuing to oppose you will only force me to sacrifice yet more of my men and resources. This endangers my mission as a whole."

"You need to call your masters back in Commieland, make sure it's okay to chat with me?" Lyons asked.

"That will be unnecessary," Lao said. "I am authorized to make those field decisions that are required for the success of my operation. This is one such 'judgment call.'"

"All right," Lyons agreed. "I'm listening."

"My men and I were dispatched by my government to kill or capture Dei Qiong, formerly a general in the Army of the People's Republic. We are further tasked by our government with the neutralization of any and all men working with Dei Qiong. This includes individuals formerly with Chinese special operations teams who have defected to work for Dei Qiong. It also includes mercenaries from Cudgel Security, a firm contracted by Dei Qiong to swell the ranks of his forces."

"Well," Lyons said, "that clarifies a few things. Suppose you tell me, what was Dei Qiong's mission?"

"First let me explain that my government is making a concerted effort to root out what it considers...obsolete components. Men whose decision making is colored by a certain willingness to engage in extralegal and hostile activities to secure what they believe are China's best interests. My nation is an emerging superpower. We do not need the entanglements created by this type of effort."

"In other words," said Lyons, "you're struggling to have the rest of the world take you seriously as an industrialized superpower, and having your government sponsor what are essentially criminal syndicates and terrorist groups works against your country's image in the public relations department."

Lao frowned and swallowed. Finally he nodded. "That is the essence of it, yes."

"So Dei Qiong was originally sent in by your government," Lyons proposed, "but his mission has been canceled and he and his people have been disavowed. You're here to make sure he gets the message and stops embarrassing your country."

"Precisely," Lao confirmed. "What I am about to tell you next is the raving of a lunatic. If any attempt is made to tie these words to my government, that is how my words will be recorded. I will be ordered to make certain it is believable, too, in that I will be told to take my own life for the good of the People's Republic."

"I'm listening."

"Our government at one time engaged in the practice of sending scouts to find and exploit natural resources around the world. Resources to which we held no legitimate claim. Those scouts discovered rich deposits of beryllium and other precious metals in the Kashmir region. They were previously undiscovered because conventional mining operations would have been prohibitively expensive. New methods were needed to identify and then to retrieve these deposits. China hired, and continued to bribe generously, an employee of an American mining and prospecting company, EarthGard. It was this man who helped us identify the resources. It was his company that was working with the Chinese government to develop a plan for the mining in Kashmir."

"Arthur Hughbright," said Lyons.

"The same," said Lao. "He continued to work in and around Kashmir, believing he was still working for the Chinese government through EarthGard, until he was killed in a local skirmish there."

"He *thought* he was working for you?" Lyons asked. "If not you, who?"

"Dei Qiong," said Lao. "Dei and his unit were originally dispatched to secure EarthGard for us. EarthGard was to be the means through which China, not the Indians or the Pakistanis, secured the resources our scouts and EarthGard identified."

"How?" Lyons asked.

"My government, through Dei Qiong, bribed the management of EarthGard. Through Dei Qiong and using

China's resources, the elaborate false front in Elmore, Ohio, was built and connected to this one. EarthGard's business had to continue as before, you see, for their company to do us any good at all. Most of their employees have no idea of the change in management, first to China, and then, when he betrayed us, directly to Dei Qiong and his unit. With EarthGard operating as before, but funneling its profits and its ores and metals to China, it was thought that the deception could be carried out at the national level without harm to China's national esteem. But Dei Qiong showed us this was not possible."

"Because he turned rogue," Lyons said. "Decided there was a lot of money to be made and that it should go to him alone."

"To him, and the men whose loyalty he bought with his greed," Lao clarified, frowning. "With the false headquarters set up and with EarthGard operating in secret in Kashmir, Dei Qiong murdered the company's management. He also killed those men in his unit who would not swear loyalty to him. To bolster his forces, he hired the Cudgel mercenaries. This, too, he did with seed funds skimmed from Chinese operational accounts."

"Where does the military flare-up in Kashmir fit in?" Lyons asked.

"Dei Qiong was instrumental in recruiting Jamali and Gera at China's behest," said Lao. "Again, he used their greed to sway them. By acting out a conflict in Kashmir, by driving India and Pakistan to war, even nuclear war, he would guarantee sufficient turbulence in the region that it would remain under the nominal control of our hand-picked turncoat generals. Jamali and Gera would ensure that EarthGard and its equipment went unmolested. Profits from the mining operation would then be split among all concerned, with the dragon's share going to the Chinese government."

"That's the share Dei wanted for himself."

"Yes," said Lao. "Originally, the fiefdom controlled by Gera, Jamali and China would have enriched all concerned. But Dei Qiong sought to cut his government out of the equation, knowing we would not be able to reach him in Kashmir and believing he could stay hidden in the United States. With control of a now false corporation, EarthGard, he would continue as before. Many of Earth-Gard's specialized employees remain on staff, oblivious to what is taking place. They accept their instructions, do not ask questions and collect their paychecks, like good capitalists."

Lyons snorted. "So China got cold feet when they lost control of the operation," he mused. "An operation that relies on destabilizing two nuclear powers to create a cover for a co-opted American corporation to mine resources, the rights to which nobody involved owns, and then pass on the profits to the conspirators who made it possible, all under the noses of the international community. An international community even now wringing its hands over the possibility of an Indian-Pakistani nuclear conflict, which has no idea the real players are a rogue former Communist spec-ops player, his hired guns, his personal goons and the company he murdered and bought to make it happen. That about sum it up?"

"It does," Lao affirmed. "My team was dispatched covertly to the United States to erase Dei Qiong, to eliminate any evidence of China's involvement in the conception of this scheme."

"A task made a little easier by the fact that China won't see any of the profits from the operation," said Lyons. "You don't think this sudden outburst of national pride, through which your superiors decided this covert op was beneath them, might not just be a little convenient?"

"It is not a question of convenience," the general insisted. "It is a matter of honor. I must find and kill Dei Qiong. He has dishonored the People's Republic. He has forsaken the oaths he took when he became a leader in our special forces. He is endangering all that China has worked for."

"You gave us quite the speech about China, its power and our debts before, Lao," Lyons argued. "Now I'd like to lay a little something on you."

"Yes?"

"Yours is a beggar nation," Lyons argued. "China built its industry on cheap labor. Cheap labor that is often indistinguishable from slave labor. Of course China has surged ahead of other nations in manufacturing. You have no pollution controls and you have the full weight of your government behind making yours the cheapest place to go for production. That's all possible because of your totalitarian Communist regime, Lao, a regime that stopped all civilian vehicle traffic during the Olympics in Beijing to try to get the massive smog problem under some semblance of control."

"I will not sit here and be insulted," Lao said.

"You will," Lyons argued, "because you've got no choice." He turned to look over his shoulder at Schwarz. "Do it," he said.

Schwarz whipped his machine pistol up and trained it on the two Chinese soldiers. They froze. Lao was reaching for his knife the moment Schwarz moved, but Lyons had anticipated that. He had the snout of his Python in Lao's face before the Chinese general realized what was happening. Lao crouched half in and half out of his chair, stopped moving.

"America is the butt of every half-baked dictator and every wailing hippie with half an ax to grind," Lyons said. "You think you're going to bring armed men onto my soil and try to murder agents of the United States government and we're just going to look the other way? You think you're going to wave around your checkbook and threaten us with your debts and then cow us? A bunch of Communist murderers? This is payback time, Lao. You stood there smug in the knowledge that you could kill us if you wanted to, that we had to comply with your demands like children whose angry teacher has just walked into the room. Teach me a lesson now, Lao, you arrogant sack of crap. Come on, tell me again about the inferior Americans!"

"Carl," said Schwarz. "I don't think this is a good idea."

"To hell with you," Lyons told him. "No, wait, I've got a better idea. To hell with Lao." He thumbed back the hammer on his Python. Lao, if it were possible for him to become any more still, did so. "I think it's time we showed China what we think of this kind of diplomacy."

"Please," Lao whispered. "Mr. Logan….this is really quite unnecessary."

"You flew helicopter gunships in my skies!" Lyons roared. "I swear to all that is holy I will put a bullet through your Communist brain for that!"

"Carl!" Schwarz urged. "Don't do this. We're not authorized to do this."

"The hell we aren't," Lyons barked. "An hour ago this asshole was ready to murder us in the street. An American street in an American city. Can you imagine that? What are we doing this for if not to stop invading foreign powers from killing people in our streets with impunity?"

"Carl, please," Schwarz insisted. He sounded very nervous now. "If you do this, it will be our heads."

"No," Lyons said. "It won't. If we report Lao killed in

battle, that's all it will be. A report. His people will disavow him. He's not supposed to be here. Our people will cluck their tongues and tell us maybe there was another way…but at the end of the day, will have killed a man who committed more acts of war before breakfast than all the terrorists on American soil combined!"

"Carl," Schwarz said. "You're not a murderer. That's what this is. It isn't a war. It's an execution."

"Then I guess I'll get to be the executioner for a day," Lyons said. "Don't tell me you haven't thought of it."

"There's another way," Schwarz said. "Lao is offering to work with us to find and take down Dei Qiong. Aren't you, Lao? Isn't that what this meeting is all about?"

"Yes," the general said quickly. "That is my goal. To suggest we set aside our differences and work together to bring Dei Qiong to justice. My government wants him killed or removed to China for judgment. Your government most certainly benefits if he is gone and his operation is dismantled. I have shown you every consideration in explaining to you the nature of the plot devised in Kashmir. All I ask is a show of good faith."

"And where is *your* good faith?" Lyons demanded. He pressed the barrel of the Python harder into Lao's cheek.

Lao rattled off a series of numbers by rote. "These are our radio frequencies," he said. "We will listen for you. You need only to communicate what it is you believe your next move to be. We can help you find Dei Qiong. I have a list of the holding companies put in place to facilitate his operation. Using that list, we can identify his location and assault it together."

"There, see, Carl," Schwarz said. "A show of good faith. Lao is giving us the means to work with him. Now all you have to do is let him live. Come on, Carl. Just let him live."

Lao was sweating. Droplets began to slide down his forehead. Lyons imagined it was no picnic to be on the other end of that gun barrel, especially since Lyons's willingness to kill Lao where he sat was very genuine. He supposed that showed in his eyes, or something. Lao looked terrified.

Lyons waited for as long as he could. Then he slowly eased back the hammer of his Python and sat back. "Either one of you so much as twitches like he's going for a gun, I'll cut you down where you stand. That goes for your little knife, too, Lao."

Lao, slowly and carefully, stood and spread his hands. He gestured to his guards. "I understand. My men and I will withdraw now. You have the ability to contact us. Do so and I will give you the holding companies. We can work together to neutralize Dei Qiong and his operation. I give you my word, the word of Chinese special forces. That may mean nothing to you, but it means everything to me. I give you my word as a man."

"Get going, Lao," Lyons said.

Lao Wei nodded. Practically grabbing his men by their collars, he led them out of the coffee shop. Lyons watched them go through the open doorway. He gave it some time more before he was willing to holster his weapon. You just never knew when someone you thought you had bested would come back after the fact to try to change the game.

It was like having a fight at a party. You didn't beat someone up, humiliate them, and then continue to enjoy the party. There was every chance that the victim would come back with a knife or a gun, and then while you were busy dancing the night away, you ended up on the floor and bleeding.

That's what he had just done to Lao. He had beaten the

man up, humiliated him. Worse, he had done it in front of Lao's men. Lyons guessed that both those soldiers would be given strict orders to say absolutely nothing of what they had seen and heard. This would not be seen as unusual by Lao's other soldiers. Men who were part of specific details were frequently told not to reveal classified information. Depending on how ruthless Lao was, and how defensive he might be concerning his reputation, it was even possible those two soldiers would end up having convenient accidents in the near future.

The effect of Schwarz trying to appeal to reason while Lyons had stuck a gun in Lao's face was psychologically jarring, certainly. It put Lao, who obviously saw himself as quite clever, on unequal footing, taking his initiative and disrupting whatever mental momentum he might have been building. It also guaranteed that any concessions Able Team gave to a temporary partnership with Lao would be relatively minor. After all, when you started from a standpoint of, "Give me something and I'll let you live in return," you weren't normally asked to throw in still more along the way. Lyons had been counting on that, as well as the preoccupation Lao would have with his own injured pride. Keep the man grinding away on those insults and he wouldn't see the bigger picture.

It was all classic psychological warfare.

Schwarz holstered his Beretta. "I think we're safe, Ironman. No sign that he's leading a charge back our way."

"Good," Lyons said. "Let's get the Farm clued in to what went on here. While we're working with Lao, I want to get together as comprehensive a list as we can of the men under Lao's command. Numbers, descriptions, photos if we can do it discreetly. I want every one of these bastards accounted for. We don't want Lao leaving any sleeper cells behind once he departs our fair shores."

"I can't believe he fell for Good Cop, Bad Cop," Schwarz said. "I mean…how old a routine is that?"

"Nobody's perfect, Gadgets. Nobody's perfect."

CHAPTER TWENTY

Outside Chicago

Dei Qiong watched the factory recede in the passenger side mirror. The staging facility for his mercenary teams was progressing as it should. From the outside, it was so much industrial space. Once inside, everything required to feed, clothe, train and sustain a fighting force of the size he required was at hand. He had invested considerable money in the operation. Between that and the investments he had made in his retirement dwelling, he had burned through the last of the money he had skimmed from his original operational budget. He had incurred significant personal debt, in fact, to see to it that everything he needed and wanted in place was established to his satisfaction.

Those funds would be recouped. Once he had established a steady pipeline of beryllium and other precious metals from Kashmir to his EarthGard processing facilities, he would have more money than he could spend in multiple lifetimes—even after spreading it around in the form of bribes at every point in the process, and after sharing it with Jamali and Gera. The continued support and effort of the two rogue generals was key to the entire plan. He congratulated himself again on his ingenuity.

Ingenuity. Flexibility in the field. A tendency to innovate and to choose solutions that were "unconventional." Thus had been the praise of his superiors in special operations. It was the reason that he, rising in his career path as one of China's covert military operatives, had been chosen by the previous leadership of Chinese special operations to head the Kashmir project.

The project was an important one. The world's natural resources were being depleted at an accelerated rate. Precious metals used for industry, such as the silver used in wireless phones and electronic devices, was in increasingly short supply. It was more urgent than ever that China, with its enormous population, continue to expand its economy. Should the Chinese economy contract, it would take still others with it. But Dei Qiong, at the time, cared little about the world. He cared about the prosperity of the nation for which he fought. China, for its economy to continue to grow, needed rare resources. The other nations of the world squandered or hoarded their own resources; therefore it was necessary to take from these nations what they had.

But therein was the difficulty. How to steal, even if it were theft in name only, while not suffering the sanctions of the insufferable UN and the arrogant Western nations, was the fundamental problem. This was the dilemma presented to Dei Qiong by his superiors. This was the problem he was told to solve.

As he did with so many problems, Dei approached it with an open mind. He was not wedded to any one strategy; he only cared about the results. So it was that he hit on an idea. His problem was one of want. China wanted resources. China did not have resources. Other nations had resources they did not require, or which they refused to share. These were all variations on the theme of greed.

Dei Qiong would use the West's greed against it.

He'd researched a number of mining and geo-location firms to find one that had the type of expertise he required. What he wanted was a private company that could help him find previously untapped natural resources, a company that could then execute the mining operations. But these operations would have to be done discreetly, by personnel who understood the precarious situation in which they found themselves. In short, he needed a company whose ownership he could bribe.

He found this in EarthGard. China's intelligence network made simple the task of investigating the financial records of EarthGard's management. He performed credit checks and examined past tax data. It became clear that of all the corporations Dei was investigating, EarthGard's management was in the worst financial straits. They would leap at the chance for freedom from debt. He would offer them salvation in the form of large payments. All he would ask, in return, was that they ply the very trade in which they were already engaged. He just needed them to do it without respect to international borders.

EarthGard's scouts turned up beryllium and a variety of precious metals in multiple sites, but the deposits in Kashmir were most promising. The history of military turbulence, combined with the remote location of northern Kashmir, made it the perfect place to exploit. If he could gain nominal military control over portions of the north, he would not even need to control the territory as a whole. He only needed to ensure that neither nation's government stopped the mining operations or the shipments of ore to off-shore processing vessels provided by EarthGard.

Once more, Dei had turned to the research that had always served him so well. He was known to be meticulous, to be thorough, but in truth he was much more than this. He was practically obsessive in his preparations. He stayed awake for days becoming intimately familiar with the military hierarchies and politics of India and Kashmir. He became an expert on their equipment, their tactics, their personnel. And he realized that there was a way to put India and Pakistan at each other's throats so badly that the two nuclear powers could well go to war.

That war, provided it stayed contained within the two nations, could benefit everyone. It would make it easier for EarthGard to take resources from northern Kashmir, while focusing the eyes of the world on the two nations in general. The world's meddling "superpowers," the Western do-gooders who always sought to bomb their way to peace, would be too busy hectoring the governments of India and Pakistan to bother much with what was happening in Kashmir. And, after all, who wanted to interfere in a stalemate between two parties who hated each other?

What Dei required was two military leaders who had a unique combination of traits. They had to be powerful enough, and charismatic enough, to bring forces of their own to a private banner. Yet they had also to be men Dei could manipulate with the promise of riches. He needed ambitious, greedy men, men who were not so ambitious that he would have to worry about them attempting to usurp his authority.

It was truly his authority, his power, and the more Dei thought of it that way, the less loyalty he felt to the nation of his birth. Why, after all, should he continue to live a life of privation and discipline just so that those in power, the Communist Party faithful, could continue to live like kings? He had seen the lavish retirement homes, the opulent party function buildings, the expensive cars, the jewelry. He knew that while they preached mass struggle, his masters sought only what they could get for themselves.

The knowledge of this had never bothered him before. As long as he was moving up in the special forces hierarchy, he had been satisfied. But now, in describing to his candidates for military usurpation the benefits he would bestow on them, the monies that would flow to these men, he found himself…jealous. Why should he, Dei Qiong, not also be enriched? Had he not conceived of the plan himself? Had he not selected generals Gera and Jamali, approached them to recruit them, and persuaded them to call to their respective banners those troops loyal to them personally? Had he not set all this in motion? Why then should Jamali and Gera be the only men to become wealthy?

Dei did not remember the exact moment he chose to betray China. He did not think the decision had been sudden or cleanly defined. Instead, his desire that he, too, should become rich, grew in his belly from day to day until, finally, he could stand it no longer.

With his course now clear to him, he was forced to take several more days, to plan for what was to come. He prepared a number of false reports; all of them intended to put the Chinese government off him for as long as was practical. Then he informed Jamali and Gera, whom he had hand-selected from among the available profiles of military leaders in India and Pakistan. He told both men that, henceforth, he and only he would be running the plan. He explained that the result would be much more money for all of them. No longer would the largest share go to the Chinese government. It would instead be added to the general profit and divided among shares for Jamali, Gera and Dei.

In their greed, Jamali and Gera were happy to agree.

Dei then sought each of the members of his special forces unit. He was confident in the loyalty of the majority of these men, but he left nothing to chance. With an empty gun in his holster and a second, loaded weapon hidden in his waistband under his shirt, he went to each man he had been assigned and told that soldier that he, Dei Qiong, intended to betray China to enrich himself and all his men. A fine life of retirement awaited all of them, he had told his troops.

Of all his men, only three tried to snatch the empty gun and use it against him. Dei Qiong thanked each man for his loyalty to China before using the loaded pistol to end the man's days.

Next, Dei and his troops murdered the management of EarthGard—but not before interrogating them. Armed with the company's most closely held secrets, and hiring mercenaries to bolster his private troops, Dei proceeded to use EarthGard as the plan had intended all along. He took those security steps he had always intended to implement, including forwarding the company's data activities and establishing a false front for these in another state. He saw to it that Jamali and Gera followed his orders and maintained their little war, sacrificing each other's soldiers on a regular basis, never surpassing an averaged stalemate level. This was harder than he had thought it would be, given Jamali's natural viciousness, but the plan worked regardless. And soon the money would start to flow.

That was all he was really giving up in going deeply into debt to establish his training facility and his retirement mansion. He was giving up money temporarily in exchange for the promise of much, much more money in the future.

He was building a money-producing system. That system was lubricated by bribes and fueled by human nature. Once up and running, it would continue running. Wealth to the end of his days would be the outcome.

He was concerned, however. He knew that some sort of interloping force, some government investigation team, had attacked several of EarthGard's facilities. These facilities could be replaced, or their processing duties reassigned to other EarthGard-owned holdings. Within the holding company that sheltered his training factory and his mansion, Dei had diversified into multiple other ventures. There would always be a way.

And because money made money, he might be able to divest himself of the EarthGard operation and its international legal issues once it had made him a small fortune. A few strategic murders to cover his tracks, a few computer records forever altered, a few documents shredded or burned, and Dei Qiong, under any identity he chose, could end his days an elderly man sought by no one. Not law enforcement, not government, not China's avenging agents.

But first he had to resolve his current issues. He knew that Lao Wei and the American team, for surely it would be Americans on American soil and not some other group, had already come into conflict. Knowing Lao Wei from special forces as well as Dei did, he could foresee any number of eventualities. Lao might well succeed in killing the American investigators, these fearsome armed men who had assaulted multiple EarthGard sites. Or, given how effective the American team had been, they might well eliminate Lao from the equation. The third possibility was that the two might cooperate toward the mutual goal of bringing Dei to "justice." That worried him quite a bit…but not enough to persuade him to change course.

All his life he had been a tool of Communist China. All his life he had done whatever had been asked of him, without complaint, without thought of personal enrichment. And now all he had to show for it, beyond what he could create for himself, beyond what he could take through his own ingenuity, was a single well-worn pistol.

Seated in the back of the car, letting his driver take him back to his mansion, Dei Qiong took the old Tokarev out of his shoulder holster and held it in his hands. He turned it over and over. He knew every millimeter of this weapon.

Every scratch, every dent, every imperfection he could re-
cite from memory.

The weapon had been his father's.

As was so often the case in China's special forces, the
enrollment was a family tradition for Dei. His father had
served with distinction until the time Dei was a young
man. Then, something had happened. To his frustration,
even after he was himself technically a general within the
special operations hierarchy, he was unable to access the
sealed records. He would never know what his father had
done. In the official record, there was no record even of
the man's name or rank. It was as if Dei Qiong had sprung
forth from the womb fully formed.

His mother had died in childbirth. He knew nothing of
her save that. He had been raised by his father and then
by the all-powerful state. He had been taught loyalty. He
had been taught hard work. He had been given specialized training. He was a special forces operative, one of
the most effective the People's Republic of China had ever
produced.

But the memory of his father was what truly had turned
him.

His father, too, had lived a life of sacrifice, of Spartan
dedication to a few goals and fewer luxuries. This had
seemed perfectly normal. His father had seemed satisfied in life, even proud of his son. And as Dei Qiong was
groomed for the military, his pride in himself and in his
father had become nationalistic pride in his nation.

That had sustained him all these years. That had mo-
tivated him in countless missions. That had been the jus-
tification for endangering his own life time and again at
the command of his masters in the government, in the
Communist Party.

But then he had described to Jamali and to Gera the

riches that could be theirs. He had been very persuasive. He had dug deep into himself and found every hidden avarice, every covetous desire, and he had shared these with the generals in an effort to bring them to his cause.

But in so doing he had awakened the memory of his father, and of the Tokarev that was his only birthright.

He had come home from his classes as he always did, late in the evening, feeling the ache of the physical education courses that were part of his demanding curriculum. Their humble apartment had been uncharacteristically dark. His father always turned on the living-room light and the kitchen light on returning home. He liked to see the place bright and cheerful, he often told his son. He wanted to be able to discuss the events of the day and see the expression on his son's face. He liked the light. He did not wish to sit in pools of darkness.

But that fateful day, the apartment was dark. Dei Qiong had let himself in and called for his father, but there was no answer.

He found his father in the bathroom, seated in the empty tub. The Tokarev the man had used to take his life was still clutched in his hand. A single bullet was all that had been required to end the man's life. Dei Qiong's father had placed his issue Tokarev in his mouth and pulled the trigger.

There was no note. There was no explanation.

Dei had taken the pistol. He had hidden it in his dresser. When men came in the morning, unbidden, sent by some knowledge or some signal of which Dei was not aware, they did not search for the pistol. They merely removed the body. Dei Qiong would understand, many years later, that it was his father's failure to show up for duty that had prompted the dispatch of the clean-up team.

With time and with the experiences a man accumulates

in life, Dei had put together more of it. The erasure of all mention of his father from the official record pointed to a disgrace of some sort. His father had been rendered an "unperson." It explained why no one was eager to examine the circumstances of the man's death. Likely, had Dei's father not committed suicide, he would have been quietly executed the following day.

His father had chosen the path of personal honor. But there was something more, as Dei Qiong understood it. His father had been unable to leave a note because there was no way to do so without implicating his son in his dishonor. He had done the only thing that he could, therefore, to say one last thing to Dei Qiong. He had committed suicide in their home, at an hour and in a way that guaranteed Dei would find his father alone.

It was a message.

Dei Qiong believed that his father had chosen to explain to his son that a man's honor was important…but that it would also lead to his death. After a lifetime of faithful service to the Chinese government, Dei Qiong's father had been thrown away. For Dei, the message was a powerful one, one that he struggled to forget, one that he tried to suppress.

He had kept the pistol all those years, even during the years that he tried not to remember his father's warning.

At best, it was a morbid reminder. At worst, the pistol might well be Dei Qiong's fate. Would he, too, be forced to take his own life, after some failure caused him to lose face in the eyes of his masters?

So it was that, as he described the benefits of wealth to Jamali and Gera, he convinced himself. And as he convinced himself, he realized that he owed no loyalty to the government that had killed his father. His only obligation was to himself. His only desire was to live well, a final revenge on the political machine that had destroyed his father.

All of his work to date was the result of that revelation. He would overcome the obstacles ahead of him. He would deal with Lao Wei, whose presence he had learned of through Cudgel's intelligence network. He would deal with the Americans, whose presence had been inflicted on him when they'd attacked his holdings. There was nothing that could stop him. He had worked too hard. He was owed too much.

He stared at the old Tokarev. He would not fail.

If he did, there would be no reason not to use the pistol on himself.

His wireless phone began to vibrate in his pocket. He removed it and put it to his ear.

"Yes," he said.

"General Dei," said the frantic voice of Lei Pan, one of his lieutenants among the turncoat Chinese operatives. "General Dei, we are under attack!"

"What? Speak more slowly, man. What are you saying?"

His mind raced. Lei was one of the men stationed at the training factory. The factory was the primary staging facility for all of his men, his combined Cudgel mercenary and loyal special forces troops. There was a small army stationed in and around his mansion, but the remainder of his forces not engaged in guarding EarthGard facilities was found at the factory. It should be the one place where he was least vulnerable, the one facility among all he controlled that was most safe from violent assault.

"A large force of men, primarily Chinese special forces, is here now," Lei Pan struggled to tell him. He sounded as though he was out of breath. This was extraordinary, as Lei was one of the fittest, most dangerous men Dei had ever met. "Lao Wei is among them. He is not alone. There are Westerners here, most likely Americans. We think it is the commando force that struck our other holdings. They are here with small arms and explosives. They are working their way through the building."

"Rally the men! Defend the factory!"

"Our defenses are smashed," Lei said. "We are in disarray. They hit us from two sides simultaneously. I have never seen such ferocity. There was a giant with an automatic shotgun… He had others with him. I do not… I do not know who survives."

"Driver!" Dei shouted. "Turn around! Back to the factory!"

"No, sir!" Lei shouted. "Do not return. Do not come back. We are… We are fallen, sir. I am concealed within one of the storage compartments in the basement. I feel heat. I smell smoke. The building is on fire. I think… I think we are defeated."

"How? How is this possible?" Dei demanded.

"I…I am sorry…" Lei Pan said.

"Lei? Lei! Lei, respond!" Dei Qiong was screaming into his phone now. "Damn you, Lei Pan, report, soldier!"

Static greeted him. Dei repeated the conversation in his mind. The curious wheezing sound he had heard through the phone. Lei Pan's shortness of breath…. The quality of his voice….

Dei realized, then. Lei had been mortally wounded. He had used the last of his strength to phone his leader, the man he trusted, the man who had recruited him. Now Lei Pan was dead, killed by an invading force that could only be Lao Wei.

"A giant with an automatic shotgun," Lei had said. That corresponded to the description of one of the Westerners, the men Dei Qiong assumed were American government agents sent to investigate EarthGard.

He had to assume the factory was a total loss. If the Americans and Lao Wei had decided to work together, that meant they were comparing what they knew, helping each other. Lao knew nearly everything about the genesis of the operation. He would be able to make things very uncomfortable for Dei Qiong if he made sure American intelligence forces, or any Western intelligence agency, discovered what was happening in Kashmir. The shotgun-toting giant could be an investigator from INTERPOL, for all he knew or cared. The result would be the same.

Curse Hughbright for getting killed in Kashmir. The moment he had learned the news, he'd known there was a chance the man would be traced back to EarthGard. Once foreign powers began poking into EarthGard, uncovering its secrets, time was short. They would follow the trail back to him. Back to Dei Qiong. Everything he had worked for, everything he had tried to accomplish, was in jeopardy.

He toyed with the idea of rallying his men, of returning to the factory to lead a counterattack. But Lei Pan's words stopped him. "Our defenses are smashed." Those were not the words of a man who thinks victory can be snatched from the precipice of defeat. Those were the truthful words of a man who knows he is dying.

"Sir?" his driver asked. "Do you still want me to return to the factory?"

"No," Dei said. "We must get to the mansion as quickly as possible. Call ahead and alert security to expect a full-scale, worst-case invasion. Federal authorities, Chinese special operations, an international team of peacekeeping investigators…it does not matter which. Any who attempt to enter the grounds are to be killed. I will be making arrangements to withdraw."

The only safe place was Kashmir. He would have to take up residence in one of Jamali's or Gera's military strongholds and hope to run the operation from there, where he was untouchable. It was considerably less pleasant than the future he had pictured for himself. Once the profits began to flow, however, he could establish a new retirement home on some tropical beach in a nation without extradition agreements. He supposed that would be acceptable. Perhaps exceptionally so. He would just have to be patient.

The thought, however, was followed by another that brought him sharply back to reality: Jamali and Gera were suffering losses of their own generated by an outside party. He did not think these men had killed Hughbright; the fool of an EarthGard prospector had managed to put himself in the middle of one of Jamali's and Gera's preplanned skirmishes, quite by accident. He had said as much when he tried to radio for help, only to be discovered by the foreign interlopers sometime later as a corpse. Jamali had admitted as much, as had Gera. The two had obviously discussed among themselves whether to admit to Dei Qiong that their machinations had resulted in the killing of an employee valuable to Dei.

No matter. They had eventually told him. That meant both generals were committed to the profits they thought Dei Qiong could wring from Kashmir. As long as their greed held, he could count on, if not loyalty, at least a reasonable imitation thereof.

Dei looked down at his phone. To his surprise, it began to ring again, once more with Lei Pan's number. He pressed the accept button on the touch screen.

"Hello?" he said.

"Is this Dei Qiong?" said a flippant voice in English.

"Who is this?" demanded Dei. "Where is Lei Pan?"

"If you mean the guy whose phone this is," the voice

said, "he's dead on the floor here. Is this Dei Qiong? Because we're sort of burning your factory-cum-training facility down. I was doing air quotes just then, since you couldn't see this."

"Identify yourself!"

"Me?" the voice taunted. "I'm nobody. It's just, you know. You're not going to get away with this. We're coming for you, Dei Qiong. Okay, now's the part where you threaten me like that will make a difference."

"I will destroy you!" Dei shouted. "I will see you drown in a pool of your own blood! I will—"

"Exactly my point," the voice said, and hung up.

Dei Qiong stared at the phone for a long time, his face red with rage.

CHAPTER TWENTY-ONE

Chicago

"Man, everything about this place screams money," Schwarz said.

"Lifestyles of the rich and the even richer," Blancanales said.

The neighborhood through which they were driving was as affluent as any Lyons had seen. Their Suburban rode at the head of a bizarre motorcade. The vehicles following the GMC were Toyota Land Cruisers. They were filled to bursting with Lao Wei and his men.

"You ever think maybe we made a wrong turn somewhere," Schwarz said, "given that we're now leading a strike force consisting entirely of Chinese special forces?"

"Maybe you should have thought of that before we hit the factory," Lyons said.

While Able Team was given a high degree of flexibility in the field, something as significant as a temporary alliance with armed, hostile forces operating in the United States without diplomatic credentials was something that Lyons had taken immediately to the Farm. This had occasioned a great deal of back and forth with Price, Brognola and the cybernetics team, as Kurtzman and his people cross-checked the information Able relayed them. On Lyons's tentative agreement with Lao Wei's proposal, the Chinese special forces leader had given them details of multiple holding companies, all of them tied to Dei Qiong's activities with Chinese intelligence and special operations.

The Farm—specifically Kurtzman and his computer team—had worked over the numbers and traced the holding companies. Then the Stony Man cyber genius had specifically appended, in a message transmitted to their smartphones, the addresses that were at the center of the majority of communications traceable to the holding companies. What that boiled down to was two sites: an old factory in the industrial area of the city outskirts, and a recently renovated mansion in one of Chicago's wealthiest suburbs. They had opted to hit the industrial zone first, theorizing that any heavy weapons or equipment used by Dei Qiong's people would likely be found there.

What they had discovered, in their first joint operation with Lao Wei's unit, was a training facility converted from an old textile factory. This had been the staging area for the majority of Dei Qiong's combined force of co-opted special forces personnel and hired Cudgel Security. It was also a maintenance and coordination facility, where troops were given specialized training. Dei Qiong had what was essentially his own private army. Those troops not on assignment at EarthGard facilities had to be housed somewhere, and it made sense to house them and train them centrally. It afforded them better control.

Lyons and Schwarz had taken point in penetrating the factory. Blancanales had stayed outside, both as backup and to keep an eye on the Chinese should they offer some kind of betrayal. Lao Wei and his men had worked to attack from the perimeter simultaneously, while the Able Team commandos worked their way through the main entrance. The fighting had been intense, but not nearly as bad as Lyons had anticipated. This was because the lightning strike, an overwhelming blitz made possible by the discipline and speed of Lao's men, had taken Dei Qiong's forces by surprise.

Working with Lao, under the auspices of Stony Man Farm and with Brognola's permission, Able Team had cleaned out the target and removed half of the equation from the battle board. That was no small thing. Lyons wasn't thrilled about an alliance of convenience with Lao, but he thought he understood the man. Lao's reputation as a straight arrow, even if he was a Communist-tool straight arrow, probably meant that he could be expected to do just what he said he wanted: Work with Able Team to take down Dei Qiong.

"Take down" was the operative phrase. It was open to interpretation. It might mean Lao would stab them in the back at his first opportunity if Able Team tried to bring Dei Qiong in alive. Or perhaps the opposite was true; perhaps Lao had orders to see Dei dead, no matter what the cost. That might get ugly if Able had the chance to take the man in alive.

Able Team had received several communications from the Farm via their smartphones. Most of these had to with operational updates and dossiers relative to Lao Wei and his people. Some of the special forces operatives had records available through the network, including Lao's file. Others were relatively new and had not yet been profiled. Where possible, Able Team would update those files. Already, Schwarz had managed to surreptitiously photograph several of the soldiers.

The opposite was probably also true. Lyons was cynical enough to believe that Lao was already compiling what he could on "Carl Logan" and the other two members of the three-man force this "Logan" led. That was a necessary evil. The Farm could probably run some interference there; Kurtzman and his group had various algorithms running worldwide, in networks across multiple nations, that routinely searched out and deleted references to Stony Man team members. Depending on Lao's exit strategy for him and his team, it might also be possible to vet the Chinese forces before they departed American soil.

Several other interesting communications had also come in. These were flagged for Schwarz's specific attention, although they were received by all three team members. The Able Team electronics whiz peered at his phone and his expression turned blank.

"What the...?"

"I'd say that's an invoice for a red dot scope," Blancanales said from the rear seat, looking at his own phone. "Why is this made out to you, Gadgets?"

"But," Schwarz said. "I don't see how..."

"Well this probably isn't right," Blancanales said. "This next invoice is for thousands of dollars. And it's made out to you, too."

"But," Schwarz protested.

"What is it?" Lyons said. He was watching the road, but he would have been lying if he said he wasn't curious about this little side discussion.

"It looks like an itemized list for every rental car and truck we've ever wrecked," said Blancanales. "Did you realize we were using the same company every time? Their fleet insurance rates must be insane. I can't imagine the processing power it must have taken to compile this. Someone on the Farm's cyber team must really have wanted to add this up."

"But," Schwarz repeated.

"Don't worry, Gadgets. I'm sure they'll just deduct a small part of this from your pay each month. Let's see. I think you can have this paid off in... When do the next eight leap years fall?"

Lyons couldn't help himself. He laughed.

"What's this at the bottom?" Blancanales asked. "Right here at the bottom of the invoice. 'Swift and terrible,' it says."

"Swift and terrible," Schwarz repeated quietly.

"All right, all right," Lyons said finally. He couldn't quite bring himself to take the grin off his face, but he sobered as he considered where they were driving…and who they were driving with. Everything had gone smoothly in the attack on the factory site, but the operation had been very bloody. Dei Qiong's men, probably understanding that prison was not the largest of their worries with Lao Wei on the scene, had opted to fight to the last man. They had been wiped out, and the factory had been set ablaze during the battle.

Lyons himself had called in a Farm clean-up crew. He had also alerted the necessary firefighting departments. It wouldn't do for the fire that destroyed Dei Qiong's training facility to spread to nearby properties.

If he was doing the math correctly, apart from any EarthGard sites still operating to mine and process ore— less those in the Kashmir area, which Phoenix Force would see to eliminating—they had successfully chipped Dei Qiong's domestic operations down to his last hideaway, this mansion among the richest of Chicago. Lyons imagined he could read what Dei must have been thinking when he secured and, presumably, fortified the place. If Lyons was the one buying the pile of bricks on which they were now closing, he'd certainly have put his private army of security professionals to good use. It reminded Lyons of the old proverb "put all your eggs in one basket" and *watch that basket*. He thought maybe Mark Twain had said that. He couldn't remember.

"Pol," Lyons directed, "call up the schematics the Farm

sent over. Give me the best possible routes in and we'll coordinate with Lao to spread the joy around. I want to take the place at every conceivable entry point. Then we'll squeeze them. With any luck we'll come up with Dei Qiong at the center."

"Roger that," Blancanales confirmed. "I'll distribute the plan to Lao's men using the frequency he gave us."

"I'm never going to get used to having Chinese special forces as backup," Lyons said.

"How do you think they feel?" Schwarz asked. "They've got Able Team for backup.

"He's right, Ironman," Blancanales said. "Having you temporarily working with them is going to give them nightmares for years."

"Hardy-har-har," Lyons scoffed. "Look." He pointed beyond the windshield, indicating a spot farther up the street. "There's the estate. He's got the whole thing walled off. Send half of Lao's people around the back and the other half to our right. We'll split right up the middle again. I like the direct approach."

"Those gates look locked," Schwarz said.

"So?" Lyons asked.

"Well, this *is* a rental," the electronics expert pointed out.

"Let's go knock on the door," Lyons suggested, flooring the accelerator. The big truck responded immediately, surging forward on its massive tires, eating up the space between the drive and the front gates. Lyons rolled down the window on his side.

"Hey, Dei Qiong!" he shouted out the window into the screaming wind. "Knock, knock!"

The Suburban smashed through the gates, flattening them. Lyons had his Python out the window on his side, while Schwarz played gunner with his Beretta on the other.

Behind them, the Land Cruisers split off to right and left with almost mathematical precision. Lyons had to hand it to the Communists; they were disciplined, if not particularly personable.

He just hoped their impromptu alliance held long enough for Able Team to get the job done and get clear of the Chinese on both sides of the conflict.

The front of the mansion had tall columns. Between these columns, as if they had been expecting military intervention, Dei Qiong's combined force of turncoat special ops and hired mercenaries had set up a series of sandbag emplacements. Behind these, gunners with belt-fed M-60s were waiting.

"This is going to suck," Schwarz said.

The gunners opened up. Heavy 7.62 mm NATO rounds chewed into the Suburban, causing Lyons to accelerate and push the vehicle even harder.

"Carl?" Blancanales asked. "You're heading right for the front of the house.

"I know," Lyons said.

"Carl," Schwarz said, "that's where the machine guns are." He ducked as rounds ripped through the hood and the windshield. Pebbles of safety glass filled the interior of the truck. Lyons, Blancanales and Schwarz got as low as they could, keeping the engine block of the truck between them and the enemy guns.

"I know!" Lyons said.

"Carl!" Schwarz argued, "we should probably go *away* from the machine guns!"

"Negative!" Lyons shouted.

The Suburban, now spewing black smoke from its engine compartment, hit the front steps of the mansion, bounced up over them and kept going.

Lyons hauled the wheel hard over. He hit the brakes

and the gas simultaneously. The big truck slewed sideways when it hit the top of the stairs, smashing one of the columns with its tail end, wiping out the machine-gun nest on that side and the fire team behind that gun with it.

The grille of the still accelerating Suburban splattered the second machine-gun team, knocking their weapon aside and splaying the men there all over the portico.

Lyons, Blancanales and Schwarz piled out of the truck. Schwarz had the duffel bag of hardware slung over his shoulder. Blancanales had his M-4 and Lyons had his shotgun on his back...but the former cop paused before they entered the house.

The M-60 machine gun was lying next to the remains of the sandbag emplacement. It looked untouched, if otherwise a bit scuffed. A full can of ammo waited with it.

"It's Christmas," Lyons said quietly. He bent, draped several lengths of the M-60's belt over his shoulders and picked up the big weapon. "Time to play action-movie hero," he said. "Gadgets, blow up the front door, would you?"

Schwarz removed a grenade from his duffel, primed it and rolled it toward the front door. The members of Able Team took cover behind the columns.

"Lao reports his men are in position," Blancanales said, checking the display on his phone. "He wants to know what the signal is going to be."

"Tell him, 'boom.'"

"Got it," Blancanales said.

The grenade exploded. The door was reduced to splinters and scrap. Lyons waited a beat to see if any fire would be directed their way. When none was, he said, "Let's go see how the other half lives."

The M-60 machine gun was like a part of the big man. As Able Team entered the foyer of the mansion, gunfire from different parts of the house began to make the structure vibrate. Lyons could feel it through the floor. The Chinese special operators were attacking from the perimeter of the house, just as he had ordered. Lao was holding up his part of the bargain.

Lyons found a hallway leading deeper into the house and took it. His Able Team partners backed him up, flanking him.

An enemy gunner stuck his head around the corner. He was holding a Kalashnikov. He took one look at Lyons, paled and ducked back under cover.

Lyons cut loose with his machine gun.

Links and shells clattered to the marble floor as the big gun thundered and bucked, chewing up the wall and the man behind it. Plaster dust and scraps of wallpaper filled the air. The noise was incredible.

Rounding the corner, Able Team was ready for whatever might come. They found themselves in a lavish living area. The air smelled faintly of chlorine, as well as blood and discharged ammunition. There was an indoor pool here just off the multilevel living room. The furniture was all in artificial leopard skin. A matching rug was laid out on the floor, the stuffed leopard's head opened in a false growl.

"Oh, yuck," Schwarz said. "Dei Qiong's decorator better be here, because he needs to be shot."

"Take a door and search," Lyons said. Multiple doors and exits opened up off the living area. It would eat up time to check them all. "Circle back and meet me here unless you get to the Chinese perimeter first. Then let us know over Able's channel. Go."

The team split up. Lyons walked past an open baby grand piano and suppressed the urge to shoot it up. That was the sort of thing kids did in video games. He had better uses for his ammo.

The ammunition for the M-60 sure was heavy, though. He needed to find more targets simply to lighten the load. He was a big man, practiced in combat, but he wasn't getting any younger.

He chose a door that he thought looked like a master bedroom entrance. When he kicked it in, he found himself in an enormous marble-tiled bathroom with walk-in showers and floor-to-ceiling mirrors.

This place is bigger than my first apartment, he thought to himself. There was another door at the other end of the bathroom. He took this and nearly got his head blown off.

The corridor he had chosen emptied into a large bedroom with an enormous circular bed. It looked bigger than a king size, as far as Lyons could tell, but he couldn't really say. He thought round beds were something you found at novelty couple's resorts, the kind with the heart-shaped hot tubs. This room did have a hot tub, and that hot tub was full of water. But there were no pretty girls to be found. Lyons felt slightly ripped off. Bad guys and drug kingpins and so on always had hot tubs full of pretty girls in the movies.

I'm starting to get as sentimental as Gadgets, he thought.

The gunmen bracing him were using the bed for cover. A bed with a dense enough mattress could stop light-caliber rounds, but Lyons didn't know of a bed in the world that could stop 7.62 mmm NATO. He dropped to one knee and blazed away, feeding the belt into the machine gun with his off hand, letting the weapon buck and dance as he braced its stock under his gun arm.

The bed was churned to fibers. The gunmen hiding behind it were blown to bits, spread all over the master bedroom. One of them staggered, bloody and dying, into the hot tub, turning the water pink and frothy.

Lyons left the master bedroom behind him.

Stalking farther down the hallway, he found a set of spiral staircases. One led up, to the top level of the giant home. The other led down, to whatever this place considered a basement. He debated which way to go. The basement level would be covered by Lao's attempt to come in from the perimeter. If he was Dei Qiong and on the receiving end of this home invasion, he believed he might instinctively head for higher ground. Maybe, Lyons thought, Dei might even think he could find a convenient choke point among the upstairs rooms. There, with ammo and time, he could pick off whomever came looking for him.

That had to be the end game in Dei Qiong's mind. The former Chinese special forces operative would know that his plan was blown here in the States. EarthGard would be on a list now, targeted for Justice Department cleansing, and all of EarthGard's personnel would likely face extensive interrogation and debriefing to separate the dupes from the willing accomplices. Dei Qiong's only hope was to get out of the country. Instead of going to an airport, he'd come here, and Lyons thought he understood why. In Dei's position he would need to figure out just where he could safely go that international forces couldn't drag him back to justice. In other words, he'd need to hole up somewhere, and that would take planning.

That's why, Lyons figured, Dei Qiong had gone to ground first at his mansion. Here he had armed men to guard him. He probably also had cash, weapons and other resources at his disposal. They were all things he would need before he could flee the country.

So you just figured you'd wait here for anyone to come try to take you, if they did come, Lyons thought. You thought if your gunners killed us all, you'd have bought yourself that much more time. A gun battle in a Chicago suburb? Who would believe it? And if you have enough money you can probably bribe your way through the locals.

Come to think of it, that answered the question of just why police response to EarthGard's various sites, and to the gun battle raging here at the mansion, had been so unimpressive. Dei Qiong had started out with cash to spare, siphoned from the operational budget for his little sleeper-cell deal here in the United States. He'd had bribe money to burn and had probably spread it around pretty generously.

Lyons climbed the stairs. When he got to the top floor what he found was a game room. There were billiards tables, video game machines, pinball machines and half a dozen other adult toys.

There was also a small army of armed men…and Dei Qiong.

The M-60 belched flame and lead.

CHAPTER TWENTY-TWO

Pakistan-India Border

The two armored vehicles hit the compound with such speed and fury that the men manning the outer gate quite literally exploded. One moment they were standing there, pointing their AK-pattern rifles at the oncoming lights of the two armored trucks. The next moment Manning was inundating them with 40 mm high-explosive grenades. When the dust cleared, the guards had been redistributed all over the landscape.

The trucks rolled through the outer gate without attracting so much as a stray shot. It was only when the MRAPs were already in the courtyard area of the encampment that they started to take serious return fire.

Unlike the fortress from which they had rescued Calvin James—not, McCarter had commented, that he seemed as if he needed a whole lot of rescuing—this was a temporary encampment. An outer perimeter of barbed-wire checkpoints and guard huts was arrayed around a central cluster of large tents that Jamali and Gera used as their mobile headquarters. This way, when it was necessary to break up the camp to maintain the image of the war between the two parties, they could easily separate.

Not for the first time, McCarter wondered how Jamali and Gera managed to control their men when it was necessary to sacrifice so many to the contrived war between them. He could conclude only that, while all Jamali and Gera soldiers might be equal, some were more equal than others. Jamali and Gera must both have had lists of top-tier and lower-tier soldiers and units under their command. They would sacrifice the more expendable men and equipment to perpetuate the war. They would simultaneously reassure their circles of elite soldiers that, of course, those men would live to profit under their warlords' command.

"All right, lads," McCarter began. "We're going to do this quickly and efficiently. Two, break left. Calvin, break right. We're going to make a large semicircle and meet at the other end. Rafe, fire up that turret. Gary, feel free to expend as many of your grenades as it takes."

"So…" said Hawkins. "'Weapons free,' in other words?"

"The very same," McCarter said.

The camp became a churning inferno. Manning was using incendiary grenades now, given the soft-target nature of the tent structures in the mobile camp. The result was that everywhere MRAP Two went, fire followed, blooming all around it among the camps of the Jamali and Gera soldiers. Encizo followed up with his very accurate machine gun. As the fires drove the men from their tents, Encizo's machine-gun fire cut them down.

It wasn't sporting. It wasn't kind. It wasn't fair.

It was war.

Several of the armored personnel carriers started moving, but McCarter was prepared for that eventuality, too.

"Now, Gary!" he said. "Cut left from Two and take them."

McCarter couldn't see Manning from his position, but the big Canadian would now be exiting the MRAP and carrying with him his rocket-propelled grenade launcher. The Briton watched intently out his windshield, following the tracks of the enemy APCs, watching the soldiers in the

APCs try to bring their own mounted machine guns to bear on the MRAPs. Hawkins was staying close to Manning, to give the Canadian a position to which he could fall back or simply take cover, but Manning wasn't worried about being defensive. He was taking the battle to the enemy.

Smoke trails from the RPG began to fill the camp. Manning took out first one, then another, then the third APC. With Encizo raking the running Jamali and Gera troops with his machine gun, the camp was soon in disarray, the troops running in every direction, trying to flee the growing, crawling fires and the spitting guns of their attackers.

"One, this is Two," Hawkins called. "I have picked up Gary. We are continuing our arc. The main tent, the biggest one, is straight ahead."

"Pull right into that tent, Two," said McCarter. "We're going to meet you there."

Meet them he did. The MRAP's big tires crunched over broken equipment and burned bodies as the two armored trucks crashed into the tent. They burst inside and nearly collided with each other at their bumpers, bursting the olive-drab canvas covering of the tent.

The men of Phoenix Force left their vehicles. Their boots crunched on the blood-covered snow.

McCarter tripped over a body. The body moaned.

"On me!" the Briton shouted. "Contact, contact, contact!"

The other team members moved in, their Tavors ready. On McCarter's signal they could have emptied their magazines and torn the man on the floor to ribbons. McCarter, however, put up a hand. There was no need for that. Except for this man and two dead guards, the tent had been empty. A casual glance around the wrecked environs told him that.

McCarter used his boot to toe over the man on the ground.

It was General Gera.

"I didn't do it!" Gera squealed. "I'm an innocent man, I tell you! An innocent man!"

"Save it, Gera," McCarter said. He hauled the rogue general to his feet. "Did your men leave you all alone, then?"

Gera looked at the ground. His gaze fell across the two dead guards. "Our forces were severely depleted by our previous losses," he said. "Mine worse than Jamali's. He has a fortress full of reinforcements."

"Had," McCarter said. "I'm afraid we got to that."

"That explains why he left," Gera said. "He must have received word."

"Left?" McCarter asked. "Where did he go? It's not like there's a commercial airport around."

Gera shrugged. He started to wander out of the tent. The men of Phoenix looked at McCarter, who shrugged and then pursued.

Gera sat in the snow outside his ruined tent. The air smelled of charred flesh and explosives. The camp was burning, spewing black smoke into the sky, raising the ambient temperature, however temporarily. McCarter felt heat on his face from the burning wreckage and tents. He moved to stand in front of Gera.

Gera had a pistol in his hand.

"Drop the weapon," McCarter ordered.

"Whether you do it, or I do it, does not matter," Gera said. "I must die. If I am returned to India I will be disgraced. I have relatives. Family members. Investors. They will force me to tell them what I know. Everything will be much worse for those I tried to help. For those who chose to ally with me."

"It's rough all over, mate," McCarter said. "You drop that gun or I'll put a bullet in your knee. You can spend the rest of your life walking with a cane and telling your fellow inmates stories about the great war that wasn't a war."

"Iraq. Libya. Romania. Revolutions that led to the public executions or humiliations of those nation's leaders. I will be humiliated."

"You're not a dictator, Gera," McCarter said. "You never got that far."

"At least tell me who you represent," said Gera. "Your men have been hounding our operation for days now, smashing it. You've proved yourselves the superior power here. Just tell me who you are."

"Us?" said McCarter. "We're justice, mate. Justice. That's all you need to know."

Gera nodded. Very quickly, he put the barrel of his pistol into his mouth.

McCarter snatched the gun and threw it into the snow. He grabbed Gera by the collar and shoved him toward MRAP Two.

"Let's get some zip cuffs on this fool," McCarter said. "We'll run him back across the border and have the Indians deal with him as they choose. Bringing him in alive will make a certain fellow in Washington very happy, too." He cuffed Gera lightly in the back of the head. "Where's Jamali?"

"He has gone," Gera said. "Vicious as he was, he kept his word and he made the plan work. He may yet still. I do not have his strength."

"Shut up and get in the truck," McCarter ordered. He watched as Manning bound Gera's hands and then guided him back to MRAP Two. The cargo compartment of both trucks had a metal cage used for storing propane and other volatile chemicals. Gera could cool his heels there.

When Gera was safely aboard the armored truck, McCarter turned to the other Phoenix Force members. Around them, what had been the Jamali-Gera camp continued to smolder.

"So are we buying this story that Jamali's just gone?" James asked. "Because that doesn't wash, to me."

"No," McCarter said, "I don't like it. Something about it is damned shady. Gera folding like that, I can see. He's not cut out for this. I think he saw power and wealth and never stopped to think about the steps that would be required to get there. But Jamali's a dictator born and bred. He's the kind of guy who'd kiss your mother and then stab her in the back if he thought that would get him what he wanted. He's just going to wander off while he's still got men and equipment at his disposal? No way. He's the sort of guy that would only hide when he thinks there's no way to fight back."

"Iraq," James said. "Gera mentioned Iraq. That remind you of anything?"

McCarter and the others turned to regard Gera's shattered tent.

"Spider hole," Hawkins said. "The bastard's got himself a spider hole somewhere."

"Watch yourselves," McCarter cautioned. "He'll be loaded for bear if he's here."

He was. In the ruins of Gera's tent, they found a rug on the ground that looked far more expensive than should be expected in such a temporary dwelling, even for a would-be dictator. McCarter stood by with his Tavor while the members of Phoenix Force grabbed corners of the rug and yanked it back.

In a shallow pit beneath the rug, wearing an oxygen mask and clutching an AK to his chest, Jamali was waiting. Instead of firing when he saw them, however, he remained completely still. This was caused by the head injury the man had sustained. He had been knocked cold by a beam from the tent that had fallen directly on his hiding spot and clubbed him in the forehead.

When he did wake up, sputtering and coughing, he tried to raise his rifle. When he discovered its magazine had been removed and its chamber cleared, he simply got up and ran.

"Uh," Hawkins said, "he just gonna run away?"

"Evidently so," McCarter said. "Secure the camp. I'll deal with our friend Jamali."

"David?" said James.

"Yes, Calvin?"

"Judging from the Jamali-employed torturer I got to know almost too well while they had me," James said, "Jamali's a son of a bitch. We've got Gera. He's the sort of guy prison will actually punish, if his countrymen don't find a way to do it for him sooner. But Jamali? He's an animal. A pure predator."

"I gathered as much," McCarter said. "Don't worry, Calvin. He'll be dealt with accordingly."

"I know," James said. "Just figured it needed saying."

McCarter set out across the bloody, soot-stained snow. Jamali was faster than he would have thought. The would-be dictator got perhaps half a kilometer from the ruins of his camp before the Briton caught up with him.

Jamali wheeled around when he perceived McCarter's presence behind him. He had an ivory-handled switchblade of some kind in his hand. Phoenix hadn't searched him thoroughly while he was unconscious. He'd been hiding that knife somewhere.

"Stand where you are, Jamali," McCarter said.

"Who are you?" Jamali demanded. "Are you a peace-keeper? Are you with NATO?"

"I'm just a soldier," McCarter answered. "A soldier who's cold and tired. And a soldier who's sick of men like you, thinking you can do whatever you want, kill whoever you want, rape whoever you want. You're a plague, Jamali. Predators like you are the scourge of the modern world. But as long as there are men like you trying to build your little empires, there will be soldiers like me to stop you."

"You…" Jamali said. Now, with nowhere else to go, his natural arrogance took root. "Who are you to tell me anything, peasant? I will be the undisputed leader of this territory. I will be a king among men! I will live out my days in riches!"

"You will live out your days bleeding in the snow," Mc-Carter replied.

Jamali lunged. McCarter easily dodged his attack and redirected it, knocking him aside. He deflected two more clumsy attacks before he tired of the game and slapped the blade out of Jamali's hand. The rogue general looked down at the snow where his knife had fallen.

"No," he said. "No. No!"

"Yes," said McCarter. "Bleeding in the snow." He held his Tavor at waist level with one hand. He snapped off the weapon's safety.

Jamali screamed and lunged for him. His fingers were curled like claws, his arms outstretched. If he could have grabbed McCarter by the throat and choked him to death on the spot, he clearly would have.

The Briton shot him, just once. The vicious Pakistani fell into the snow, on his back, staring up at the sky.

McCarter turned and, without another word, left him to die there alone with his sins.

CHAPTER TWENTY-THREE

Chicago

The M-60 machine gun thundered. It rocked. It rolled. Lyons sprayed the room with enough firepower that he felt like an avenging demigod. He powered his way through the throngs of armed men, feeding the belt into the M-60 with his support hand, moving slowly, methodically in and around the obstacles arrayed in front of him. There was not a stick of furniture in this upper recreation level that afforded even a little cover from the machine gun's heavy rounds. Bullets cored through sofas, chairs, a wet bar, a massage table. Bodies fell. Weapons hit the floor. The resistance mounted by Dei Qiong and his men was completely ineffectual. They were not ready for what they faced.

The rogue special forces operative and his combined force of loyal underlings and mercenary soldiers had been waiting, arrayed through the room, to shoot whoever came up the stairs. It was Dei Qiong's arrogance that had prevented him from giving the order to fire immediately. Had the enemy started shooting as soon as the top of Lyons's head came into view, they might have had a fighting chance. But Dei Qiong had apparently felt confident in his numbers. That overconfidence had cost him the battle.

When every one of the men waiting on the upper level had been put on the ground, Lyons kept firing. The M-60 sawed away at the room, at its contents, at the walls, at the floors, at the ceiling. The vibration of the weapon began to make Lyons's arm go numb. Still he didn't stop. He didn't stop firing until the last of his ammunition had been eaten by the big weapon, didn't stop firing until the final links and shells had struck the blood-soaked carpet, didn't stop firing until he was convinced that he had wrung from that M-60 every last bullet.

Then the only sound was the ringing in his ears and his own heavy breathing. He threw the anchor-like weight of the M-60 aside. It had no belts now. It was useless. He drew his Python.

"Carl to Able. Carl to Able," he said, speaking for the benefit of his earbud transceiver. "Able, report."

"Pol here," Blancanales said. "I'm on the southwest corner. Enemy fire is neutralized, but so are all of Lao Wei's men. I repeat, I have nobody moving down here."

"Ditto for the northeast corner," Schwarz said. "I've got bodies on top of bodies. Lao and Dei Qiong's men have annihilated each other. It's a slaughter."

"I know the feeling," Lyons said, gazing out over the corpses he had just created. "Secure the ground floor perimeter and keep an eye out for Lao. If he survived, I want eyes on him."

"What about you?" Schwarz asked.

"Dei Qiong is down," Lyons said. "I'm about to confirm."

Carefully, mindful of the danger he was putting himself in, Lyons began working his way through the pile of dead men. It was slow going. The M-60 had done its dreadful work only too well. The 7.62 mm NATO rounds left little room for argument when they found a target.

Finally, he found Dei Qiong.

The Chinese operative's eyes were closed. His clothes

were bloody, but there were no visible wounds. Lyons gave the man a shove with the toe of his boot. He leveled the Colt Python at Dei Qiong's face.

"Dei Qiong," he said, "you are now in the custody of the United States Justice Department."

Dei's eyes shot open. He surged forward, grabbing the Python, shoving the barrel aside as Lyons fired. The muzzle blast dug a vicious furrow in Dei's cheek, but he kept fighting as if he hadn't felt it. He practically climbed Lyons like a monkey and began hammering away at the bigger man's head with edge-of-hand blows. Lyons was no pushover, but the sudden explosive assault drove him to his knees as Dei slammed his hands into the sides of Lyons's neck.

You can't pass out, Lyons thought to himself. If you pass out, he's going to kill you.

He felt the sudden throbbing in his head that told him Dei had hit the carotid artery, maybe more than once. The blow caused a head rush that made his temples surge. He knew he had to fight through it. If he went down, he would never get up again.

He lost the Python in the scuffle. His shotgun, strapped to his back, might as well have been back in the truck. As Dei Qiong mounted him and began raining blows down on his head, Lyons covered up with his off hand.

This was where people died, on the ground. Getting mounted by an enemy was about the worst thing that could happen to you in a fight. The shotgun mocked him, pressing into his back painfully, pinned beneath him.

The big former cop's right hand found the folding combat knife clipped to his pocket.

"Stop!" someone shouted. Lyons was a little groggy from the beating he had been taking. Dei Qiong stopped hitting him, though, and his head rapidly began to clear.

The awful headache that was now clawing into his brain was that much clearer inside his skull, too.

Dei Qiong was looking at someone who had just come up the stairs. Lyons, painfully and awkwardly, followed his gaze.

Lao Wei was ascending the steps. He held an AKM assault rifle in his hands. It was pointed Lyons's way, but that meant it was also pointing at Dei Qiong.

"Do not move," Lao ordered. It was not clear if the Chinese operative spoke to Lyons, to Dei or to both of them. Lyons decided he would hope for the best.

"Good work, Lao," Lyons said. "Get him off me." The last part he said for the transceiver. It would give his Able Team partners some idea of what was happening.

"I said do not move!" Lao Wei ordered. "You are both prisoners of the People's Republic of China."

"Lao," Lyons argued, "we've been over this."

"Silence!" Lao ordered. He moved to within a few paces of both men. "Dei Qiong, step away from the American. Place yourself facedown on the floor. Interlace your fingers behind the back of your head. Do it now or I will shoot you immediately."

Dei Qiong stepped away from Lyons. Lyons took his hand off his knife. He didn't know if he'd yet need to use it; he didn't want to call attention to its presence. He stood and took a step sideways, moving him farther from Dei Qiong and forcing Lao Wei to choose one or the other of them to cover with the AKM.

"Stop moving," Lao ordered. He finally settled on pointing the rifle at the Able Team leader.

So much for cautious optimism, thought Lyons.

"So," Dei Qiong said. His hand went to the pistol holstered on his belt. "You have chosen sides, after all."

"Do not draw that weapon," Lao said. "I will kill you before you do."

"Lao Wei," Dei Qiong said. "How long have we known each other?"

"Years," Lao answered. "Not well. But for years I have known of you. Your work was once something of which you could be proud. Now it is like ashes. You have destroyed it with your betrayal of the People's Republic."

"Wake up, Lao," Dei urged. "You are a puppet of our government. But you do not have to be. Join me. Join me and together we will reap the profits of the mechanisms I have put in place. My plan can yet work. Escape the United States with me. Your men can join my own."

"My men have joined yours," Lao said. "They are all dead. They have been killed to the last man, just as the members of your private army have been. So much waste. So many good soldiers have given their last breath to salve your ego."

"This is not about my ego," Dei said. He was angry now. "This is about what is just. What is right. Why should I not profit after so many years as the tool of the People's Republic? Why should *you* not profit? Have we not both given up enough? Suffered enough? Worked hard enough?"

"Enough," Lao said. "I am taking you back to China. You will face judgment for your crimes."

"You could be a rich man!" Dei said. "Come with me and we both win!"

"No," Lao said. He turned to Lyons, careful to watch Dei out of the corner of his eye. "I release you, Logan. You are not my prisoner. You may take word to your government. I appreciate the honesty you have demonstrated. You have proved yourself a worthy soldier."

"That's mighty bright of you," Lyons said. "But there's the little matter of *me* taking *you* into custody."

"I do not think so, American," Lao protested. "I have showed you honor. Show me the same. I will leave with Dei Qiong. He will be punished for what he has done. As for my own crimes against the United States...I have lost every last one of my men. Is that not payment enough?"

"It's not about payment," Lyons said. "It's about justice."

"A familiar refrain," Lao said.

There were footfalls on the stairs. Blancanales and Schwarz ran up the steps two at a time, their weapons in their hands. When they saw the tableau awaiting them on the upper level, both men dropped low and trained their guns on Lao and Dei.

"Stop right there!" Schwarz shouted.

"Lao! Step away!" Blancanales ordered.

Lyons put up a hand. "It's all right, fellas," he said. "Lao here is just going to leave with his prisoner."

"I am sorry," Lao said. "As I said, you have conducted yourselves with honor. I regret that I must betray you now. But Dei Qiong cannot be taken into custody by your government. My mission was to bring him in or make certain of his death. Alive and free, he is an embarrassment to us. His activities have severely compromised the new China's image on the world stage, or could, if he is permitted to go on. Therefore I must take him from you. If you try to stop me, I will be forced to shoot you. I would regret that action."

"Oh, you're going to have just enough time for regret," said Dei. He snapped his arm and caught something that flew from his sleeve. It was the size of a small garage door remote.

"No!" Lao shouted.

Lyons got ready to spring. He would tackle Lao, take him to the floor, then pry the remote from the Chinese man's fingers—

Dei pressed the single switch in the face of the remote.

Lyons closed his eyes, waiting for the explosion that would send them all to oblivion.

Nothing happened.

"It is a dead man's switch," said Dei Qiong. "It is wired to explosives in the roof. If I let go of this remote, you will all die."

"You'll die, too," Lao said.

"I'm dead anyway," Dei explained. "I will not let you take me back. Torture and execution are all that await me back home. If I must die to escape capture, I will do so on my terms. This is your last chance, Lao. Join me and we can leave this place. Turn your gun on the Americans."

"You do that," Schwarz warned, "and I'll shoot you down myself."

Lao sighed. "There will be none of that," he said. "Dei Qiong, you leave me no choice." Lao raised his weapon to his shoulder and aimed it, not at Lyons, but at Dei.

"If you shoot him," Blancanales said, "the roof comes down."

"He is desperate," Lao said. "He is bluffing. He said so himself: If I take him to China he will suffer. And this I know. He will suffer terribly. He is a traitor, like his father before him."

"What do you know of my father?" Dei demanded.

Schwarz made eye contact with Carl Lyons. The electronics expert jerked his chin toward Dei. Lyons offered Schwarz an almost imperceptible nod. At Lyons's signal, the electronics genius took another step forward.

"I was quite young when it happened," Lao Wei said. "But I have seen the records. I began my career in the archives, working my way up to field training, then to field work, then to command. I have always remembered those early lessons. The most powerful of the things I learned came when I first began exploring the secrets of special operations. Among them was the tale of Dei Zhao, Dei Qiong's father."

"I wear on my belt," said Dei, "the only legacy of my father. It is his pistol. It is the weapon that he, for honor, took his life."

"Honor?" Lao spit. "No. Perhaps this is the lie you have told yourself through the years. Frankly it is a miracle you were permitted to continue in special forces, after the disgrace your father committed. The sins of the father should fall upon the son when they are this great. You have proven yourself to be just like him. Your greed has destroyed you. Your greed has killed many. Just as your father's did."

"What's he talking about?" Blancanales asked.

"Tell me what you know!" Dei Qiong demanded. He had completely forgotten the Stony Man team was in the room, and that was just what the crafty Lao probably had in mind. Schwarz took another step closer to the two Chinese operatives. Lao very carefully did not turn his head to look at Schwarz. He kept his gaze fixed on Dei's.

"American intelligence possibly knows of this," Lao said. "Or perhaps it does not. It began first with lead in the paint on toys exported from China to America. It continued with other chemical corruptions. Glycol in toothpaste and pet foods. Fillers and poisons in milk substitutes. Plastics in rice. Time and again it happened, each time shaking our American customers' faith in the products China exports to the United States. As outrage grew in the U.S., the demands for someone to pay for these crimes escalated in China. Eventually, several high-ranking Party officials, men in charge of things like export of goods, or agricultural inspections, were publicly executed. The executions were meant to assuage the ire of the American people. But we underestimated your long memories and overestimated your stomach for such cruelty."

"What has this to do with my father?" Dei demanded. Schwarz inched closer.

"Your father was a revolutionary," Lao stated. "He was part of a cabal of men who thought that the best way to end communism in China was to strike at the heart of what made us powerful in the world—our ability to sell, our manufacturing capability. The conspiracy was quite involved, judging from the records. Many were heavily redacted. Except in the most secret of sealed archives in special operations, your father and his fellow conspirators were…unmade. Their identities were dissolved and all records of their existence were purged. Family members over a certain age were eliminated. Had she survived, your mother would have been executed. Had your father been discovered but a year later, you, too, would have been killed."

Dei was pale. "My father died for honor."

"Your father died of shame," Lao Wei corrected. "Your father died because he knew that before his death, he would be interrogated. He chose to take his own life because he did not wish to face the consequences of his actions. How many innocent people, I wonder, including infants and children, did he injure or kill in his attempt to sabotage the Chinese economy?"

"I will kill you," Dei swore. "I will kill us all—"
Schwarz tackled him.

The electronics expert threw himself through the air and smashed Dei Qiong to the bloody, corpse-strewed, bullet-pocked carpet. He lost his Beretta 93-R in the process. Dei fought back, trying desperately to release the remote detonator. Lyons joined the fight, however, clouting Dei in the head several times. He found his Python on the floor and scooped it up, then used it as a club to pistol-whip the increasingly dazed Dei Qiong.

The sound of a roll of duct tape being unwound was very loud. Schwarz was wrapping the detonator in tape against Dei Qiong's palm, fixing the remote, its button and Dei's hand in place. Still the former Chinese special forces operator fought back, despite the beating Lyons had delivered.

Lyons heard Blancanales shouting.

The big former LAPD cop looked up in time to see Lao pointing his Kalashnikov.

"No!" Lyons shouted. "Don't fire!"

The metallic hammering of the AK was as final an argument as one got. Lao fired only once. The bullet punched through Dei Qiong's forehead and blew his brains out the back of his skull.

As Lao fired, Blancanales did, as well. The round from his M-4 took Lao in the shoulder and spun him around. The Chinese operative stumbled back, putting Lyons and Schwarz between himself and Blancanales, preventing the Able Team commando from making a follow-up shot.

Lao threw his gun down. "I am done," he said. "I offer you no aggression."

"Gadgets?" Lyons asked. "The bomb?"

Schwarz looked down at the dead man's duct-taped palm. "The contacts are still safely closed. We'll need bomb disposal in here. A local team or, even better, professionals from the Farm."

"Pol?" Lyons said. "Get the Farm. Get all the backup we can handle in here."

"I regret that it was necessary to do that," Lao Wei said. "I know you had hopes of taking him alive. And I realize that debriefing him would have been of considerable value to your intelligence agencies. That is why I could not allow it. China's affairs will remain China's affairs."

"Lao," Lyons said.

"We worked well together," Lao declared. He paused as if Lyons hadn't spoken, looking down at the dead men littering the floor. "This is…quite the slaughterhouse. Is this your handiwork, Mr. Logan? No matter. I regret that I lost my entire unit. Their losses will weigh heavily on my record. My superiors will not be pleased. But Dei Qiong's recapture or death, costly though it was, has always been my primary mission. Having him held by your people was unacceptable."

"Lao!" Lyons roared.

Lao Wei stopped. He looked back over his shoulder at the Able Team leader. "What is it, Mr. Logan?"

"You're under arrest," Carl Lyons said. "Put your hands on top of your head and interlace your fingers."

"I will not comply," Lao said defiantly. He turned and paced into an area of the floor that was reasonably free of debris and dead men. There he adopted a fighting stance. "Do you think you are capable of defeating me?"

Lyons was familiar with a particularly brutal offshoot of Shotokan Karate, among other systems. He would need no martial arts to take on Lao Wei, however. He walked slowly to where the Chinese man stood, flexing his big fists. His fingers tightened and relaxed, tightened and relaxed. Lao Wei frowned.

"You will regret this," Lao warned. "I am a master of Praying Mantis Kung Fu."

"And I'm really pissed off," Lyons countered.

When the two men were within reach of each other, Lao dropped into a much lower stance, hooking his fists and striking out with a vicious, whipping kick.

Lyons ate the kick. He took it squarely in the gut, his

face turning red as air rushed from his lungs. Instead of "celebrating the hit" or letting the pain faze him, he grabbed Lao's leg and bore down with all his strength. The big Able Team leader's steel grip crushed the joint, causing Lao to scream in agony.

The pain made Lao stick his head up in a futile attempt to take the pressure off his knee joint. Lyons looked at him, released him and fired off a tight hook punch with a closed fist. The punch caught Lao right in the knockout button, where his jaw met his skull. The Chinese operative hit the floor and stayed there. His injured leg twitched slightly.

Lyons took a plastic zip-tie cuff from his pocket, knelt and strapped Lao's wrists together behind the unconscious man's back.

The mission had been a hard one. But it was over now. He would leave it those in charge to run the tally on how much they had won and how much they had lost. As he surveyed the room full of blood, corpses and spent shells, he shook his head.

Justice had been done. But justice was never free.

EPILOGUE

Washington, D.C.

Hal Brognola stared at the headline in the newspaper, shaking his head. He was walking along the Potomac toward an office building few visited. Indulging himself the morning paper, he stopped to sit on one of the benches along the river walk and scan through the articles. His eyes kept going back to that headline, though.

General Gera, the subject of a highly publicized show trial in India, had been found dead in his cell overnight. Word from the Indians was that this was a suicide. Brognola had his doubts. It was possible Gera had taken his own life by hanging himself with a bed sheet, sure. It was equally possible someone in the Indian government hierarchy, or even someone as low on the chain as an overzealous guard, had decided that Gera needed to have an "accident."

Regardless, the India-Pakistan border was settling down. As the dust from the wipe-out of Gera and Jamali's operation had cleared, the desire of the two nations to go to war just now had also evaporated. Brognola supposed that Gera's death behind bars was a good thing. It drew this particular chapter in India-Pakistan relations closed with that much more speed. Perhaps that had been the motivation for Gera's death. Why, it was even possible Gera himself, out of some last, late impulse to do right by his nation, had killed himself to spare his countrymen further indignity.

You never knew what people would do, once they were caught. When a man lost hope, he was capable of nearly anything.

There was another, smaller article in the business column that alluded to government raids on the offices of Cudgel Security. He saw nothing about EarthGard, but those offices and branches, too, had been swept clean. The Farm had seen to it that the appropriate government agencies, from the Labor Department to the EPA to the IRS and even various union officials, had been alerted to the numerous legal violations for which the management of both companies was responsible. It would probably take years to sort it all out, but by the end of that process, neither company would exist. Okay, so maybe it wasn't a clean sweep. It was pretty dirty. But Cudgel and EarthGard had been broomed. They would be no trouble to anyone ever again.

He finished the paper much more quickly than he would have liked. Newspapers were dying all across the country. Print editions were harder to come by, and those that were published were anemic shadows of their former selves. Brognola snorted. He wished he had a birdcage to line with most of them.

Rising again, Brognola looked around for a trash can before realizing that all the public trash receptacles had been removed to combat terrorism attempts. He sighed. What a world we live in, he thought, when they have to take the trash cans out because someone might put a bomb in there.

He continued his walk, feeling the weight of the gun on his hip under his jacket. The .45 ACP-caliber Glock was as serious a piece of hardware as any he'd carried in his professional life. Strapping it on each day, he felt protected, yes, but he was also keenly aware of the escalation in violence that had occurred over the years. More than once, this gun had saved his life. And he was a bureaucrat, a desk-rider. He could only imagine what it must be like for the men and women of the Special Operations Group under him, facing the direct line of fire every day.

Still, Brognola refused to let such dark musings ruin his otherwise positive mood. Pakistan and India were no longer threatening to nuke each other. That counted for something. It was material evidence of the good that Able Team and Phoenix Force had done during this operation.

He was about to be confronted by another piece of that evidence.

The decrepit office building was just another crumbling façade from the outside. Within, there were several security checkpoints. Brognola checked his gun and took a concealed elevator to the subbasement. There, he was ushered into an interrogation room that boasted two chairs, a stainless-steel table and a single bright light overhead. Seated on one side of the table, wearing an orange prison jumpsuit and holding his head in his hands, was General Lao Wei of the People's Republic of China.

Brognola sat. "Hello, Lao," he said. "One of us is in big trouble." He slid the folded newspaper across the table. Lao did not touch it.

Lao grimaced. He rubbed at his shoulder; it still pained him, evidently, although the medical report indicated a clean through-and-through wound with no complications. He would heal. According to his medical jacket he was still wearing a brace on his knee for a very nasty sprain and hyperextension. That, too, would heal.

"I am a citizen of the People's Republic of China," Lao said. "You will release me. Immediately."

"You are a foreign military operative who was caught

attempting to murder federal agents on American soil,"
Brognola said. "You also murdered Dei Qiong in cold
blood. Don't try to con me. I'm well aware of the dangerous game your government has been playing with mine.
This isn't the first Chinese incursion across our borders.
It also isn't the first act of war you and your special forces
brothers have committed."

"You are a debtor nation—" Lao began.

"Stuff it, Lao," Brognola said. "I've heard your speech.
My teams have the ability to record everything they hear.
Your shtick is old and tired. I've listened to enough angry
Communists for a lifetime."

Lao glared. "What will you do with me?"

"Well, Lao, as you're so fond of saying, times change.
My government holds a substantial amount of leverage
over your own. But you did help us with Dei Qiong. I'm
told you conducted yourself honorably and you stuck to
your word. That means something. The Justice Department and its personnel have earned quite a bit of respect
here in Wonderland. And with that respect comes a certain
amount of *flexibility,* as you once put it, when it comes to
breaking the rules."

Lao's eyes narrowed. "What do you mean?"

"I mean," Brognola continued, "that this prison isn't
a prison. It's more like a local jail. From here, we trans-
fer you to the deepest, darkest hole we have. Someplace
so secret I don't even know its exact location. And once
you're there, you won't ever leave again unless I say so."

Lao hung his head. "What do you require of me?"

"I'm going to have you debriefed, Lao," Brognola said.
"Wow me with your interview, give me everything you
can think of on Chinese special forces operations past and
present in the United States, and it's possible that I'll set

you up for a prisoner exchange. You know. An *eventual* prisoner exchange."

Hearing his words used against him, Lao grimaced.

"This is the best deal you'll receive," Brognola said. He stood. "I advise you to take it." He left the interrogation room. The door slammed shut behind him, echoing down the darkened corridor.

Brognola smiled and continued on. He had a lot of work waiting for him back at his office, and plenty of politicking to do on the phones. Even that could not sully his mood. He enjoyed these visits. He enjoyed leveling ultimatums at the sort of people who were so fond of presenting them to others.

Lao Wei would cooperate or he wouldn't. Either way, an enemy of the United States had been brought to justice.

That was, after all, the mission of Stony Man Farm.

It always would be.

* * * * *

JAMES AXLER

DEATH LANDS®

Desolation Angels

JAMES AXLER

DEATH LANDS

Desolation
Angels

Dawn reveals the
terrible new truth...

Bad to the bone...

Violent gangs, a corrupt mayor and a heavily armed police force are hallmarks of the former Detroit. When Ryan and his companions show up, the Desolation Angels are waging a war to rule the streets. After saving the companions from being chilled by gangsters, the mayor hires Ryan and his friends to stop the Angels cold. But each hard blow toward victory proves there's no good side to be fighting for. As Motor City erupts into bloody conflagration, the companions are caught in the cross fire. In the Deathlands, hell is called home.

Available July wherever books and ebooks are sold.

AleX Archer
THE DEVIL'S CHORD

The canals of Venice hide a centuries-old secret some would kill to salvage...

In the midst of a quarrel on a Venetian bridge, the Cross of Lorraine is lost to the canal's waters. Suspecting a connection between the cross, Joan of Arc and Da Vinci, Annja Creed's former mentor, Roux, sends the archaeologist to search for the missing artifact.

After facing many difficult situations when retrieving the cross, Annja discovers that the artifact is fundamental to unlocking one of Da Vinci's most fantastical inventions. But the price Annja must pay to stop this key from falling into the wrong hands may be her life.

Available July wherever books and ebooks are sold.